Meet Me in Mozambique

E. A. MARKHAM was born on the volcanic Caribbean island of Montserrat – bearing strong resemblance to his invented neighbouring territory of St Caesare – and went to school in London. After working in theatre in London and the Eastern Caribbean, he lived mainly in continental Europe in the 1970s – Sweden, Germany and France, where he was a member of the *Coopérative Ouvrière du Bâtiment*, building and restoring houses in the Alpes Maritimes. E. A. Markham is Professor of Creative Writing at Sheffield Hallam University, a programme he has headed for the past fourteen years. His work has been widely published – with eight collections of poetry, three collections of short stories and a novel. His collection *A Rough Climate* (2002) was shortlisted for the T. S. Eliot Prize for Poetry.

Meet Me in Mozambique

E. A. Markham

**Tindal
Street
Press**

First published in October 2005
by Tindal Street Press Ltd
217 The Custard Factory, Gibb Street, Birmingham, B9 4AA
www.tindalstreet.co.uk

A CIP catalogue reference for this book is available
from the British Library

ISBN: 0 9547913 7 1

Typeset by Country Setting, Kingsdown, Kent

Printed and bound in Great Britain by Clays Ltd, St Ives PLC

Contents

For Teacher Morgan

(1910–2005)

of Harris', Montserrat, sceptic and savant

Once, Teacher Morgan refused all urging to punish a boy in his charge for a minor misdemeanour, because the boy's account of the incident was inventive – and growing more so. 'But the boy's lying,' urged an exasperated onlooker.

'I know he's lying,' said Teacher Morgan, 'but he's lying intelligently.'

Part One

The St Caesare
Connection

A Woman in Her Daughter's House

She was here for her protection, protection against her own foolishness and protection against worry about things like Ransley's dog; and she was working to overcome these disadvantages.

Once, Mother Stapleton had her own home, inherited from her mother, and servants; and the children did what she asked, though, towards the end, they showed reluctance, which was natural enough, as they were preparing to be immigrants. The move to England may have masked something which she would have had to punish as disobedience on the island. But all that was past; she was here now – thirty years or more: how time had passed! – relegated to a room in her daughter's house, even though she had the run of the house: did she really have the run of the house? She had been, her life had been, in a sense, confined. Not that she was complaining, she still had a perfectly good house on the island, which she had not seen, which no one had lived in for over thirty years; she had maintained the repairs. She complained, but she wasn't, as it were, complaining. They were, all things considered, good to her.

There was nothing wrong in complaining, as often complaining was merely a way of remembering what you once had, and of recognizing what you now had. It was said –

not *said*, as such things in the family were never said, merely communicated to the children, first by their father even from a distance, then by the children themselves – it was hinted at that she was not very intelligent. She didn't deny it. She had failed examinations in those far-off days when success in examinations proved whether you were intelligent or not: some who had made it despite failure in examinations were never allowed, fully, to compensate, not like these days when you could so easily turn the tables and embarrass those – no name mentioned – who had excelled at their studies, leaving them behind.

She was proud of their intelligence – though she was confused. There were others more intelligent – from poor families, even – and that couldn't be helped. She was confused because of incidents like the time in Ladbroke Grove when Pewter had embarrassed them all; a man with a degree not being able to do Bell Parson's sums, some little nonsense they taught her at night school, so that she could pass the Post Office test. But they had shouted her down, denying they were embarrassed, shouted her down in their own way, shouting without raising their voices, telling her that a degree in a different subject didn't enable you to do simple sums in maths, which was another subject. And despite their confidence she remained embarrassed. (More embarrassed than when they proved incapable of doing practical things, like mending the dripping pipe in the kitchen, or building a shelf for her bedside light to make it easy to read her Bible at night: these things needed not brainpower but muscle, and that could be left to others less clever.) Nevertheless, she thought that intelligence and long years in England where even the lowest of the low were improving themselves would teach her children simple things like maths, and the ability to explain things that confused the less fortunate.

Spending so much time in the house alone – who would have thought, growing up in a yard full of people in St

Caesare, a house with servants, of such punishment? – she couldn't help thinking about these things, wondering if what the clever ones told her was true. Because they had got it wrong, all of them, years ago, including the doctors who said she wouldn't recover from the stroke; and she had, she didn't even need to walk with a stick any more: she could go downstairs and make herself a cup of tea. Now, she did that more when they were out of the house so they didn't have to notice how slow she'd become. Her only real worry was fire: lots of fires in the news. In fires you had to move fast. The old and the very young usually got burned. The men who were strong and mindful only of themselves usually escaped. You could see them in the newspapers next day grieving over their burnt women and children. She didn't want her menfolk to be so embarrassed. She did her fire drill when no one was looking, and concluded that she would be burned several times over before getting to the front door, which had two locks – the key to one on a high shelf – or to the back door, which had a bolt that was too stiff for her fingers. But the others were clever; they must have thought of that. (The smoke alarm didn't work properly, they said, so they turned it off.) They must believe it when they assured her there would be no such fire in the house.

With so much time on her hands she got to thinking about other things as well, of Muriel, for instance, Avril's cat. (Why a big woman like her daughter needed to have a cat in the house, she couldn't imagine.) You had to put up with these things when the house wasn't yours, and make sure that the door to your room was locked against the cat. In the rest of the house she had to get along with Muriel. In no way, as she saw it, did she have the run of the house, even though she was alone there most of the day when the others were at work. Cat-hairs mingled freely with her clothes. She had to pretend, even, not to be repelled when the animal tried to lick her hand. If people who knew her at home saw her reduced to this, they wouldn't know where to look; so to save everybody embarrassment she told no one that the animal succeeded from time to time in licking her hand. Now she didn't even always notice when it was happening till it was too late.

But it was something else about Muriel that intrigued her. It was Muriel's way of getting into the house when she was locked out at the front, there being no cat-flap on that side. She would stand outside and scratch on the paint-work. This made a horrible sound, but it was one of those sounds that you didn't pick up at once, and even when you heard it you weren't quite sure what it was; and only later did it dawn on you that Muriel was trying to get in to the front door. And the cat kept it up as long as she knew there was somebody in the house, knowing that eventually she would be let in. Rebel thoughts came to Mother Staple-ton, thoughts which had Muriel scratching at the door of an empty house, but this didn't make sense: if you did that for days and weeks with the occupants gone on holiday or in hospital or . . . you would wear out, your paw would be bloody and useless; it would be on the *News at Ten* that cats had been doing this, and they would pass a law against it. But nevertheless she sometimes played a little game with Muriel, turning off the radio and remaining very still; but the cat was not to be fooled; and in the end she had to hobble to the door and open up, grateful that Muriel was not the fire she feared. She liked to think she learned something from the animal: if you kept your nerve and continued to scratch, help would arrive; and that's exactly what she did one day, in a manner of speaking, to get the plumber when a plumber was needed.

It worked. She was as effective as phoning the *Yellow Pages* and it cost them nothing; the man even refused a cup of tea. (Funny, they should make so much, later, of the man refusing a cup of tea, and of his being in the house; and play down the fact that he had fixed the radiator.) She had had to do something in a hurry to stop the front passage flooding. But she wasn't going to lose heart over their lack of appreciation. The man was just passing by in the street; she had no way of knowing if he was a plumber, so she had to ask. Before him she had had no luck with two people going by, who made their excuses and went on their way; but this one responded to her 'scratching' and came in and stopped the water spurting out of the radiator: maybe, when it mattered, she would be able to stop the gas, the fire.

She had talked to the plumber about her sons (she always forgot to talk about Avril, whose house it was), about how well they had done for themselves, embarrassed, though, that their expertise didn't extend to doing Bell Parson's maths and simple plumbing in the house – though she wasn't really embarrassed about the plumbing; and the man, without saying so, seemed to understand her position. But, of course, you had to be loyal to your own.

She had discussed some of these things with Pewter, the clever one who had come out less well than some who had failed their exams. He had studied something at university which she had difficulty in remembering, but he had studied English, too, so she called him an English graduate, though she knew he was prouder of the other thing, which she couldn't remember unless someone said it first. She had reprimanded him for falling into new ways, new fashions, things that would have shamed the family on the island. He would sometimes eat in the street, along with his friend – a pleasant girl with lots of hair who frightened Mother Stapleton a little. In the old days in Coderington, in the big house, where they did the baking, where her mother supervised the baking, Pewter would never have dared to be caught in the village, eating. Now he gave the impression that these things were all right, maybe because he had passed his exams. When he got older he would be out of control. He wasn't young any more. She feared what would happen when he got older.

But these visits from her son helped, and she was sorry he spent so much time abroad, but then when he was in England he didn't visit often. Once, she embarrassed him by admitting a fear she had. It may have been a fear or it may have been a dream, she couldn't remember. But he was reckless; or maybe he was unlucky, and it just came out before she could take it back: she asked him not to die before her. And he didn't want to hear her talk like that; so he turned the conversation round to other things. He liked to treat her as if they were still on the island, and often she had to put him right, because he had been a child then. When they talked of old times, as if they were equals in age, she had to be careful in case he was setting a trap. They would discuss, again, the mystery of Ransley's dog – something she wouldn't dare to talk about with others – and he would make her laugh. Ransley was a man from the island, from their part of the island, near Coderington, but he had gone to the north to work in the French Sector where he did well, and bought a car, and a dog, which he drove around in the car, as if he were a Frenchman. The dog would sit in the passenger seat, as if it were Ransley's wife (though Ransley didn't have a wife he was married to), looking out. And that's where the mystery happened. One day as they were driving along one of those mountain roads, the dog's head exploded out of the blue and taught Ransley a lesson. There was no shot, no accident, the dog wasn't ill, Ransley hadn't been drinking. The dog had been calmly looking out of the window and suddenly there it was with no head. No one, then or now, had been able to explain it. The incident reduced Ransley, a confident man, to a nervous wreck, and when he finally escaped the island everyone was relieved because of what the man had become. After all these years and degrees, Pewter's explanations for the dog's head exploding were no more intelligent than Mother Stapleton's. She laughed at that.

Such things confirmed her doubts about Pewter. But in recent years she clutched at signs of hope: if Pewter, who had studied that other subject at university, was still ignorant about these matters, and it didn't seem to bother or depress him, and didn't seem to make the foreigners among whom he worked think less well of him, maybe she, herself, could own up to one or two lapses and not be punished for them, things she had not got right in her life and were as mysterious to her as the exploding head of Ransley's dog. But could she be sure of Pewter?

Then one day Pewter came clean and confessed. He had nearly been killed crossing the street, run over by a van. It was when he had had a holiday job, doing something fairly menial in the West End of London. He had a bag of ladies' belts that he had to deliver somewhere; and as he was crossing the road, the van actually caught the bag, missing him. Pewter being Pewter used this example to reassure his mother that she needn't worry, his luck was in; he promised not to die before her – unless, of course, she insisted on living to a hundred and fifty. In which case they'd have to discuss it.

They used to talk in her room upstairs while the rest of the house was watching television downstairs; and he used to tease her and tell her that she was the classiest of them all, though that didn't stop her disagreeing with the things he did, like eating in the street (which he did, she knew, to provoke her), and living in a house and sharing a bath with strangers, or a swimming pool abroad with people who were not family. He accepted that you shouldn't eat and handle money at the same time, because money was dirty, but she suspected that even then he was using the word dirty in a different sense than she meant.

On one of his visits they had managed to agree about queueing. They agreed that it was a good thing, one of the good things they had gained from living in England, though, as usual, they agreed on it for different reasons and that meant, in a sense, that they didn't agree. He liked queueing because it saved time, and put pressure on those in front, those at the head, not to hang about. (He was thinking of things like public telephones: she didn't use public telephones.) For her, it was a different matter. She was never sure of her place, of her status, here, in this country. She had never quite believed what they said, that you were equal; they didn't treat you as if you were equal; that's why she liked the queue – *there* they treated you as if you were equal. A few years ago when she was more mobile, she would make up to three trips a day to the shops, just to check on them, just to confirm that they were still treating you equally. When he heard that, Pewter was impressed. It was years before she owned up to that because you learned, after years of living in a strange country, living in someone else's home – and having had a stroke which, though you'd got over it, no one was happy to let you get over it – you learned to protect yourself. But Pewter was delighted and called her a fighter (he was a fool, she didn't know one end of a gun from the other), and it was all she could do to restrain him from telling them downstairs and spoiling it all. But now, she felt confident to confide something to him which he must in no way pass on. She felt she had to speak because he was going abroad again, and who knows . . . ?

It was about the time she had left his father. The children were very young, babies; she herself was young; maybe that's what had unsettled her. He came and went, the father, often leaving the island; she couldn't imagine this life, this coming and going – being left like this while someone came and went – for the rest of her life. And yet she knew, when she looked around at other people – most of them stronger than her and able to cope – that that's what her life had in store. And she had packed a few things and left him. Left them. Now, you had to understand that, on an island in those days, when you lived in the house of your mother, in very favourable circumstances, with status and servants – and only the husband sometimes missing – it's very difficult to know where to go when you decide to leave home. And as she walked down to the market – pretending she was just taking a stroll – and accepted a lift into town, it dawned on her that she had made a hash of the packing, because really, none of the things that were hers and spelt home could be packed – her rocking chair on the gallery; the screen on her bedroom window to keep out the lizards, that had come from Germany; her grafted mango tree in the garden: you couldn't begin to count. So of course she went back just to discover that it had all been in her mind: she hadn't even packed those few things that would have been useful; and everyone treated her as if she had just popped out to visit a friend. The fright of that moment was like living in a foreign country.

And then the humiliation. After an argument over something unimportant, it was revealed to her that she had, indeed, packed to leave home; and they had unpacked the things she had packed (how stupid, how stupid to forget to take the suitcase with her!), and *he* had involved the entire family in this; and to save her embarrassment, it was agreed that no mention should, again, be made of the incident. For it clearly was a moment of foolishness; and foolishness was allowed in the family. Now, all these years later in England with Pewter about to go abroad again where he was more likely to be hit by a van as he crossed the road, Mother Stapleton wondered if she had transferred her madness to him. What if they asked him, over there, to explain the mystery of Ransley's dog?

She was sorry he was going abroad again – all these separations – and for a while was muddled and couldn't quite work out his real age: he was the sort of age now that she had been when she had come to this country over thirty years ago, and she had brought skills with her which the country hadn't needed, and gradually she forgot what they were; and she feared that the same would happen to Pewter in his new country: she feared that those who didn't need his skills would say that he was not intelligent, despite his qualifications; and that would be worse than if you didn't have qualifications.

She would urge him not to be depressed when that happened, and secretly hoped he'd come up with a better way of explaining things. She had kept her sanity though she had failed the odd test early in life: she never managed to master the horse, even though Ruby was docile and the groom held it steady. But sitting on Ruby, looking down, she couldn't get used to being so far off the ground. Naturally, she may have learned in time, but you couldn't bring the horse to England with you. Here, horses on the television did strange things, which confused her, and made her regard not riding as a blessing. Other things she didn't learn at the right time were swimming and riding a bicycle and learning to drive a car. Oh yes, she hadn't managed to play the piano either, despite the lessons.

They couldn't take that life away from her. But of Pewter: what did he have to fall back on when he could already do most of these things? – though he couldn't play the piano, either. Or sing. Maybe she could tell him about that time that she had pretended to leave his father.

2

A Place to Hide

'He spent the night before the execution writing a prayer
in the form of a poem. With it he achieved posthumous
fame abroad.'

G. Cabrera Infante, *View of Dawn in the Tropics*

I

To recall the studied casualness of the start of E. M.
Forster's *Howard's End* – that throwaway line by the
narrator – one may as well begin this story of the painter
da Firenze with his controversial demise. It is known that
he walked out of the house in the middle of a hurricane,
the night he died. Da Firenze was, arguably, the one major
visual artist to have been produced by the island of St
Caesare, and the endless tacky images of wreckage from
hurricane and volcano with which we now associate the
place show how much, as an artist, he must be missed. His
work would not have been 'scenic' – a term used by an
American surveying the wreckage by helicopter the day
after the 1989 hurricane. The volcanic effect, five years
later – no longer broken-backed houses and churches, but
town and villages disappearing under sand – was duly
scenic. I was affected, of course, being from St Caesare,
even though I left the island as a child. I was depressed at
the thought of the island's 2,500 people yet again having

to flee their home. I looked at the local photographs and the TV images of devastation and felt that da Firenze might have sought to escape all this before it became, well, an aesthetic burden.

So it wasn't *just* the fact of suicide that disturbed: I'm not trying to minimize the act of suicide, for the combination of desperation and sense of abandonment (either personal or cosmic) that this must entail doesn't bear contemplating. Oddly enough, I can't off-hand remember that many painters who have committed suicide – only Modigliani's mistress comes to mind. And Van Gogh, of course. But there were writers galore, from Virginia Woolf and Plath and Sexton and Berryman to our own Eric Roach in Tobago, who in a fit of weariness (wariness, perhaps) swam out to sea, in 1974; and there is the fashionable sub-genre of literature that explores artistic sensibility and suicide: how to talk about da Firenze without adding to that literature?

Da Firenze's action, in the 1989 hurricane, has been compared by some in the region with Eric Roach's embrace of the sea. And yet, the comparison leaves me uneasy. Not just that Roach was a man of a certain age, his considerable life's work more or less behind him, whereas da Firenze, at fifty-three, was just beginning to make his reputation, startling us with invention, even as he went through what must have been one of his periods of self-questioning. It is also true that the degree of recognition he began to enjoy abroad (something in which, he was graceful enough to say, I played a part) hadn't endeared him to some at home; but that was to be expected. I come back to the question of da Firenze whenever I'm struck by the thought – which might be a trifle crude – that what our painter from St Caesare had thrown away was more than what, say, the Tobagan poet had sacrificed.

But there was more to the anxiety than this: the Caribbean

sea, rough or calm, was, if you like, a source of food off-shore, and promise of what lay beyond, but it was, too, an environmental gaoler, always there, hemming you in, making you invent stratagems for escape: at best it kept you insular, bred distrust of your neighbours – often near enough to be sighted – on the other side of the shore. It was also the graveyard of your ancestors. To take this on, *to open your arms to this*, is to make a statement both too-large-for-us *and* despairing. OK, let's call it ambiguous: I will die, but at the same time, freed of the burdens of today, there is no reason why I shouldn't get there, get there in my mind, get there in my head; or physically just get to the other side. In a work of fiction I would get there. In a normal world I would get there. More theatrically, perhaps: this big water containing me – *containing me* – has to be challenged. My own success in negotiating it is irrelevant; what's important is to make the attempt. Here goes. I am of sound mind, etc.

On the other hand – this is beginning to sound like a *Guardian* editorial – on the other hand, to die voluntarily in a storm, to walk out of the shelter at the height of the hurricane, seems different somehow. There are those who would downplay the incident, who would find *reasons* for it: the man was an artist, therefore odd. So he was famous in Cuba and Manchester: well, bad luck, he didn't live in Cuba and Manchester. He just couldn't cope with the St Caesarean reality. From there, you trace the bitterness and eventually, the madness. (Remember poor Horace, whom the same island drove to madness?) Walking out to greet Hurricane Hugo was a sign of that madness.

The madness line was also adopted by some who were more sympathetic to da Firenze. He was a real artist, they say, trained in Italy; he had the heightened sensibility of someone for whom a storm wasn't just rain and winds at 150 miles an hour; a storm was environmental disturbance;

there was something psychic about a storm; *a storm fired the sublime imagination*: this connected with the artist's antenna, and set him off: at that moment, when he opened the door of the shelter and walked out, it was like a lover going to meet the beloved: no, rather the beloved being drawn irresistibly to the embrace of the lover: this was the stuff of romantic poetry; this was an operatic moment, when a St Caesarean joined the cast of the world's doomed lovers. Even though I'm pleased that the death of a St Caesarean artist is accorded such . . . grandiloquence, I'm equally suspicious of this interpretation. For I'm not convinced that da Firenze wanted to kill himself – and to kill himself in that way. When I say the problem was that the man, at a crucial time in his life, his art, felt he had no one to talk to, I don't mean this as a jibe at inflated ego; and certainly not as a slur on the people of St Caesare. (Though why he didn't draw support from his fellow captives in the shelter in Barville puzzles me; for they, too, would have been in a heightened hurricane state, praying to their god, reciting poems, planning new identities should they survive this one.)

But am I claiming to know da Firenze better than others did? Yes and no. No, in important ways in that there is no intimate memory in my life of the smell of turpentine and linseed oil. No, in the more general sense that we were not particular friends, we were never close, we met infrequently. But, yes, in that I knew him, and we talked art. I knew him in the days before we left the island in '56 when he painted pictures of the house we were about to abandon for England, and humiliated my mother, in paint. I remember him saying to my mother, yes, he would paint us on the veranda, getting in bits of front lawn, and the edge of the flowerbed; showing everything at its best; pristine. Yes, he would paint one of us sitting on Ruby, the horse, and all that; but what he really wanted to do was to paint her (my mother) or my sister, indoors, in the dining room, say at table, or upstairs playing the piano. Better still, why not paint the Sunday afternoon gathering in the drawing room after lunch, with C. J. Harris and Parson Ryan and Uncle G from town sipping iced lemonade and coconut juice and munching on Nellie's coconut tarts; why not just capture the Sunday afternoon conversation? (What impressed me at the time, having little experience of painters and painting, was how you painted 'conversation'. It was much later – in England – when we talked about art, that da Firenze explained that his purpose back then had been to capture something of the intimacy of our *interiors*, and that's why he had painted my mother without her shoe.) I, too, had misunderstood the point he had been making.

Maybe I overcompensated; for when the opportunity came I took up the case of da Firenze, not 'the boy who was so worthless that he didn't even finish the picture and paint the other shoe' on my mother's foot, the ankle strained and bandaged from the accident coming out of church, but of da Firenze, the painter, pursuing his artist's vision of 'interior space'. In the 1980s, when I edited a black arts magazine in London, we devoted a lot of space to the visual image; and here was an opportunity to do something for our man from St Caesare. The Whitechapel Gallery was mounting a 'retrospective' of his work – highlighting the new-to-me 'Cuban' panels; and I volunteered to write the introduction to the catalogue.

We had 'reconnected' in the mid-1970s when we both found ourselves working in Manchester. I was teaching at a college and da Firenze had come on some sort of art fellowship. We didn't see much of each other. I lived in Manchester and he was staying in London with family and came up to Manchester maybe one day a week; but we met from time to time at the Danish café in Piccadilly, or at the Royal Exchange, for a snack, a meal, to see a play, or maybe just to have a drink in upmarket company. Da Firenze was very much into theorizing (while I, in a writerly environment, was perhaps guilty of betraying the opposite tendency), and we engaged in the usual sort of art talk.

So we talked round the subject: the old theory – that West Indians tended to shy away from their interior space – still stood; even the writers who like to claim something different lived it; and when he added me to his list of 'subjects', the point seemed to have been made. He had chosen to paint me in my rented room upstairs in Mrs Leaning's house in Higher Openshaw; and we agreed to disagree about what point was being made. It was much more interesting to talk about the new work informed by the Cuban revolution.

Two things made me uncomfortable with this da Firenze contact in Manchester. I'm sorry, but I must come back to the painting he did of me. (I am, it seems, very easy to parody. 'When a black man has grey hairs it's because he is old and free of cares' was to be the eventual caption. I would be hung beside the Cuban dandy in the white three-piece suit, in a hat; but not, thankfully, with the murderers.) Trapped in a dark space that was my room (the one window at the back not letting in enough light), the effect was something more than I could explain away as a dark, northern environment; it was, for him, my hiding space. And in this hiding space I was wearing something suggestive of a military jacket. Gone was the old innocence of my 'temporary' room which never quite threw off its winter fuzziness of the one-bar/two-bar electric fire, which didn't much matter because I had stumbled into it by accident, and would soon be moving on; it was not something I was *comfortable* with. The picture captured me at my typewriter, papers piling up on both sides, me in profile (unflattering), a different shade of dark from the rest of the room, the whole giving the sense of a man in some sort of solitary confinement. The jacket, hinting at military activity or at military posturing, seemed to suggest that one had lost either the sartorial moment or the rebel's luck; and was now, yes, writing about it in solitary. On reflection, I had to accept that this was a legitimate enough way of seeing.

Da Firenze was, in a way, persuasive. No, this was just part of the old narrative, the same old argument of our visual sense not having an 'interior' dimension (think of the rationalizations at home about outdoor living and sun and sea and carnival, etc.); that made it easy to be into denial of our real interior spaces even when we came to live in a country, like England, where life was geared to living indoors. (We even had to re-create carnival.) You couldn't fault his examples: Look, he said, what about visiting any Caribbean household in England, in the evening, how the family is unprepared to put on the lights with the curtains open; look, during the day even, how the curtains are usually closed, how someone inside peers through a gap in the curtains when the doorbell rings. If you can't, after twenty or thirty or forty years in a country, in a house that you own – if you can't just open the door when the doorbell rings, you are effectively hiding. You still suspect that what's out there is potentially dangerous; at the very least, is likely not to be benign. Clearly, if you are in this position, which is being mentally or emotionally under siege, you are not going to open up your interiors to investigation. No criticism intended. But are you at the same time preserving your secret history, as those grim fellows in the Soviet Union used to do while putting on their false, official version? Or are you still in denial? Are the painters invited in to capture that intimacy

19

which you fear the enemy might get to see and misread? Where are our Bonnards and Vuillards and Persian courtyards that we alone know how to interpret? This could be our secret weapon, our form of resistance. (A middle-class woman, painted in her Sunday best, one leg outstretched in the drawing room, the ankle bandaged, was not evidence of satire, but an intimate statement of someone, secure, at home.)

That was all very well, that was in the past; but why the military touch, why paint me in a military jacket, twenty years later? Da Firenze clearly wanted to express an attitude to those of us who could still be described as anglophone; *he* had discovered Cuba. Or, more particularly, he had discovered the Cuban writer, G. Cabrera Infante, and had illustrated scenes from one of his books. The paintings were all military, almost pornographic, to do with defeat, killing, mutilation, all, we like to think, non-West Indian virtues. The experience of those 'exteriors' began to influence, to seep into the earlier 'interior' vision, to the point where I, in my dark room in Higher Openshaw, sitting at my typewriter writing an unpublishable novel, am shown wearing a mock-military jacket.

Da Firenze was to say elsewhere that his theme was denial in its widest sense. In our *not* putting on the military jacket when we in the Caribbean were at war, or should be at war – for land, for hinterland, for resources, for the right not to be exoticized, etc., and for not being able to live aspects of our lives, economic, medical, intellectual, social and psychic – *at home*, how could we *not* be at war! Our desperation to educate our children to live abroad, while treating 'abroad' as not their place, was part of the schizophrenia of our condition. Not to fight to reverse this was to be in denial.

The hint – the military jacket in the domestic space – that the violence outside that we deny would be reflected inside if we admitted to having interiors – was a sophisticated development in da Firenze's thinking. When he proclaimed that our native scenes were both macho and violent and it was churlish and irresponsible to protect the domestic image from this reality, I began to realize that I needed to look again at those 'interiors' which I had thought, if not benign, at most just mildly satiric. I was relieved, in a sense, that he had not permitted himself to live to see the disaster pictures of St Caesare after the hurricane and, more terrifyingly, the volcano; for his version of the 'disaster literature' which had sprung up everywhere would not have been 'filmic' nor, in a heroic sense, comforting.

Another point he had made in passing that I didn't really pick up in the catalogue: the 'truth' in a painting capturing the moment between artist and subject, frozen and living for ever, as an honest exchange between the two, *and* a sense of harmony with something not seen, beyond the canvas – never got into my analysis. Maybe next time. Maybe this time.

II

The panel that caused the sharpest comment – probably because it was released as a postcard – was the *Le Déjeuner sur l'herbe* parody. This painting of death was almost obscene in its primary colours, suggestive of over-abundant nature, and ripe fruit. Too green. Something over-ripe. The entire text (in Spanish), which the painting illustrated, was reproduced (reminding me of Goya's captions for the *Caprichos*).

Although the three of them are lying in the grass, it's not *Le Déjeuner sur l'herbe*. One had a hole in his forehead, another a hole in his face, and the third a hole in his neck. The other

one is face down and there's something wrong with his head.
Perhaps it was beaten or shot up. The third one, a shirtless
mulatto, received at least ten shots in his chest and stomach.
In the foreground you can see a strip of asphalt which must
be the highway, and behind it a segment of beach or the coast,
the sea.

They don't move because it's a photograph and because
they've been dead for hours and were left near the highway as
a warning.[1]

[1] *Vista del amanecer en el trópico* (1974) by G. Cabrera Infante
(translated as *View of Dawn in the Tropics*).

III

Still, I had a go at the introduction to the catalogue; for I
shared many of da Firenze's concerns, if in a slightly
milder form. I, myself, had written a review of the 'disaster' literature of St Caesare and Montserrat, warning
against being seduced by the muse of hurricane (and, I
would now add, volcano) to the exclusion of all the other
impulses that inspire and provoke expression of a people's
passion for life; a people's art; for, with a history of others
caricaturing us, we had to be careful not to assist them by
typecasting ourselves. So I made a point in the catalogue
about da Firenze not being a 'disaster' artist (despite the
Cuban period, which was, perhaps, more than a 'period');
and made a – perhaps strained – comparison with Goya's
Caprichos, claiming that Goya's nightmares came less
from a war with nature that you couldn't win than with
the man-made and still medieval condition of late
eighteenth-century Spain.

The objective of bringing artist and sitter (or subject)
together into some sort of harmony so that the result,
trapped, would continue to be 'honest' was a line of argument I hadn't developed in the introduction, perhaps for

fear of being thought pretentious. But, of course, after a man's suicide you tend to weigh things he said differently.

And that's really why I return to the night of his death by hurricane. If you are an artist and this subject (wind, rain, panic, chaos) presents itself to you, how can you not store images for the canvas; the odd groupings, the revealing body language of people caught off-guard – the strange dignity of someone embracing loss or displaying the opposite, defying the gods, God? Whose worn face is calm and suddenly beautiful? How can you *not* want to paint this? When, next morning, or the days following, you *imagine* the photographs of the amateurs, the pictures of damage (nearly all exteriors), the commentary by the man in the helicopter the morning after, freezing this aspect of the people's history, how can you resist providing the corrective? *You are the artist, you have imagination.* You don't just walk out and abandon the scene to those who would make it, forever, banal!

OK, there was another theory. It was of the first-hand-experience variety, the Odysseus having himself strapped to the mast of the ship in order to resist the sirens of Scylla and Charybdis. Then why didn't da Firenze have someone tie a rope round his waist to pull him back after he had experienced enough hurricane to capture its texture on canvas? Or – I ask selfishly – why did he deprive us of that last, defining picture (or series of pictures) of the St Caesare artist killed by hurricane? For, you know, this is what interests us now about da Firenze. How different was his thought process, at a crucial moment, from that of the poet Eric Roach? At what point did he think (not Macbeth-like – 'I'm in't steeped so far', etc. – for he may not have seen himself as culpable; Macbeth is my image, not his), at what point did he think: that's it; might as well keep going. Or: damn: miscalculated again. *Damn damn damn.*

And now I make another point when I talk about da Firenze. You might call it lack of hinterland; lack of living space; lack of a place to hide; lack of interiors. What if da Firenze was unwilling to paint his fellow victims in the shelter? What if at the height of the storm he found them on their knees praying to their gods or some God (*the woman kneeling, Goya-esque . . . arms clasped in prayer to some nightmarish figure of a monk's robe hung on the skeleton of a dead tree, the rest of the company lined up behind her*)? How to stop the images crowding in from nearer home: women, children, men, on their knees in some God-fearing American or South African apartheid town, a bandit with a whip, a sheriff with a gun humiliating them? This town, that town, this America, that Africa. What if he refused to collude with this scene, refused to transmit it to canvas, freeze it for ever, showing his sitters, his subject living in an age earlier than himself: what if he thought he would not be an agent to this form of pornography? Well then, there was no point to it but to walk out into the mindless storm.

3

Grandmother's
Last Will and Testament

Sarah was giving my grandmother her bath and for
once, waiting outside in the drawing room, I didn't fall
asleep over my book. *Robinson Crusoe* was an advance
on *The Pilgrim's Progress* in this respect. It was the middle
of the week and we three were alone as before in the big
house in Coderington, now that my grandmother's crisis
had passed. My mother had gone back to the old routine,
staying in town during the week with my elder brothers
and sister, who were at the grammar school. Then we'd all
be together for the weekend, from Friday evening, when
they came with news and presents.

The wick wasn't burning well in the lamp, darkening
the shade on one side, but I could see to read. I had been
trying, alternately, to feel the pain of Crusoe hitting his leg
on the sand as he was washed ashore, and to figure out
why he had two surnames, Robinson and Crusoe, at the
expense of a Christian name. I had three Christian names:
I was ahead of him there! (The only person I could think
of with no Christian name was my friend R. T. Harris. RT
was the son of 'Professeur Croissant' down in the village.
But then Professeur Croissant was a historian who didn't

believe in God – and wasn't even French. On top of that PC had a drink problem – two things against him which meant that he would never become our headmaster.) During all this Sarah came in to say that my grandmother – her bath over – wanted to see me. A quick check. No panic. She had called me a heathen just this morning, but that was because I hadn't cried at the funeral: it was just her way of speaking. She often called Professeur Croissant (whose real name was Teacher Harris) a heathen because he wouldn't say DV, *deo volente* – God willing – when he made plans for his or his children's future. So the fact that I was now a heathen, a member of my cousin Horace's gang, dedicated to the worship of Satan both in the pulpit at the Methodist church in St Anne's and the Anglican church in Coderington, was something she couldn't know about.

I checked for more obvious things: yes, I'd washed my hands and feet. Hadn't cleaned my teeth yet, but I wasn't ready for bed; I hadn't forgotten, I was OK.

But as I entered the room I found her, not under the mosquito netting, but sitting on her commode in nightdress and dressing gown. She had an expression as if she knew something. But I liked the smell of bay rum in the room, so much better than the Canadian Healing Oil which she sometimes used and which got everywhere, the smell lasting for hours. I thought about the joke we'd been doing to death since last weekend, about my grandmother's new servant. She had got a letter from the governor, in connection with registering some land at Mulcares, and he had signed it: 'Your Humble Servant'. We liked the idea of the plump, well-dressed fellow, all superior and fat-cheeked, descending from his official car to fetch my grandmother's ewer of water or to feed the pigs in the animal pound last thing at night. My grandmother, herself, protesting, had been tickled by the idea. This was a bayrummy sort of joke that her present aspect seemed to invite, not the Canadian

Healing Oil explanation for wrong-doing.

'Yes, Mammie.'

'The teeth still hurt?' she asked me. I was tempted to correct her: you got the same treatment for one tooth as for three, so there was no benefit in having more than one go bad at a time; but I let it pass in case she felt I was checking up on her grammar. Anyway, that was all in the past; that was this morning when I thought there might be a chance of being let off school.

'You too small to always have teeth hurting. Get the glass.'

'The glass?'

'The glass, the glass.' The glass was on top of the dressing table. At the same time she was reaching towards the press – she didn't have to move from the commode to do this; she had a bad leg, she was lame – reaching for the hidden bottle. The press also contained books to do with magic I was not allowed to read, so I was already thinking of its new name – wardrobe – to see if that would help to open it up to me.

And then she handed me the bottle.

'Here, here. Open it, open it. You teeth wearing out and you don't even grow up yet. The Lord works in a mysterious way. Judge not His ways.'

I braced myself for the sermon, but she had finished.

'Pour, pour.'

So I poured brandy into the glass, and looked around for the water that she diluted it with when occasionally she had to take 'the medicine' for her asthma.

'Now, you must gargle.'

The brandy was for me. This was a trap; I had to be careful. There was already talk in the village about two or three of my friends from school – particularly RT, 'not even at grammar school yet' – who were addicted to toothaches. It was well known that when you had a toothache in the middle of the night – or at a time inconvenient to go to the dentist in town – the only thing to do to relieve the pain was to gargle with brandy. Because he was now so far gone RT had long been taken off brandy and put on rum – and white rum at that, the kind that shrivelled raw liver in a saucer – the sort of low drink that no one but a heathen like his father and the men in the rum shop would let get past their throat. But RT, writhing and moaning (with his parents rowing over it), always ended up *drinking* the medicine and having either to miss school or Sunday school because of the state of his breath. So there was talk, and I had to be careful; because it was hinted that if neither brandy nor white rum worked for the toothache, we would have to go back to taking the traditional castor and cod-liver and Canadian Healing oils.

I sipped the brandy and made a face, a face intended to indicate that the brandy was unpleasant, not that the tooth-ache was unbearable. So it wasn't an extravagantly ugly face, just a moderately ugly face; and that seemed to satisfy my grandmother, a shrewd judge of these matters. She chuckled a little. And as I gargled I felt the full force of the medicine which, as medicine, didn't have to be diluted with water.

'I'm going down, you know,' she said, as if I was an adult. So I had to pretend not to understand. 'Going right down.' The only thing to do was to take another sip of the brandy and pretend to be in pain.

'Then, you children will be without me . . . Baby and the rest of you.' ('Baby' was my mother. It embarrassed me to have her referred to like that.) But then my grandmother grew philosophical:

'The Lord will provide,' she said.

To which I felt obliged to counter: 'The tooth's really getting better.'

'Things turn upside down.' She wasn't listening to me. But her mood might be lightening. 'Bright ones turn out bad. Your great-uncle turn out bad. And your father.'

I didn't say anything.

'You know?'

'Yes, Mammie.'

'Who tell you?'

'Don't know,' I lied.

'Your father was one of the bright ones.'

'Sorry, Mammie.'

'And you just as stubborn. When I hear that you refuse to cry at Bess Chambers' funeral . . .'

'I forget. Forgot,' I said. But of course I hadn't forgotten. Our gang, the Heathens, decided not to cry at funerals because we hated to see adults in our family cry. Horace, our Leader, went one further and vowed he would *laugh* at them; and sure enough he managed to laugh at Bess Chambers' funeral, which was the first one that had come up after the vow. But Horace was clever, that's why he was our Leader. (Or, truth to tell, that's why he wasn't challenged when he announced himself our Leader.) He had a way of laughing that those adult mourners, who weren't in the know, confused with crying. That's why you always had to be careful when you went along with Horace: he got away with things that the rest of us couldn't.

'A funeral is a funeral,' my grandmother was saying. 'You have a hard heart. To forget.' Then she sighed and changed the subject. 'Why that child taking so long with the hot-water bottle? Go and see what Sarah doing with the hot-water bottle. And tell her to bring a glass from the dining-room cabinet.'

I was relieved to be doing something, so I went for the glass myself. I had to open up the trapdoor between the corridor and the 'boys' room' to the dining room downstairs. Sarah must have used one of the outside steps to get down to the kitchen and bread room underneath my grandmother's room. From the dining room, I called to tell her that my grandmother was waiting for the hot-water bottle; and she answered by sucking her teeth, saying something about the fire in the coalpot going out.

Back upstairs, we settled down to our drinks. My grandmother's consisted of very little brandy drowned in water and mine was, as before, undiluted. I now gave up the pretence of gargling.

She was daring me, testing me, pouring more brandy into the glass each time I finished. Now I was emboldened to smack my lips the way Professeur Croissant and the men in the rum shops did. I calculated that my grandmother had already made up her mind not to punish me. And if I had a hangover in the morning, she would have to explain it away. So I continued to drink, silently, 'To the Heathens'.

'Your grandfather never touched a drop,' she said simply. 'But God take him, nevertheless.' And now she was direct, dropping the roundabout approach: she wanted to die in peace. Many of the best didn't die in peace. There had been a doctor in the family. And a lawyer. And many parsons; one of them ordained, even. But these things didn't hide godlessness. She was frightened for me. I was even beginning to look like my father. There was talk in the house that I should go on to become a doctor or a lawyer or a priest. She was frightened of such talk; for such a position, when you were stubborn, could lead to the wrath of God and pestilence. Her brother, Ned, managed to remain a Christian even though he was a doctor. But he wasn't stubborn and wilful. Like me.

In the end I assured my grandmother, as she demanded, that I would not go on to become a doctor or a lawyer or a priest: as a ten-year-old I didn't see what I had to lose by promising that.

'You swear?'

I swore and raised my glass.

Finally, Sarah came in with the hot-water bottle and took away the glasses to wash them; and I got myself ready for bed.

That Sunday evening Parson McPherson preached in Coderington and visited our house to eat and pray with my grandmother. This time when I was called in after her bath, there was no promise of brandy, my grandmother was lying under her mosquito net and the room smelled of Canadian Healing Oil.

I would be given a chance, she said, not looking at me, her voice registering a new distance between us; for no one was so far gone that he didn't deserve a chance.

What sort of chance?

I learned that a heathen among heathens might still find the Lord merciful. If they were all heathens together and didn't know any better, the Lord might not see fit to punish them.

I wanted to own up that Horace and I and the gang were *knowing* heathens; that we went into the pulpit of the empty church and opened the Bible at Deuteronomy and loudly preached a sermon to the many breasts of Fatima, the Queen; and to the gold in her nose and the bracelets on her ankle; but I knew that was not what my grandmother was referring to. No, she had spoken to Reverend McPherson and would alter her will to put a little money aside to send me to a heathen country for a short time where God might not notice me in the crowd. And then even I wouldn't be so brutish as to learn their ways. But the choice had to be mine: they couldn't banish me from a Christian house. I had to choose my heathen country. I had to kneel down and ask God for advice. What heathen country would I go to?

'Russia,' I said, without thinking; it was the only heathen country I knew about; they used to preach sermons about it.

'What you say?'

'Russia.'

'You stupid or crazy?'

To my discomfort she insisted on an answer to the question – not of which heathen country, but whether I was stupid or crazy. So, eventually, I said that I was stupid, as craziness would not have been allowed in the family. Then her breathing changed; she was asleep.

During the week, I naturally consulted Horace on my choice of heathen country, and he said there were many countries like America that were heathen, but the best of the lot was China: what they had *forgotten* about heathenness in that country, Russia didn't even begin to know. In a roundabout way I sounded out Professeur Croissant, and he confirmed that the Chinese were serious people. So, China it was.

It was difficult, though, to get to my grandmother; she was worse and, until my mother could arrange to come from town, a woman from the village was now living permanently in our house, and trying to keep me from the sickroom. But I still managed to convey to her that China is where I would go and become a good heathen.

'They have coloured there?'

'Don't know.' I didn't trust Horace enough to say yes.

And she seemed to lose interest. She talked from time to time about her passing on; of not being able to take things with you: 'The Lord taketh away. We are just instruments, after all. Poor vessels at that.' But she returned to our pact.

'And what you will do in that place?'

'Don't know. Study.'

'You determined to study their heathen ways!'

'No no, not study; work.'

'What work you could do?'

'I could look after the goats and . . . Or I could weigh the cotton.'

'No one sending you anyplace to come labourer.'

'No, I mean . . . something really big like . . . flying an aeroplane.'

'Like father like son.'

'Not preaching or anything like that.'

'Don't bring any more disgrace on your poor family,' she said at last. 'They suffer enough.'

And that was the last time I heard her speak.

PART TWO: CRICKET TO THE CHINESE
(30 YEARS LATER)

The on-off, much-planned trip to China – six weeks from Beijing to Xian to Shanghai – would, of course, change the history of the world. I had to avoid ostentation, to lie low and play a waiting game; to cultivate the virtues of patience. Though, towards the end, in Shanghai, sitting night after night in the Peace Hotel listening to 'live' traditional jazz, I couldn't help wondering if I had been set up. Which of the musicians in the seven-person band (the pianist was a woman) would turn out to be the emissary from Mr Bao, his contact from the State Physical Culture and Sports Commission? This obviously was the meeting place for foreigners not in government pursuing diplomacy with the new China; and it was hard to tell who was getting anywhere. Two who seemed to fancy their chances were from the ABC – the Australian Broadcasting Commission. They had come to help the Chinese write more professional radio scripts, and had learned their craft, it appeared, in Papua New Guinea, working for the Department of Primary Industry. They speculated about power struggles in Beijing while they waited; and passed the time drinking and dancing with the Shanghai ladies – more adventurous than their Chinese escorts whom they deserted from time to time, to jazz with the foreigners. Then when the Australians made their 'kill', I couldn't help feeling I'd missed out.

Their man, apparently, had direct contact with (remember the name) Long Xinmin – the man from the Peking Television Studios, and he had a line to the Beijing political hierarchy . . . Now it could all be admitted: no one really believed all that 'radio scripts' stuff: the powers that be wanted to show how far they'd moved from Maoist orthodoxy and were planning a nationwide beauty contest to be called 'Girl of Youth and Elegance'. The Australians, over cognac, reckoned they knew something about that. I couldn't help thinking that my mission was so much more politically reputable that it couldn't fail to find some takers up there where it mattered. One slight irritation was that I wasn't actually staying at the Peace Hotel but at the Shanghai, a much more sedate establishment some distance away; and so I had the sensation of missing the real action, when I went home for the night.

I had been less impatient in Beijing. There, the first stop, it had been possible for me to enter into the spirit of the thing with a raw curiosity, playing the tourist, observing the flatness, the dryness, oh, the straightness of the boulevards and the rows of trees growing alongside them – the endless lines of people working (sitting, sleeping, cooking – and working) at the side of the road; the rush-hour bicycles six abreast, etc. There, everything seemed possible because I was buoyed by the feeling that I was in the vanguard of an idea whose time – as they say – had come. As with Kissinger and Nixon in 1972, sport was the lever; only in Deng Xiao Ping's China, we played diplomatic cricket, not ping-pong.

There I had sat in the Jianguo Hotel waiting for Mr Bao to turn up. I had tried to build up an image of him on evidence gleaned at the hotel: would he be dressed like Peter May, Chairman of the English Board of Selectors, sitting down to breakfast, fastidiously, at the far end of the vast hall with its dozens of round tables laden with what seemed the remains of last night? Or of lunch the day before? Would he censure the waiters, waitresses, like rebellious Gattings, for being so impressively shabby? Or would he commend them for making a political statement in, in effect, *wearing* their Peking duck as part of the uniform? By the time I reached Shanghai this game had begun to get a bit stale, and as I left the Peace Hotel each night I half-expected to bump into Clive Lloyd on his way in (or, perhaps, a military gentleman from Pakistan, associated with cricket) and miss out on the real negotiations. For *their* credentials would not be in question.

Then Miss Wu had introduced herself. She said that though she wasn't Mr Bao, she was acquainted with my situation and would keep me informed of Mr Bao's thinking on the matter. When I asked if she was a member of the State Physical Culture and Sports Commission she said no, but she was a graduate of the No. 18 Secondary School in Qingdao, which was famous for its field and track sports. Three high jumpers in her year had cleared two metres; and she proceeded to tell me how many world and junior championship records Chinese athletes had broken or equalled in the past year.

Was she, I felt I had to ask, interested in cricket?

Everyone, she said, knew that the South African, colonial, racist hold on world cricket had to be smashed. She spoke without anger; indeed, she seemed a bit distracted, anxious to get away. She was delicate-looking, an attractive figure in her very early twenties, wearing a smart plaid skirt, startlingly different from all the other Beijing women wearing loose-fitting trousers. Miss Wu was distracted because she had to double as a tour guide to a group of Americans and Canadians 'doing' China; and she invited me to join the tour while I waited for Mr Bao.

Naturally, I wanted to see Beijing – my first time there; but my real curiosity was to take a good look at the tour group to see if there were any ex-Test players posing as Americans and Canadians. After three days we had done the zoo (and seen the pandas); done the Wall (and reflected how breachable it seemed, even if it could be seen from the moon); done the Ming Tombs (magnificent); the Forbidden City (off T'ien An Men Square, with its portrait of Mao – the only one seen in public in six weeks in China): all that marble in the Forbidden City, marble, marble everywhere (what must it have been like back then; all these halls of harmony and goodness!). We had had our fill of temples and friendship stores – and no Mr Bao. So I decided to spend more time in the hotel doing my homework on China, reading everything from *China Daily* and *Beijing Review* and *Chinese Sports* to assorted English-language publications to do with life in post-Cultural Revolution China.

One night I dreamt about my grandmother materializing to ask me if I was stupid or crazy. Next morning I was sure I was both. I had been sitting upstairs in my room waiting for Miss Wu (who seemed unconscious of the inferences the Americans and Canadians on the tour coach were beginning to draw about the two of us), filling in time writing postcards. On one I had written: *Sitting in the Jianguo Hotel, waiting for Miss Wu. Waw!* Would this get the poor girl into trouble? After all, she wasn't exactly Mr Bao with friends on the Central Committee. But I quickly censored these 'First World' prejudices. The embarrassment about the card was its hint of indelicacy.

Losing interest in the cards, I opened the fridge and reached for a bottle, but decided that at half past eight in the morning, I had to desist: that was the sort of thing people in old films did when they were stranded in the 'East'. Healthier to take a walk. (An odd thing about the hotel, which came back to me as I got out of the lift, was the row of banks on the ground floor: they seemed never to do any business; you never saw anyone coming in or going out of them; it was as if they were just put there to hold up the building.)

A walk at this late hour – 8.30 a.m. – filled me with a sense of my own sloth and bourgeois decadence: the clean-living Chinese had long put in their health stint. I would get up sometimes as early as five o'clock to peer down on them at their *taiji* – in the street. Old people. Middle-aged. Even older people than the old people (though not many of China's youth) shuffling along the pavement to take up their positions. Then, as if to some unheard music, arms loosely outstretched, turning, slowly; arm, leg, neck; bending, stretching, over and over again, so slowly that it hurt to look; no sense of competition – a view of Old China at six o'clock in the morning. Would Miss Wu – the smart, confident Miss Wu whose very efficient English could deliver an Australian joke with something of the accent – would Miss Wu fit into all this? I began to see callisthenics as a sort of public confession of indulgence, an athletic equivalent to the political self-criticism sessions, apparently still in vogue. Could I risk such observations on Mr Bao? Or Miss Wu? Somehow I had the feeling that she had already taken steps not to develop into something arthritic and stiff. And her mouth, at aged seventy, certainly wouldn't have fallen in. She had the most perfect set of teeth I had seen in all Beijing.

*

Mr Bao came one day and looked more like the coach driver than a high bureaucrat; he got my name wrong and was very polite. I was a bit disappointed that he took me to lunch at the hotel where I was staying. However, he briskly signalled that his business was cricket by making a joke about English cricket commentators. I hadn't anticipated this. The joke involved 'the Englishman', Brian Johnston, and his one-upmanship in having chocolate cakes sent to him in the commentary box at Lords, or wherever – supposedly, from the public. I was impressed that Mr Bao had done his homework. He said this attempt by Brian Johnston and other members of the ruling class to show that the English public supported the present set-up of cricket was cynical and flawed.

I asked if he thought that was why England were doing so badly at cricket.

Mr Bao laughed and took a picture from his pocket. We looked at it for a bit while we picked at the ten or twelve dishes of what might be breakfast, lunch or dinner.

'They call it Fred,' he said, to help me out.

It was a bowling machine.

'Ah! I've heard of Fred,' I said, trying to work out just how high up in the State Physical Culture and Sports Commission Mr Bao was. His dress didn't, of course, give out any clues.

'The name of this is Fred,' he said; as if I was missing something.

'Ah, Fred. I see.'

'What is the background?'

I didn't understand.

'The name, in English. What does it represent? From what pedigree has it come?'

I was under-prepared; I'd been learning the names of people on the Standing Committee; or was trying to work out the present line on dissidents – whether people like

Fang Lizhi – 'the Chinese Sakharov' – were in or out; I'd even had a translation of Deng's 1981 paper: *Resolution on Certain Questions in the History of Our Party Since the Founding of the People's Republic of China* checked and annotated. What I hadn't prepared myself for were questions on the genealogy of a bowling machine called Fred. In fact, all I could think of was Fred Trueman, and I didn't want to speculate how his ancestors related to Ming and Tang and Sung.

'I believe Fred is not from a ruling family,' he said at last.

'No, wrong class,' I said.

'Not like Raffles.'

'What?' I was completely taken aback.

'You know, the gentleman burglar. Cricketer.'

'Ah! The um – fellow in the stories.'

'Ernest William Hornung. Went to Uppingham Public School. Was a member of the MCC.'

'I see what you mean by class,' I said.

'The curse of your society.'

'Ah, it might be changing a little now.'

'Class and race: which is worse in your society?'

'Ah. That's a question Confucius could answer.' I was enjoying this.

'Many classes in your society.'

I wasn't going to deny it. I wasn't going to criticize his 'one class' society, either.

'With many classes, you are lucky. Passions run to object quickly.'

I didn't understand.

'. . . without time to get out of control.'

This man was maybe worth listening to. 'I see what you mean,' I said.

So he told me what he meant. He explained that with passions running against objects (i.e. class) everywhere, there was no space left in the society for them to get out of control. I was warming to him.

So, about Fred. Again, we studied the picture of the bowling machine. I held back my thoughts about the merit of bowlers over batsmen as a way to strike at the English class system – the miners from the north, etc., winning out over the public school boys from the south; and let Mr Bao take the initiative. I'd waited for him long enough. At last he said: 'I think we give it a Chinese name.'

'Good idea.'

Then he grew suspicious. 'Do they have Fred in racist South Africa?'

'I believe they have everything in racist South Africa,' I told him. 'Except the obvious.' I didn't let on that I knew about Chinese trade with racist South Africa.

Mr Bao collected his photo and became fatherly. 'You mustn't be despondent,' he said to me and winked. I liked and didn't like the wink. Then he proceeded to tell me a story about an Albanian tennis player. The story was so strange, and at the same time so not unexpected, that it made me feel, stupidly, hopeful.

This is the story about an Albanian tennis player who didn't actually play tennis. The man had started out playing tennis and, having honed his game in the usual way, decided with the help of the Party – and with the thoughts of Comrade Enver Hoxha, then head of the Party – to tune up his game, *ideologically*. At this point Mr Bao actually began to seem inscrutable. He continued in the same vein. The Albanian player studied the effects of competition in sport and realized that this was to take a risk that somehow should be built in; an uncertainty that should be countered by *thought*. So he studied the accidental side effects of the tournament circuit – the fact of travel, of playing on different surfaces, the weather, of different types of ideology informing the umpires, linesmen, ball boys and girls; of the personality of the crowd, etc. And he decided – with the help of the Party and the *Collected Works* of Comrade Enver Hoxha – to counter these things, not by excess of temperament as with players in the West and the Soviet Union, not by luck, but by the purity of thought. In the end the tennis player's preparation was so complete, his mental attitude so correct, that it was deemed unnecessary, even crude, to pit him against an actual, human opponent. So he was simply proclaimed the Tennis Champion of the World.

Mr Bao delivered this without comment; the perform-ance was so finely balanced between joke and revelation I couldn't work out if he was putting down the Albanians (who had long broken, ideologically, with China), or if it was his way of saying that China, liberated from Marxist ideology, could now go one stage further and actually *play* some games of cricket.

When I said, cautiously, that China had more flat land than Albania for cricket, Mr Bao laughed, reached into his pocket, and brought out a review of a book on cricket to which I had contributed.

About three years before I'd given some talks on Radio 3 about the new world order in cricket. (The talks weren't, of course, called that; but a couple of them had been put in the book.) My premise was the uncontroversial one about world cricket breaking up under the pressure of racism. There was the proposed re-entry of South Africa to the international Test arena. The break was going to be along racist but not strictly racial lines. Australia or New Zealand, West Indies and two of the sub-continental sides might be in one camp; Australia or New Zealand, South Africa and the other sub-continental side in the other camp; and England in between unable to make up its mind. A few people were (un)kind enough to write in protesting. Then, out of the blue, I got an invitation to visit a building near Hyde Park to discuss the issue of world cricket. That led to other meetings, at the end of which I was convinced that not only were the Chinese interested in getting into cricket, but they were ready to promote a democratic alternative to the present 'colonial, racist set-up'. This would eventually involve matches in China (hosts), Albania (representing Europe), Iran, Tanzania and Angola, etc., with people dispatched to all these places to study the politics. I, as a privilege, got to go to China.

So, sitting in the Peace Hotel in Shanghai, alarmed that this was week six in China, going over and over in my mind why things had gone wrong in Xian, with the guides and tourists to Qin Shi Huang's Tomb no more than that – my conviction that one of the terracotta soldiers would step forward and hand me a note from Mr Bao, unrealized; and having to settle for a new tour guide telling the same Australian joke that Miss Wu had told in Beijing; and here now in Shanghai having to suffer the confidence – and the cognac, they were generous – of the real Australians of 'Girl of Youth and Elegance' fame, I felt less confident. Old habits began to reassert themselves. I would rescue something from this trip, even if it was just another series of talks for Radio 3. I could say something about jazz at the Peace Hotel; about the lads outside my hotel offering to exchange money for yuan; of the jade and carpet factories I had visited. But this was enough; this was defeatist; this was almost bourgeois thinking. *Think of the Albanian tennis player*.

Now was the difficult part. I was back in London and had to meet some people near Hyde Park to report on my trip. I'd had a meeting with others who had returned from

Tirana, Tehran and other cricket-ready places round the world; and as there were rumours in the press of an impending cricket revolution I feared that some of my opposite numbers had had more success than they were admitting to.

But the difficult part was the night before Hyde Park. This was when I found myself on a train to Upton Park to report to my mother. That's how it felt. She knew nothing about China (as far as I know), or about cricket, or about diplomatic activity; but somehow I felt that she was the nearest thing to what my grandmother had represented when I had promised her to go to China, so that my heathenness wouldn't be punished.

I had confused the family over the years by promising much and delivering little. There had been a few plays performed, here and there; but where was the break-through in the West End? I had taught in various places, without distinction, written this and that, had failed to make any cricket team. When they heard me on the radio even friends said it didn't sound like me. Oh, yes, and where were the wife and children?

So I would have had long practice in my decision to play down China.

My mother was pleased that I had come, because I could collect the present she had been saving for me, as I was out of the country on my last birthday. That led to the sort of chit-chat we were both comfortable with. But it couldn't last. Then:

'Where's Whatsername?' she asked.

I knew who she meant.

'At home,' I said, evasively.

'Your home?'

I pretended not to hear.

'You see her?'

'Yes.' And more strongly, 'Yes.'

And here she sighed. 'You should see her.'

'Ah, well.'

This led to the familiar talk about what I was doing; whether I got paid for the work I was doing; whether I ate the food when I was abroad; whether the people abroad were clean . . . till she drifted off to sleep. Then she woke with a jerk and continued the conversation.

'They play cricket in China?'

'Well, they're thinking about . . . Well, not yet.'

'You not too old for that?'

'Well, I'm not going to play.'

'Cricket is a young man's game.'

'In China fifty is young.'

'You know about cricket?'

'Well, I might change the rules a bit.'

'You have to be careful.'

'When I was in China . . .'

'You went to China?'

'Sent you a card, didn't I? Sent you a card from China. At least two cards. Didn't you get my card from China?'

'I don't remember.'

'Maybe the post . . . Sent you a card of the Great Wall of China. You can see it from the moon. The Great Wall of China.'

'You go to the moon?'

'And I sent you one of the zoo.'

'I don't get any card from that place.'

'It'll come.'

'They have black people there?'

'Only a billion. More than West Indies and Africa put together. But you should have got one card at least. From Beijing. Peking. Had Peking duck in Peking. Beijing.'

'Maybe they throw it away.'

'No, it'll come.' A change of subject. 'Anyway . . . you're looking well.'

'So they say. I still can't find that present, you know. Your birthday present. You never here on your birthday. I lost the present.'

'Ah, I'll get it next time.'

'Next time you not here. You never in one place. Everything get lost.'

'Sorry. Next time I'll be here. Promise.'

I managed to prevent any more reference to Whatsername.

4

Irish Potatoes

I

He wasn't going to dwell on this, this feeling of . . . this wasn't the main part of his purpose here, that would be next week, that would be the Kigali meet . . . meeting. So his conference paper this morning was . . . a preview to the main event. Not that it went down badly, but he had a feeling . . . He snapped shut the book he could no longer focus on reading. Since when was a guide book something you couldn't concentrate on? Granted this was The Brandt Travel Guide doorstop, and he couldn't find the information about Uganda that he was searching for, nothing under 'Ireland' or farming nuns and priests; he needed a break after all that, what? – information about 'Batwa Pygmies' and 'Genital mutilation in Kapchorwa' – important though he suspected it was.

Michael knew he had to snap out of this, for wouldn't they say to him – the mythical *they*; wouldn't they say: your next task is to take on the enormity of Kigali – 800,000 dead in three weeks, the weapons of mass destruction being the bush-knife, the knife, the hoe, the pitchfork, the digging-stick, the axe-handle, the stone, the big stone? Facing that enormity, what is the loss of *one* family far away just because it happened to be yours; and what do you mean by *loss* anyway? Three people dispatched, dispatching themselves without bloodshed, no scars on the body, no blows: calm, civilized, loving words of regret with their – proportional – accompaniment of tears; as if a shadow orchestra were miming the music; making the right gestures to show that some ways of destroying the family are better than others. ('You'll be missing your books more than us.') *No*, he promised himself he'd do better than lapse into . . . if he were writing up his recent life he'd cut out the indulgence.

So, Michael Carrington decided not to feel guilty sitting here missing the next session which the loud-speakers were blowing from the conference room across the way. It was all a blur, of course, he was on the other side of the pool, ground level, and the temptation was to put words in the mouths of the conference worthies. But they were humanists; they would probably be indulgent and absolve him of bad faith.

He felt he had been operating without nuance; he felt others had been operating without nuance: *should Human Rights be nuanced*? Each person here seemed to have understood him differently: either he had fifty or sixty 'understandings' or he was misunderstood. He had posed as *messenger* (with a lower-case 'm', this being a humanist conference) between one group out there, in the diaspora, and people here, at home, so to speak. A trusted messenger was, of course, expected to modify the message to suit the occasion. Either he was making statements that dishonoured Africa or he was the one affirming the right of Africans not to be infantilized; so the thrust of his speech this morning, which was about taking responsibility, was probably lost: was the norm by which the human was measured to be seen as different in Africa, different from in the West? His answer was no, as long as you decided which measurements in the West made sense. And if you got that wrong . . . ? In the Shakespeare play, Cleopatra rained blows down on the Messenger because she didn't like his message. Ah! if only . . .

There was a very fat boy swimming in the pool at the edge of the tables and Michael's first impulse was to disapprove of a boy so fat. And then he thought: why, in Africa, should I disapprove of a fat boy? With the men in power, now that was a different matter; the word for them in the Caribbean was Fatbellymen. Not the case here in Uganda but you see them, these men, on the television, at the international conferences, particularly where aid to developing countries is negotiated. So many Fatbellymen representing under-nourished people. Was irony a Western thing, then? If not an American thing at least a European thing. He would probably pose the question to his American friend at the conference, a lively man who he hoped would calm down a little. The man had one of those one-syllable names which stood for something larger, but Michael had already dubbed him 'Too Sweet', a character from a play he'd heard on the radio, Too Sweet being some sort of jazz-player or dancer doing the clubs in Brooklyn. Too Sweet was wearing another very colourful shirt today, and gave the impression of impersonating either 'An American' or 'An African'. But then he was a black man attending a conference in Africa. Like Michael. And Michael felt that his talk this morning had embarrassed Too Sweet.

He would get a taxi and go into town, into Kampala, maybe change the rest of his travellers' cheques for his trip to Jinja tomorrow, and buy some postcards: if he didn't show some little independence he might be seen as too locked into the conference; and he was here by invitation, not membership; he didn't want to pretend otherwise.

*

He was right to have had the feeling of being upstaged, even by people at the conference; there were some impressive acts on show: he had already identified the secular priest from the century before last, full of goodness and harm, the Peggy Ashcroft character in *Happy Days*, and Too Sweet. The organizer was young and massively but discreetly effective, prompting thoughts of what the country may have lost in Idi Amin's Asian cleansing of thirty years ago – though the man himself was from India not Uganda, and lived in Europe, in Brussels or Switzerland. But Michael couldn't help being impressed by the white-skinned delegates: so it *was* possible to be old and not smug or sour, or an example of selfishness or bafflement. *These* old humanists didn't have to prove anything other than to conduct themselves as they were already doing; anything more was a bonus. Their eccentricities didn't irritate; you could believe they had lived lives of thought and reflection and risk – lives worthy of a Rembrandt portrait, maybe. But here Michael checked himself: he was becoming inauthentic. The painting image was not his own; he had slipped into thinking like his old friend Pewter Stapleton, who had a weakness for this sort of fake imagery. So, even from afar, his friends were keeping him honest.

But he was talking about being upstaged . . .

II

When he got back from Jinja, from the source of the Nile, Michael learned that the police had paid a visit to the hotel, the CID, no less, to talk to members of the conference who were reported to have been encouraging homosexuality in Uganda. The speeches yesterday had done it. There had been something in the day's newspaper to this effect; but no one thought the police would get involved.

(This took precedence over other things that were fresh in his mind, like ways of overcoming the impossibility of using your Mastercard in Kampala and the difficulty of acquiring Ugandan shillings.)

One newspaper, *The New Vision*, living up to its title, probably, had run an article on the humanist conference. They'd got the balance wrong, playing down the broad human rights theme and emphasizing the detail of the delegates' support for gay and lesbian rights; and pointed out the presence of homosexuals – one of whom was named – attending the conference. They had quotes in the paper which the man in question said were accurate enough. How to respond?

It was poor journalism: the title was offensive and the opening paragraph was made up; and the general balance of the argument was wrong; but it got the conference reported. And it was good, in a way, that a subject not normally discussed in public here in Africa – homosexuality – was being given an airing in the national press – alongside headlines about massacres by the rebels in the north, and of the president's doings: yesterday Musaveni had created a new batch of generals, and had approved a new seatbelt law, the law coming about because of the death of a popular government minister in a car accident somewhere outside Kampala. The conference report was on an inside page, but not buried as it faced the comment page, where readers debated whether Musaveni should have a third term, after eighteen years in power, etc. So, how should one react to the misreporting of the conference?

Naturally, the person named as a homosexual or those who had spoken out – including a very impressive woman lawyer from the university (educated in America) who had talked about a woman's right to choose – couldn't get involved and draw attention to themselves. But the organizers would sort it out: naturally the main concern was less for the foreign delegates, than for the Ugandan humanists who might be harassed (or worse) when the foreigners left. Today's follow-up cartoon in the same newspaper had carried a new threat; specifically to this group, daring them to proclaim their homosexuality – a practice banned by law – under the banner of 'human rights' after their foreign 'donors' had gone home. The threat had to be responded to; and Michael was relieved that the conference organizers were quick to take it up; so he wasn't called upon to do anything. He could go back to his private concerns of preparing himself for Kigali, and making himself useful as a sort of roving, unpaid consultant in an African country. Yesterday, at the source of the Nile, outside Jinja, he had drawn up a plan – back of an envelope sort of thing – on how Uganda might gain foreign currency by making others further down the river pay tribute for its waters. Because if the Nile started here, in Lake Victoria, surely the portion of Nile water through Sudan and through Egypt couldn't be divorced from the *source* in Uganda. Not that one wanted to be a water terrorist, as was the case in the Middle East or with Saddam Hussein in his own country, with the Marsh Arabs. But even when there was no punitive intent – as with Spain, say, diverting the waters of the Ebro towards the arid south – there was the ethics to be worked out. Give him a weekend and his laptop. (And why, pray, should Egypt and Cleopatra have appropriated the romance of the Nile at the expense of, what, Nubia?) Michael wanted to distance himself from those Africans in the diaspora who wanted to freeload on Africa, or who were emotionally needy and came to Africa to seek their 'root' – he'd given up his books, dammit, his real *root* – or just those who came to get material for *their* books and films: this was the new Africa-watch.

By the end of the week he had come up with an 'initiative' of producing a catalogue for the National Museum.

He was in a good mood, having had an excellent response to a lecture he had given at Makerere University, lecture and drama workshop. (The whole place had been buzzing: in the afternoon someone – a visiting Malian-American academic and film-maker – had given an outstanding talk about politics and film; politics, aesthetics and film, etc.) The woman who taught drama in the literature department had said that she had a selection of Michael Carrington's plays on her shelf –

'The Pewter Stapleton edition.'

'Pewter Stapleton, yes.'

'An old friend.'

'Ah!'

– and she had been pushing to have one of his plays included on the syllabus, alongside Soyinka and Sembane: now that he was here she would love to pick his brains. She was a slim willowy woman (the term Nubian came to mind), magnificently clothed, with headdress to match; and her questions about 'appropriation' in his writing had to be dealt with, before he went on to talk about adapting Shakespeare.

So some of this must have informed his 'initiative', later, at the museum. He had enquired at the desk for any literature on the exhibits that might be available; and there was none. When he realized the excellence of the collection, the care of display, the knowledge of the guide – a young woman who spoke beautiful English and, during the course of the guided tour, joined the resident musician on the drums: the musician himself playing a stringed instrument, singing – Michael had offered to compile a catalogue for them, in return. It was a desperate gesture – if he were now homeless, he could choose to be anywhere, sort of thing – but it was also buoyed by the exhilaration he felt from the university meeting: it was as if he had crossed some barrier and was beyond being a tourist; he could now do the tourist things without being a tourist. (There was no defensiveness in visiting the Baganda tombs on the edge of Kampala, or the source of the Nile; he even felt he was beginning to talk *differently* to the taxi drivers.) If he had had second thoughts about going on a cruise of Lake Victoria which the conference delegates were organizing for the final day, these reservations now vanished.

III

At the university, at Makerere, he had wickedly sought to drop his old friend Pewter Stapleton in it. It had been a good session where he talked of the early days of making theatre in Britain, the 1950s, then in the Caribbean – putting a black image across, what sort of black image you put across, sort of thing; and he talked them through his own approach to adapting the classics, Chekhov, Shakespeare . . . Just as Soyinka and Mustapha Matura had done. (The Carrington *King Lear* was in the collection that the woman had on her shelf.) He had worked with Pewter Stapleton on other adaptations, notably the *Lysistrata* of Aristophanes, though that one had never come to light. He reminded them of the anti-war theme of that play, where the good women of Athens, led by a Lysistrata in her prime, staged a sex strike against the war that the men were fighting (were losing), spurning the 'eight-inch toy' until the men came to their senses and made peace. In their version, in the Carrington–Stapleton version, the scene was shifted from Ancient Greece to a French provincial town, and the men now were Muslim clerics convicted for using sacred texts to justify the subjugation of women; the punishment was to have a group of moderate Muslim women, with the consent of the state, beat the men till they recanted or died. The play never got to production, and with current developments in the world it might now be too politically hot to handle. Michael couldn't decide whether to charge his collaborator for sensationalism on the one hand or, alternatively, for intellectual timidity in not volunteering *all* religious pranksters to submit to a sound beating.

He had said enough, so he changed tack and talked about the challenge of adapting *Antony and Cleopatra* for a modern audience.

At lunch on the last day – the trip on the lake had been cancelled for some reason – Michael picked up on something he might have done earlier. At the buffet lunch in the hotel garden, two days running, he had passed up on the rice and matoke for the 'Irish potatoes' – partly because of the name.

'Why "Irish" potatoes?'

'That's what we call them. They not sweet.'

'Why not English potatoes?'

'Sometimes we call them white potatoes. Or English.'

'Like in my country. Like my place in the West Indies.' And he had to explain.

He could be back in his childhood Montserrat, on the other side of the world. This wasn't the quirk of one hotel or one clan. At Jinja, at the source of the Nile, they had also offered him Irish potatoes. It was unlikely that this was a sort of general historical prejudice, associating the Irish with potatoes and the memory of ancient famine and migration; so the Irish must have had some connection with Uganda, as they had had with Montserrat.

There had always been talk of African survivals in the Caribbean, and Michael, for a moment, thought of the influence travelling the other way, from Montserrat to Uganda, as the Irish had been in Montserrat since the 1660s, had in fact colonized the place, a fact well documented, not least by Montserrat's leading historian, Sir Howard Fergus. So maybe the book he should be researching was *The Irish Connection in Uganda*, though he was sorry to deprive Montserrat of its singularity as the place where English potatoes were called 'Irish'.

*

Then it was time to write the postcards. He was sitting alone in the new curtained off section of the conference room that was now used for breakfast. Some of the delegates had gone home so there was an end-of-season feel to it all. Even the white cloth on the tables seemed autumny.

Writing postcards was like taking an exam: would cards to the children and a card to the mother assume parity, and hence bad taste? And then there was the *type* of card: nothing too joky on the one hand or too educational on the other to confirm suspicions that this was post-marriage. So you couldn't say: *Done Uganda, done Kampala, off to Kigali. Ciao.* So he put aside the (possible) cards to family and started on his Done Uganda, off to Kigali cards to friends.

He thought his elder daughter – her loyalties not yet shifting – would like a Ugandan stamp. Not the boring one with the athlete, or the one with the bird with the somewhat menacing beak and stern eye; but something more 'made up'. She would be interested in being add-ressed as a grown-up with a reference to the source of the Nile, or even the riddle of the Nile – and something about Cleopatra? No, that would be for her sister.

While he was working this out he dealt with other cards, to people he hadn't seen much of in recent years, to people who had acted in his plays; to friends. This one was to Pewter Stapleton:

Pewter Man,

*Yes, they want me to take power here but what's the
point? Makerere still works. Beautiful woman and
nun (in full habit) guarding the drama shop. Brought
a list of questions to the wise women. Are you
interestingly tattooed? Do middle-aged men of your
acquaintance, as in the West, have stale breath?
What's your view of the handsome Scipio Africanus?
Etc.*

Cheers. See ya. Michael.

(PS: the Police came to tea.)

After that, the real business of writing the cards.

His daughter would have moved on from his own earlier
musings. *Nubia, nubile*: it was good that he couldn't
stretch this image further to the source of the Nile, then to
someone in Cleopatra's court; so even though he was proud
that this child had a structure of thought that acknowledged this type of parenting, he had to ease up, he had to
stop oppressing his own. He'd merely tell her that a couple
of days ago he had dipped his hand, his finger, in the
source of the Nile; and that there was a Russian saying that
if you did that in a river in the Siberian spring, you were
likely to add one year to your life. So, to the mother.

She must wish him less than well, surely. She wasn't a
saint; and he wouldn't have her be a saint. How to atone?
He would have to do something heroic and stupid.
Women liked men doing heroic and stupid things. Like
Jack Hawkins, in an old film. Like Alec Guinness in *The
Bridge on the River Kwai*. He was off to Kigali. That was
heroic and stupid. But they didn't like you to be too
stupid. So stress the heroic. Uganda had a problem in the
north. Go up there and solve it. Like a nineteenth-century

Englishman in funny clothes and with a charmed life. Go up and stay calm amid the frenzy. Go up there and take the man out. One bullet one sword juju one rival bible. He had no gun but one bullet. Collapse of resistance; peace to the region, peace to the . . . peace to Nubia. Nobel Peace Prize. Women.

He would have to explain to her that he wasn't advocating violence. For his new humanist friends would disapprove of violence. Though old George Orwell would have approved. ('Someone's got to go to Spain and kill the Fascists.') Good man, George. Fine woman, Sonia. Now, he would risk a card.

Before that, he wrote another card to Pewter Stapleton with a new thought for the *Lysistrata* – as well as a comment on Too Sweet. Then, finally, a simple card.

Kampala. 29.5.04

Dear x,

Another place. Another part of the world.
Wishing you safe in your part of the world.
You walk through my dreams
(looking good). Do I walk
through your dreams?

Love. M x

PS: they talk of 'Irish' potatoes here.

5

Old Brisket and Madame

'What're we going to be? What're we going to be?' 'What're you going to be?' Hard to tell, they were already gangsters, pointing their guns at me, so I raised my hands in recognition. But they weren't impressed by this.

'*What're we going to be?*'

I glanced round, glanced at the old house which seemed half-deserted, the yard overgrown and patchy in parts, the dwarf coconuts untended, only a dog on the porch keeping watch – and when I answered, it came out of the side of my mouth.

'Gangsters?'

They weren't amused, they weren't even contemptuous; they looked at me, expressionless, and without getting excited about it, shot me at close range, both of them. And when I was down on one knee they said, both of them said, though not together:

'Victims. We're going to be *victims*.' And with that they turned round and walked slowly away; they didn't even holster their guns: they didn't hurry, they walked slowly away, in broad daylight. I couldn't work out their age; twins, certainly, but I couldn't tell whether they were boys or girls; they were in fancy dress, gangster clothes; and they headed towards the house (dragging something dead behind them) – the house that belonged to Old Brisket and Madame.

*

'They must be the grandchildren,' someone in the town said, a few minutes later. I had popped into the Quatre Chemines, the liveliest café in town, that had changed hands since my last visit, for something cool, a drink or ice cream; and was told that I shouldn't be surprised at what went on at Old Brisket's – or rather, at Madame's, particularly now that Old Brisket had passed on, and Madame was – as they say – a law unto herself.

Someone pointed out that Madame had always been a law unto herself.

'It's not the question of kids playing with guns,' I said, hoping that I wasn't over-reacting. 'It's the fact that they weren't *playing*; there was a deliberateness as they shot me. The slowness with which they walked away, for Christ sake, without even bothering to glance back! What if I had a gun concealed on me somewhere, and then shot them in the back?'

'You can't if you're dead.'

I wasn't getting my point across. The children weren't asking you to call them gangsters *when they grew up*. They were already gangsters, that was old hat. 'Victims', that's what they were going to be. *Victims*. These privileged kids.

Someone said that nobody trapped on this little island could be considered privileged.

In the café, people looked at me puzzlingly. 'You've been away too long, Pewter.' Before they got bored with this and turned to other matters someone said: 'Madame's keeping the old frontier spirit alive. Madame's just nostalgic for the old days, the days before she killed Old Brisket. You remember Old Brisket?'

Well, I did and didn't know Old Brisket. If I did, I didn't remember which one he was. There used to be two or three old men of that kind, that class, brown-skinned, with long, unruly hair – what was left of their hair was long and unruly. Except that you confused yourself this way because one image I have is of a full shock of hair, and another is of a few unruly strands; yet there couldn't have been more than two or three men like that in Barville in the 1970s (though those who remembered him from the 1950s would do better). I remember vaguely, visiting, driving along the new development above Barville, and seeing this man, who I took to be Old Brisket, sitting on the porch of a big, old house, scratching his head. I remember it because most of the other houses along there were new, villas. And again, I have an image of a man sitting in the back of a car – this is from the 1950s – one of those little Morris Minors, a man sitting bolt upright in the back looking a bit odd in an open-necked white shirt – no tie – ignored by the rest of the family as they took their Sunday afternoon drive together: was either of them the same man who used to walk past the grammar school tugging at his hair, appearing to pull bits of it out? I didn't remember hearing him *talk*; that's why I can't pinpoint him. That's why Madame was more real to me. Madame even came to our school once to talk about her own 'Family Tree'.

Madame was, as they say in St Caesare, 'something else'. She was held in some quarters to be a figure of fun, or to be crazy; except that to us, children, in the 1950s, she seemed often to be thinking along *our* lines; in fact, she had the knack, if reports were true, of saying in public what we told ourselves in private. Except perhaps when it came to America, then we were ahead of her there. Her name was Finola Brisket. Better known as Madame.

Madame wasn't liked in some quarters because she boasted too much. Some of the adults went even further and said that she 'made things up'. The business, for instance, of her brother in St Kitts, who was a general. That was a case in point, that was plain stupid: where were you going to hide something as big as a general in a little place like St Kitts? If she were going to manufacture a general, surely she should send him to live somewhere big, like Guadeloupe or Puerto Rico or maybe Cuba. (Once, on a Sunday, in order to get out of Sunday school, I dawdled outside Uncle George's house in the village and worked up the courage to ask about Madame's brother, the general. Uncle George – in fact, Great-uncle George – was on the verandah, looking out, on the other side of the house from his friend, Rodney, both of whom had spent much of their lives abroad; and I asked if they had ever run into the general on their travels in Panama or Aruba or places like that, hoping they'd say yes and tell me a story that was more serious than the stuff in the catechism; but in the end I had to go on to Sunday school, disappointed.)

But Madame was right all along, because when the general at last visited St Caesare, in the early 1970s, he was altogether more convincing about his status than his sister had been on his behalf. His early campaigns, he said, with an impressive recall of place names in two languages, were in Haiti and in the Dominican Republic; he had fought, as a young man, in the famous Massacre River campaign of 1937 – on the Haitian side, of course. But as he was not a Haitian national – he had neglected to get the papers sorted out – he was at risk from both sides. He had been acclaimed general by the remnants of his army, that weekend on the river; his was the only contingent that had not only stood and fought but had made repeated sorties into the ranks of Trujillo's murderous madmen, the only successful engagement on this side of what came to be known as the Persil War (Parsley in English; *Perejil* in Spanish). But back in Port-au-Prince, the Haitian government was so ashamed of its performance, its failure to support the valiant workers and immigrants fighting its cause on foreign soil, that the one successful general – General by Public

Acclaim – had had to choose between civil war and exile. Naturally, as a man of honour, a St Caesarean of good family, he chose the latter. It had taken thirty-three years and a change of government to get him officially reinstated. Of course a military man of his rank was always going to be a threat to governments in these islands, so he kept a low profile, ending up in St Kitts, pretending to be something else. (He was saying this in the 1970s when he no longer had to keep a low profile; he could wear his military coat again, and people could call him General openly as he walked down the street. He would nod in appreciation, and if he was in a particularly good mood he might even permit you to 'Stand easy. *PRESENT* ARMS. Stand easy'. Behind his back they called him Persil; but when he visited the schools and talked to them about 'discipline, DISCIPLINE' and the 'Lessons of Adversity', etc., it was always 'The General'.)

So that was the general. Now, of the children, Madame's children, one son was a doctor, one daughter was a scientist working for the UN and another son taught at Oxford, in England – though, it might be accurate to say, not at the university. Only one child (of those who survived) fell through the net, so to speak; and it's unnecessary to focus on him. Anyway, he found a nice woman to give him children, so that worked out OK. (The doctor was called Francis.)

A couple of other children had died in infancy and Madame was blamed for that, and had to take herself to bed (the first time for *two and a half years* and then again for six months) – though, it is rumoured, that's not all she did – to avoid the worst. But Madame had long survived – as the smarter grammar school boys used to say – her credibility problem.

Her method worked. We were all at school over in Montserrat, then, when she made Francis, her first son, a doctor, years and years before Francis qualified as a doctor. Say it took seven years to become a doctor in those days; well, Madame made Francis call himself Doctor a good seven years before the *start* of those seven years. And now Francis was a perfectly good doctor practising in some hospital in the north of England. It stood to reason that if you've been called a doctor virtually all your life (with people, in the end, beginning to approach you with their minor ailments as you walked home from school) there would have to be something *wrong* with you, after all that, to bring humiliation and shame on your family, *not* to qualify as a doctor. After all, they weren't asking any more of you than any leader, any president or king anywhere in the world asked of his own children. No one says of a king's son: I wonder if the boy wants to be king when the old man goes? No one says: maybe we should just wait a little while, see how it goes, see if he passes his exams, see if he's not better suited to the *ballet*, or to running a Chinese restaurant, than being king. And the world has proved, more or less, that succeeding to the role is not a difficult thing to do, if you put your mind to it – *and have someone like Madame to help you deal with the opposition.*

Now, to ask a boy to be a doctor, a boy who is already in school, is not an unreasonable thing to do. Particularly in a place like St Caesare, where people might give you custom out of loyalty, even if you failed the exam. And people had now, after maybe a little scepticism, come round to the view that Madame was right about the children all along (for the two that had died in infancy might well have died anyway, crossing the road, or eating bad food, or through obeah).

The children, as we say, were all right; it wasn't the children whom people were sorry for; it was Old Brisket, a mild man who was forced to suffer openly, before finally he couldn't take it any more, and just sat down on his porch, and started to scratch himself in public. Can you blame him, they say: it was bad enough that the first child, Doctor Francis, wasn't his. It's one thing having a doctor son who isn't a doctor, you could live with that; but having a son that wasn't your son – that must have been difficult.

Madame had never hidden the fact of who did or didn't belong to whom. It had all happened, she told those who needed to know, when she was a woman young and free and had set off to broaden her horizons, and to meet with royalty into the bargain, and that sort of thing. As you would imagine, it would be said on the islands that it wasn't her 'horizons' that Madame had ended up broadening; and that it wasn't even likely that she would succeed in meeting royalty as her Grand Tour had taken her first to Guadeloupe, then to wherever it was that her brother, the general, was in hiding before St Kitts, and finally to France. And you will note that this was a long time after 1789 (or 1793) when French royalty were themselves more or less in hiding – or worse. Anyway, Madame came back to St Caesare, a *Madame*, with young Francis (who maybe wasn't a doctor yet), and married Old Brisket (who wasn't old then), a man of good family who was something of an accountant or book-keeper, keeping books or accounts for the big companies in Montserrat and the warehouse owners in Barville; a respectable man who wore a tie to work. But Madame wanted everyone to know from the start that Brisket wasn't doing her any favours in marrying her, Francis or no Francis; and that she would make Francis a doctor while he was still at school to show that her own pedigree (with a general in the family) was second to none. Because when you came down to it, a job adding up other people's figures was no big thing, particularly when you got the sums wrong, as Brisket sometimes did; though when you were an accountant or a book-keeper, you got to know people's secrets, and that protected you in the end; because they couldn't sack you, however many times you got the sums wrong.

We, as children, had no problem with these things; they seemed normal enough. Madame wasn't doing anything to her children that our parents weren't doing to us – and we didn't aim to be book-keepers or accountants, either. No, it was the intimate side of the Briskets' life that fascinated us. First of all there was Madame's brooch. She wore a *frog* on her blouse. The crappo sprawled, legs spread, climbing up the woman's left breast as if they were man and wife: if you watched it closely you could see it *move*. And the frog was in *gold*, which made it worse: it was known throughout the island that Madame could go wherever she liked night and day, do what she liked, and no one could lay anything on her because she was *protected*. It was even said – and more than one servant would swear to it – that in the days when Madame and Old Brisket used to do their business, their man and wife business, Madame used to transfer the frog from her breast to a little golden chain round her neck, and that the poor man, Old Brisket, had to perform on the woman and frog *together*, right there in her own bed. And that was before the man started to sit on the porch, scratching himself in public.

I made an excuse to visit Madame again. She seemed in good shape and was relaxed: some old people were never as old as you thought, really. Maybe she was only about twenty years older than me. From inside she had called the dog to order, and the dog had a perfectly normal sort of name, though I can't remember it now. Madame asked me which branch of the family I belonged to and I told her; then she asked which of the children I was. When I told her, she said she remembered my brother. And I accepted the offer of a snack.

'You just missed Neighton,' she said, 'and the children. They shouldn't be long. Neighton is in hiding from some bad people.'

Noting my surprise she said, 'Oh, there's lots of bad people around. You remember Neighton?'

Only vaguely, but we talked about Neighton. Then she turned the conversation back to me: was I a doctor or a lawyer or a professor?

Surprised at the abruptness of the question I stumbled; and said yes, without specifying which one.

'Everyone who come out here from England is a doctor or a lawyer or a professor.'

It sounded like an accusation, and then I realized that it *was* an accusation. She said it was a bit rich for those of us who had had the advantage of living abroad, and being put through schools where they spoon-fed you; and even when you failed your exam they passed you anyway, because the government had to have its statistics just so; and whether you could add up or not you got your maths; and you got your chemistry and your German and whatnot; and of course at the universities it was the same thing: the government ordered them to admit everybody, whether they had one eye or one brain cell and couldn't use a knife and fork. In all these years she had hardly come across anyone coming out from England who wasn't a doctor or a lawyer or a professor; the few who weren't doctors and lawyers and professors had all been in leading positions in their companies and had armies of people working under them; and the government was busily offering them this or that title which, out of modesty some of them felt they had to decline. And it was people like her, now – though she didn't count because of her age, but people like her grand-children, never mind poor Neighton – who were the under-privileged in this world.

So I apologized for my condition of privilege and

thanked her for the drink and the cake; and wondered if it was rude to take my leave so soon.

'Expect you've been to Africa,' she said.

I said, 'Yes.'

'Now, there's a continent of privilege.' And she told me about the privilege of Africa. For people liked to talk of deaths and starvation and this and that in Africa; but when you looked at it almost everyone who survived those first few years had a chance of getting to the top and becoming a general or a president with a Swiss bank account. Not like the old days in this part of the world where a General had to know what's what to become a general; and then to have to go into hiding for his pains. And more. And more.

As I was leaving I saw the two child soldiers returning, pulling the carcass of something they had killed: it was a dead weight and I tried not to look at it; but I heard Madame first praise them, and then ask them to take it outside the house.

6

On the Death of C. J. Harris

I

The incident with Pilate would have to be worked in somewhere. Pewter Stapleton tried not to see this as a chance to be seized – writing a friend's obituary, sort of thing; though there could be no sense of satisfaction in having outlived an older man. No, the risk was of appropriating the event, a lapse in taste. C. J. Harris was very much older than Pewter, a man of a different generation, so that was OK. And in this case Pewter would be doing something that needed to be done, talking about the man, thinking about him, *writing* about him; and as a result bringing a certain visibility to a remarkable life that had been lived, if you like, *invisibly*. Pewter had a very clear image to start with; it was of Pilate, the barber, in the yard in Coderington in front of his little house cutting CJ's hair. It would be a Sunday morning and neither Pilate nor CJ would be going to church, Pilate because he was deaf and dumb and it would be no point his going to church if he couldn't hear what was going on; and CJ because he was anti-Christ. CJ used to tell them that long ago, over there in Europe, they used to have a Pope in the Roman Catholic Church who was anti-Christ; and because this man was so rich and brazen, and also because it was in Europe, you didn't need to be afraid of things you couldn't see; so this Pope used to boast about being anti-Christ till he ended up calling himself Antichrist, written with a capital A, a sort of new title to vie with the old Christ. Only in these backward places like St Caesare people didn't know how to pull these things off and that's why you saw them dressing up, dressing up and flocking to church on Sunday, come rain come shine, and having to walk back home in the hot sun after the minister did his foolishness from the pulpit. So, on a Sunday, as Pewter and his brother and sister with their mother walked past CJ's house on their way to church – whether CJ was inside the house at the window looking out or whether he was sitting under the tree in the yard having his hair trimmed by Pilate – there was likely to be a 'good-humoured' exchange with Pewter's mother, which was worth quoting.

'So, Mrs Stapleton, you all going to church to stock up on the goodness of Christ?'

'Don't listen to him,' the mother would hiss, out of the side of her mouth; and she would pick up her stride, so the children had to hasten to keep up.

'Mrs Stapleton, I hope you not badmouthing me there to the children.' And Pilate would say something in his private language and adjust CJ's head, and continue the clipping.

'No harm meant, Mrs Stapleton, no harm meant,' CJ would shout above the laugh, though his head now would be turned a little away, under Pilate's direction; and it's only then that the mother would utter under her breath: 'Jackarse.' And the children were supposed not to hear the swear word; so they couldn't react to it openly.

And maybe on the way back from church, if CJ was at his window looking out, he would apologize to the mother; and she would ask him if it was he or the rum that was talking; and would say to no one in particular, that some people in this place love canejuice too much; and she didn't hold with people who called themselves teachers and who were slaves to the canejuice – she didn't hold with them pretending to stand up in front of the class and set a bad example to other people's children. And CJ would say that yes, she was right, Mrs Stapleton was right, the spirit was willing but the flesh was weak (a phrase he would repeat); but never mind that, never mind that; and would she like to come in for a minute with the children for a glass of water or something cold to drink, after the long walk; before the climb up the hill?

And sometimes the family would go into CJ's house for a few minutes, for the shade; and have a drink.

*

Michael Carrington, sometime colleague, friend, rival of Pewter Stapleton, would end up doing the eulogy for C. J. Harris – even though he didn't yet know that the man had died. Carrington is en route to Africa and hasn't heard the news. His mind is switched on to another wavelength. If asked he would deny that he was going to Africa. Carrington was from the island of Montserrat in the Caribbean and lived mainly in Britain and America. Though his present address was Trieste, Carrington was, if you like, the island's leading dramatist. He was, by his own admission, at a low ebb, having lost his family (or, his family having lost him, depending on who you spoke to), and was, so they say, turning to Africa as a form of therapy. Michael would put it differently: he was shifting his thinking up a gear, so that he could bring in the intellectual thing to balance what he hoped was a temporary malfunctioning in his emotional running order.

So he rejected the notion of Africa and tried to focus on the particular country in question, which was all, he said, a man from a small island was permitted to do; for who could have the temerity to take on Africa's fifty-plus countries and maybe 800 million people. He started, idly, to draw some analogy of identifying Africa country by country with Aristotle's approach to the *Laws*, an empirical rather than rationalist project, but soon lost the thread of it.

So he wouldn't fall into the trap of all those other fellows whom we all know, who got up on their moral soapbox about Africa, about colonialism colonialism colonialism and the rest. Or, on the other side, those who came with their pre-packed questions: why are you into denial about Aids? Why aren't you allowing your women to do this and that? What about the child soldiers? And what about the institution of President for Life?

Well, he was off to a country in Africa which didn't have a President for Life. So when he got there he could risk talking straight, and no side needed to patronize or lie to the other. He'd done his homework, had his UN and World Bank statistics and knew this country wasn't doing so badly, all things considered. And he was trying to find a way of talking about those other areas where they weren't doing so well, without being a boorish guest or without putting himself at unnecessary risk. So, all in all, he was satisfied that *this* African country he was about to visit was – if this were a track race – all kitted out and on the starting line; they'd got through the preliminaries: when the pistol went off, the runners would be ready.

II

In Sheffield Pewter Stapleton had convinced himself that he would be asked to deliver the C. J. Harris eulogy; so he was already mapping out the lines of argument. (i) *CJ as atheist-savant.* (ii) *CJ as philosopher-historian.* (iii) *CJ as seminal writer.* He felt he knew better than others how to speak to this agenda.

CJ had actually taught him in the little school in Coderington and was therefore tolerated – though distrusted, because of the drink, and because of his godlessness – by the family. CJ was the adult who told them about the world *out there*; he had the trick of slipping foreign phrases into his conversation, and not always translating them. Of course his detractors hinted that the phrases were just made-up words, nonsense; so even when he translated, you didn't know if the translations fitted.

'*Souviens-toi du vase de Soissons.* Remember the vase of Soissons' – that he would translate.

And now Pewter could imagine talking to him decades later; visiting him in the Home on the island. On the last visit CJ was already past his eighty-ninth year, and Pewter was writing a memoir about growing up on the island, contrasting growing up there in the first part of the 1950s with growing up in London in the second half of the decade; and going to school in both places. And the two great teachers he would profile (for you had to have great teachers in any memoir of growing up), the two great teachers were C. J. Harris of Coderington, St Caesare, and Mrs Yetton of Kilburn, London. (Yetton, he planned to be less kind to than CJ, maybe because Yetton had accused him, all those years ago, of not being able to appreciate Jane Austen's irony; that was after he had written an essay in the A-Level class hammering *Emma* (or, more accurately, Emma); after which it was impossible not to focus on Yetton's facial hair, and then that was just a short step to associating her with her nearest neighbour in the Himalayas, the yeti; so that they became in his mind, interchangeable – Yetton, yeti – and in his memoir a composite creature emerged, called the Yetton, *the Yetton*.)

So there he was visiting CJ in the Home: CJ's in bed wearing designer socks (he's had a stroke but he's wearing designer socks; *that's the measure of the man*), and they're talking about this and that; about the madness of England (of which CJ approves), about the christianizing of black people (of which CJ disapproves), and of the sorts of people from the community, both here and abroad, who could properly make it into fiction, and those on the other hand who would have to settle for the carnival – carnival on the street or carnival in the church. And finally, CJ and Pewter would be talking about a book they could both agree on: *War and Peace*.

He's had it on tape, CJ says, but he likes to have visitors read bits to him and hear how they stumble over the Russian names, for if you could say Nikita Sergeyevich Khrushchev and Eduard Ambrosyevich Shevardnadze why couldn't you get your tongue round easy names like Anna Pavlova that had been around for over a hundred and thirty years. Pewter is thinking of whether West Indian cricketers presently in England were more likely to make it into fiction than to the Notting Hill carnival. But he's also thinking, looking at CJ lying there in his designer socks, of the old perverse Prince, whatsisname, Bolkonsky, on his estate miles outside Moscow, doing his carpentry and his joinery and whatnot. (For everything is contemporary to a man of eighty-nine: you are present at the incident with Clovis and the fifth-century vase, just as you are out there with Tolstoy's reclusive Prince Bolkonsky, still clued up on what was going on in the world of Napoleon. He relates to the Old Man.) In the book Andrei, come to drop off his wife before going off to the army, can't figure out how his father is so up-to-date with this information. *The dad is so up-to-date with his information because* we *supply him with that information.* And yes, it would depend how the boys do this summer in England against Mike Atherton's men whether they deserved to be put into fiction or to take to the streets in funny clothes.

So if this scene were happening now Pewter would have

to scan the day's headlines for an update: the fraud Milo-sovic in the Hague pretending to be too ill to attend his war crimes trial; or he would be lamenting Portugal's loss to Greece in Euro 2004 – defeat of the artists to the seven-foot-high spoilers stonewalling in defence; and of course, he and CJ would touch on Sharapova, the six-foot-tall, seventeen-year-old Russian model defeating Serena W. at Wimbledon ('She don't fraid the father; losing like that? I would fraid that man, you know!'); and then the talk would come back to West Indies' chances in England this summer against (this time) Michael Vaughan's bits 'n' pieces men. (And how good, really, was Flintoff?)

At some point before Pewter's departure CJ would tell the story again of the foolish Clovis, King of the Franks – bright enough man but made foolish by his conversion to Christianity – Clovis, who was so mad when one of his soldiers stole something from the bishop who converted him, some little vase, that when he later came across the villain – that is, the soldier not the bishop, a man named Soissons – when Clovis came across the villain he took out his sword and split the man's head in two with the immortal words we now like to quote: *Souviens-toi du vase de Soissons*.

Pewter would have to find a way of bringing this up in the eulogy.

*

But this wasn't a race; the idea of standing in line was foolish. He was thinking of a conversation he had had last time he was here: he hadn't acquitted himself well. He came on as the inquisitor, the man from the West with a mind already set: *So why are you in denial?* And he had to be told, and was embarrassed to have had to be told:

'There might be reasons that we could give you, but you're not interested in them, because you've already made up your mind that I am – that the whole continent is – in denial. So those things that I might say to you will be brushed aside, won't be heard; so why should I bother to say them? And you will think because I don't say the things you want to hear, they're never on my mind. So, be my guest, my brother from the 747.'

III

Pewter was not going to sulk or feel hard done by; for someone didn't die just to give you an opportunity to preen; and he had to accept that he wasn't the one to give the Eulogy. He had got on to them on the island, the family, and they were fulsome in their thanks that he had rung; and seemed genuinely delighted when he said he was planning to come to the funeral; but that didn't lead to an offer to participate; instead she said, the woman on the phone said: would he by any chance know how to reach Michael Carrington; for it would be nice to have Michael, if he were around, to come and say a few words on her father's behalf. Just like that. And Pewter said he thought Carrington was in America; then he relented and gave his friend's Trieste number.

His depression – which he denied was depression – lifted when he realized that they had chosen Carrington over him because Carrington was the safe choice. Fearless, iconoclastic Carrington was held to be safer than bookish Pewter; and that was compensation enough for Pewter. He hadn't worked it out but he could be said to have an agenda, and they would know it. He more than suspected that they were already in the process of rewriting CJ's life; they would end up *christianizing* him before he was buried. And they couldn't be sure that Pewter would play along: *hence the call to Carrington.*

Pewter wondered if he, too, had been underselling CJ,

the way he had been thinking of him: all that high camp stuff about Clovis of the Franks, and Tolstoy's *War and Peace*.

That was literary bullshit; that was his idea of how to report CJ's table talk. That was almost to deny that a man of eighty-nine, dependent on helpers, old and in pain, still managed to hold on to his atheist's faith. It was as if he were turning CJ into a mere stage baddy to frighten the children: he would revisit the scene, these scenes. That last time, for instance, at the Home, just before they were struck by the 'hurricane'.

They were having the usual banter about this and that, about life after the volcano on the island, of the loss of the libraries; of the malice of nature rendering everyone on the island *democratic* in their lack of reading matter. Then, there was the talk about the success of black religious sects in England, all encouraged by a clever government in order to keep control: they even allowed the sects to call themselves 'communities', for heaven's sake. That's why CJ could never live in England: he would want more social depth in his community, etc. – all usual themes of CJ's. So visitor and resident were at this familiar play when they were struck by the hurricane.

This came in the shape of a woman bustling and announcing her presence. Though she halted, surprised to see Pewter. She'd been dropped off by somebody Pewter didn't see, someone who had roared away as if he were of a different generation. The woman, panting, said it was good to see Pewter and asked about his family in England: apparently, she prayed for them and wished them safety and good health. So Pewter thanked her for that.

So, she was a bit pressed for time today, she just came to say a few words from the Good Book to this old man here who was still pretending to turn his back on God. But God is not fooled. And she turned to CJ.

'God is not fooled, Maas Clarence, innit?'

CJ's eyes were closed.

'Like I say, Maas Clarence. The Lord is not fooled.'

'I hear you.'

'You hear me, Maas Clarence?'

'Nothing wrong with me hearing. Nothing wrong with my hearing.'

And to Pewter she said: 'The Lord is not fooled.'

'So Skerrit not coming in?'

'He have to go and fill up the car. And he come back for me. He don't have time today. No, sir, the Lord is not fooled.'

'So if you goin pray, you better pray and get it over and done with.'

'The Lord is merciful.' She turned to Pewter. 'The Lord is merciful. Or some people would be dead, dead long time now, innit? He keeps sinners alive for a purpose: I tell you that that man there can't dead till he repent. He giving them time to repent. That's His purpose.' And with that she launched into a prayer.

The two men listened in silence (with Pewter thinking that if God kept you alive until you repented; and you refused to repent, and therefore got to stay alive for ever, then that was the best argument for God that he had ever heard). Meanwhile, the woman was praying, and when she had finished praying she said Amen, and CJ said Amen, and Pewter said Amen.

'The Lord is merciful,' she said again.

'We've had all that,' CJ said, dryly.

'I not going to argue with you today, Maas Clarence. I just want to pop round the corner and say hello to Miss Becca, see how she doing. So I going say goodbye now. Mister Stapleton. Maas Clarence, I go see you soon. Praise the Lord.'

'I here. I'm not going anywhere.'

When she had gone Pewter commiserated with CJ: it must have been hard to suffer this sort of frustration.

'No, it's not hard.'

'I mean, people who won't take no for an answer.'

'Easy, man. I occupy myself when they start talking their talk. Sometimes I listen to see if they getting it right. If they start to misquote I don't bother with them.'

Pewter was intrigued: *getting it right?*

'She a regular visitor?'

'Oh, Chrissie. Chrissie harmless, man. She just trying to forget that she still have big breast and don't know what to do with them, any more. Big breast seem to give these women a lot of frustration.'

Pewter wondered how normal it was for an eighty-nine-year-old man to be thinking about big breasts. He recalled a poem about breasts written by Frank Collymore, the Barbados man of letters, some time ago – and Collymore must have been in his eighties then.

But CJ seemed to have fallen into a sort of reverie.

'When she overdo it I don't mind Chrissie,' he continued without prompting. 'You just have to close your eyes and think of Chrissie up there in the pulpit. One of those, what I call Leviticus women. Always quoting Leviticus: "And you shall count seven weeks of years, seven times seven years, so that the time of seven weeks of years shall be to you forty-nine years," and all that kinda foolishness. Either that or Leviticus 20. Man lying with his father's wife, and man lying with man instead of woman and all that sort of thing. I don't bother with Chrissie.'

And maybe that's where Pewter was thought to be suspect; being too determined to make something of these scenes: though he didn't see what was wrong with that one with Pilate, the barber – should he be asked to say a few words. He had gone public, but then so had Carrington. That night, in his borrowed villa, Pewter had started turning

C. J. Harris, still living, into fiction, really, to rescue him from the family, from Chrissie. The WOMAN, naturally, played a part, came in to do her Leviticus. At which point CJ (OLD MAN) promptly switches off and starts reciting to himself the opening paragraph of a well-known novel, maybe *Pride and Prejudice*, then on to some Shakespeare, maybe the food of love speech from *Twelfth Night*, and ending up with something American and out of the side of your mouth. Dashiell Hammett. *The Big Sleep*. Not *The Big Sleep*, it was *The Thin Man*:

I was leaning against the bar in a speakeasy on Fifty-second Street, waiting for Nora to finish her Christmas shopping, when a girl got up from the table where she had been sitting with three other people and came over to me.

Amen.

She was small and blonde.

Amen.

Amen.

Amen.

At which point CJ would say something writerly. How about: *Isn't she exquisite? And how she carries herself! For such a young girl what tact, what finished perfection of manner! It comes from the heart. Happy the man who wins her!* etc.

Maybe this – portrait? – was too funny; maybe this wasn't funny enough.

*

The lights are out on the plane, but Carrington's eyes are open. He can't sleep on planes at the best of times; and this isn't the best of times, as he thinks he might have handled things differently, back there. The sinking feeling comes from the consciousness that he's now facing the other way: mission completed but not accomplished. He rather liked the taxi driver from the hotel. Young man, thickset, like one of those West Indian fast bowlers who didn't quite blossom at Test level, someone like Wayne Daniel. (Nice touch, calling your son Wayne, John Wayne's masculinity turned round, made feminine.) But the African, whose name was Sam, wouldn't be typecast in this way. Carrington's head didn't hurt but this thinking wearied him; yet he wouldn't succumb to the temptation to turn on the light, and read.

Hours and hours and hours later; a glass of water and a glass of orange juice from the people at the back, later; a visit to the loo, later, and what can he do but count sheep in his own way?

So, he is rewriting an old scene, substituting for the Caribbean comic turn an African, by name of Sam. The scene is the one in which our Memory Man (no skills, the employer recognizes, no credit to his London school) nevertheless proves himself an asset to a gang up to no good. He can remember numbers numbers numbers, upwards of two hundred and fifty numbers; combinations of numbers, numbers of all kinds, which would let him into this building, that building, however securely locked. And the big scene is where the gang boss tests this possible new recruit. After the viva they drive him off into the night and dare him to get into one of those locked buildings. Then another. And a third. They are all nothing-much buildings, or buildings with nothing much. Schools. Libraries. A mosque. Nothing is stolen. It's just a demonstration of something strange in the West Indian psyche: *we can do it if we want, but we don't really want.* It is this scene that Carrington is rewriting on the plane home. For the West Indian, substitute the African, Sam. So, instead of playing the fool – take this man of hinterland, who can imagine himself standing in the middle of his own place, and can sense hundreds of miles of land in front of him, and the security of territory on all sides, beyond the horizon, as if he doesn't need to be armed; *as if in a sense he's armed.* This memorizing of numbers has to have a point; so the owners will know, the enemy will know, the country will know that the building has been entered. *Sam is serious. Sam is a skilled driver. Sam is serious-minded in company. Sam's face gives nothing away at the too large tip. Carrington feels he must turn the plane round and go back and resolve things with Sam. But he can't turn the plane round; he's not even armed. You're not allowed to be armed these days. You are disarmed. Disarmed.*

He got up.

7

A Pigeon in the Fishpond

I

Someone said – at an early stage of this story – that the title was too cryptic; that this was another story about the death of C. J. Harris; or one concerned with the jostling for position by the two main characters, Michael Carrington and Pewter Stapleton. Or even – given its setting – that it was just an opportunity to sound off about the trip to Budapest.

And, yes; it *is* set in Budapest, and the more knowing remarks about that city – comparing the 'residential' aspect of Buda to the more bustling Pest – need to be toned down, though one might retain the name of the odd bridge across the Danube. And what about Messrs Carrington and Stapleton?

In one version the shorthand for them was the Native and the Tourist, but the attempt to send up Carrington's pretence of knowing the city and Stapleton's frank admission of being a tourist scavenging for 'material' became too strained, and increasingly blurred the distinction between the two characters. So, in the end, they reverted to being Michael Carrington and Pewter Stapleton, playing themselves, if you like.

And the interesting thing is that these comic characters managed to serve their purpose of providing the jokes without entirely trivializing what others have said was the subject of the story – the death (or the burial service) of C. J. Harris on a tiny island in the Eastern Caribbean. When the new title, 'A Pigeon in the Fishpond', was suggested, both characters could be held to agree that this was a good way of deflecting undue reverence from the kind that death and funerals are bound to impose – not least on a dead man who would, if he knew, have scorned the notion that his life had had significance. So Carrington and Stapleton raised their glasses, though neither man spoke the toast.

They were sitting in an outdoor café/restaurant in Budapest, on the Buda side of the river. The detail of sparkling water in one glass and red wine in the other registered with Pewter; and that connected with another thought which led to a process which gradually took the story away from Michael Carrington, so that this version would end up as Pewter Stapleton's take on the story.

So Pewter is the one sitting facing the river; he is on his third glass of red wine because his doctor, unlike Carrington's, hasn't yet diagnosed diabetes; and in looking over at Pest, his glasses off to demonstrate the success of his cataract operations, Pewter knows he must play down this points victory; so he forces himself to take in the surroundings, the traffic along the main road, the yellow toy-like tram rattling and grinding now one way (up), then the other way (down), like a relic amid the wheeled traffic, creating a shadow barrier between them and the strangely quiet Danube. He's beginning to name things; he is the tourist. The café is called Angelika Kávéház and it's on Batthyány Tér ('Tér' meaning Square). Over on the Pest side of the river is the ornate – and rather splendid, by the looks of it – parliament building, which he'd probably visit. It was there – middle of the afternoon, at the Angelika Kávéház – that Pewter renamed the story 'A Pigeon in the Fishpond'.

*

At the side of the table where they sat was a little fishpond with a few red and pink fish moving about; and a pigeon lighted on one of the stepping stones, and was having a drink. (It was a hot day.) Neither man might have noted this but for the fact that at the next table sat a Bulgarian princess elegantly at work. She was, as it turned out, judging a poetry competition in English, and a sudden gust of wind blew a few of her poems into the fishpond. The men – and an American woman (with her partner) at another table – rushed to the scene to rescue the poems. This was when Carrington began to lose a grip on the original story, for the American woman's gesture made him think he must be more charitable towards characters like her; and that immediately had him imagining her in situations other than this; and that gradually drew him away from the story that Pewter was pursuing – that of the other woman sitting down again dabbing at her wet poems. The association he now found was with an early John Updike story about a Bulgarian princess, a little book that Pewter had read maybe thirty years ago and liked at the time, but couldn't remember clearly except for the suspicion that the princess was made up. And this princess, who was English and brown-skinned and beautiful-voiced and beautiful-featured, seemed real enough.

Naturally, the flight of poems into the pond had occasioned the flight of the pigeon; a matter of less significance now than the princess sitting in the sun in the café sipping still water with her back to the Danube. Princess (summery top showing off the tones of her skin) judging a poetry competition in English: this seemed more fitting a narrative on a day like this, than the old story of the death and burial of C. J. Harris.

*

So, where are we? This being Pewter's story now, Carrington will be seen from the outside, and in another tense. Carrington had come back from the C. J. Harris event in the Caribbean; and surprised Pewter by revealing that he had been living in Budapest – since his separation from his family, who were still in Canada. Pewter's last address for Carrington had been Trieste (Joyce's city): a man clearly on the move. But it was from Budapest that Carrington had invited Pewter to visit an art exhibition of their mutual friend, Leon da Firenze, the first in Eastern Europe. Carrington's interest in fine art was new to Pewter; but the artist in question was someone they would both wish to promote.

'Is whatsername coming? Celia.'

'Madame Celia. Of course.'

Celia was the artist's cousin, in charge of his estate. (Da Firenze had committed suicide.) She lived in Kilburn, in London, and was said to be busily creating 'lost' da Firenzes.

Both men tried to sound neutral about the artist's cousin.

Pewter said he didn't mind her, really. He wished they all had someone like that, like Celia, to protect their literary or professional interests. Though it seemed vaguely odd to him, the prospect of three Caribbean exiles getting together in Budapest, on an art mission that none of them knew much about. It crossed his mind that that was a fun way to give old C. J. his send-off. Curiously fitting: the work of the artist who had died young, to mark the end of a committed atheist – one who had lived on into his nineties, both signalling the pointlessness of it all – paintings floating in space, light and guiltless.

Pewter was being put up (and very elegantly, too) at the parent Art'otel just a few blocks down, on this side of the river, near the Chain Bridge. Carrington, too, was staying in Buda, in an ornate, 'period' establishment with marble pillars in the foyer and American voices in the café/restaurant, what, four, five stops down on the tram.

There were massive thermal and leisure baths next to that hotel and Carrington said he could recommend the massage. At the mention of massage Pewter summoned up the Bulgarian princess, but dismissed the image as . . . too close to raiding someone else's goods.

Pewter was pleased to think that this was how they did things in the new Eastern Europe, the hotel turned into an art gallery. The renovation was imaginative: a group of buildings of different style and period – including two or three two-storey cottages with balconies – was incorporated into the grand design, forming a couple of courtyards, one covered, and the other, a garden open to the sky, with tables for sitting out. And on all the public walls, the art was displayed. It was all the work of one man, Donald Sultan, an American whose '600 pieces' gave a hint of industrial design, but nevertheless seemed appropriate. Sultan's three main motifs seemed to be a variation on buttons (this in the main hotel foyer), playing cards (hearts, diamonds, etc., along the corridors to the guest rooms, a theme taken up on the carpets), and a series of 'self-portraits' in the covered courtyard – his figurative phase: here we had the man standing in space, the man on a motorbike, the man lying on his back, an object of some kind floating above him; the man standing breaking the line of others (sitting in armchairs), his back to us; most of them had their back to us. This was at the Art'otel on Bem Rakpart, where Pewter was staying. Carrington's project was an attempt to do something similar with the da Firenze paintings and prints at the new Art'otel on the other side of the river.

They were not having one of the fancy ice creams or the *Cappuccino torta* cake or whatnot at the café in the square across the river. Carrington (theatrically) underplayed his surprise that Pewter didn't know that this café was famous the world over for its cakes and ice creams; and the menu soon confirmed that the Gerbeaud, located 'in probably the nicest square in Pest', was known and acknowledged worldwide. Because they were both watching their health the men steered clear of the 'famous treats' that other tourists were tucking into, and it did make Pewter wonder why the other visitors didn't seem to have health problems; and he put this thinking of health matters down to the effect of the recent death of C. J. Harris.

Carrington was talking about possibly missing the Antibes Jazz Festival later in the month, and Pewter refrained from asking if he had planned to go as a performer or as a tourist; and Carrington must have picked up something of the signal, so he switched to telling a story, as if he were deliberately sending himself up, of a night he had spent in a hotel in Brighton.

Pewter was part-listening and thinking that it was increasingly hard to pin Carrington down to any particular part of the world, and wondering if this is what would happen to them all, including himself, floating, deracinated men, with or without families: England. America. Toronto. In his friend's case Trieste, Budapest, forays into Africa and the West Indies. Globetrotting men, men globalized.

So Carrington's story was about a night in a hotel in Brighton, and not in a dump, but in one of those places that took group bookings, and that was the source of the problem. The noise, the rowdiness, the – to coin a phrase – yob culture in action.

So he's kept up all night, Carrington, by the noise, the shouting, the abuse from upstairs, what sounded like the breaking of furniture. So, in the end Carrington phones the night manager, not once, not twice but three times; and of course nothing happens. The man may have been up once because the shouting stopped for a few minutes, but only to start up again with the same force. And meanwhile there's some other nut knocking on his door calling out some woman's name. Nightmare. In the end – and by now the man above is pissing out of the window, pissing down on Carrington's window; and what makes it worse there's a bit of flat roof outside Carrington's window – pissing down from above and *singing*. And that's when Carrington pulls out his gun and kills the bastard.

'Yes?'

Shoots off his cock and kills him.

So now Pewter has to listen to the story. It beats the one he was imagining, the parallel story of Carrington getting up and going downstairs and remonstrating with the night manager, a middle-aged, overweight man at the bar still serving drinks to the kids; this at four o'clock in the morning; and the night manager, wanting to be one of the boys, alternately blustering and self-pitying (what d'you want me to do, sort of thing; I've been up twice already . . .). The night manager hates Carrington for seeing through him; so Carrington makes his complaint, calmly, explaining why he won't pay for the room where he has been unable to sleep (yes, he's prepared to fill out a form); and without resistance (for Carrington is supposed to be telling this story) – without resistance he checks himself out of the hotel at five o'clock in the morning and goes for a walk on the beach, killing time till the first train back to London.

But now Carrington has reclaimed the story by killing his man; and Pewter has to respect that.

'Killed him, did you?'

'What would *you* do?' This isn't a question, more a weary shrug.

And after a pause: 'Killed him with what? Smith and Wesson?'

'Nah, just the little . . . Luger, y'know, the woman's . . . Luger Parabellum thing that the women use. Semi-automatic.'

'Killed him, did you?'

'Any man who messes with me . . .'

'Who pisses on your . . . whatsit.'

And then the conversation switched to talk about the philosopher G. E. Moore and Goodness; or rather to C. J. Harris talking about G. E. Moore and Goodness. ('Philosophy is a lot of damn nonsense, but it keeps the mind occupied.') And then they were trying to decide whether you ate well or just well-enough in Budapest; and whether it mattered.

The next day . . .

Celia was expected next day. The opening would be delayed by a week; Carrington would be busy with labelling the pictures and prints: he presented the labelling as an artform in itself, a witty commentary on the big theme, which was eggs. (Why not? Donald Sultan had buttons.) Da Firenze had given some of his people eggs for heads.

People on the island had said that he was stupid, that he was crazy, or that he couldn't paint faces. Then after his stock began to rise abroad (after his suicide), the smart criticism was that he was being clever to substitute eggs for these black people's faces; for those who were ugly would be spared too faithful a representation; and with eggs he could avoid the pitfalls of representing people's pigment too exactly – either too light or too dark – white, brown and speckled being a good colour-coding compromise. And you could take this art criticism further, building your interpretation around the sort of egg (hens, guinea fowl) and the size of egg (ostrich? Not an island bird) to argue the artistic originality of da Firenze.

Carrington – with a rather heavy reference to René Magritte: 'This is not an egg' – seemed to be taking it seriously and pretending not to take it seriously, in his gallery notes.

Pewter would miss out, too, on the jazz scene that Carrington promised at one or other of the hotels.

So they both ended up taking credit for the de-christianizing of the death and burial of C. J. Harris, and of giving a new meaning to the meaninglessness of human (and other) life. And Pewter found himself saying to someone that two men of sensibility sitting in a Budapest café refusing to hijack a life was a way of paying tribute; for they weren't ignoring the Harris thing either, and sitting around talking the usual stuff about politics and corruption, or students and plagiarism or of doctors and policemen and punishing women whose glances slid past them as if they were old, old men; nor were they talking about the current crisis in West Indian cricket. So all this must be put down to C. J. Harris for not jolting the world the wrong way when he fell out of it; and that meant that the man, despite everything, was a star.

While he was saying this, and much else, to someone or other, Pewter had an image of something he could mourn in a more conventional way. It was like a flash at his looking out of the window, looking down from his hotel room on the garden below. This was just as he was about to check out after breakfast. He had come down early, to breakfast, and was now packed; and was just looking down on the pleasant garden to take in the scene one last time. And there she was, the Bulgarian princess, sitting at her little table. The waiters must have cleared away breakfast, for all she had left was her pot of tea, and a cup, elegant, with the hotel's playing-card design. And spread out on her table poems, poems (he supposed) in English. She didn't look up.

This could have been a better story than the death of C. J. Harris.

8

The Mosley Connection

That night my neighbour came to the university and complicated my life. He was Geoffrey Hamm, Oswald Mosley's 'right-hand' man and he lived next door to us in Ladbroke Grove. By next door I mean literally in the next house in Bevington Road. And here he was in college – *he had followed me all this way to Wales, and it had taken only a year for him to catch up with me* – he had been invited to talk to the society tonight. I forget what society it was; it wasn't the Literary Society, which had put on Eliot's *Murder in the Cathedral* and would mount my own play later in the year. Professor Chanderman, the historian, played the THIRD TEMPTER in the Eliot play, bringing the house down with his regional (actor's) accent as he admitted to being 'a country-keeping lord who minds his own business . . . a rough straightforward Englishman' and a self-confessed 'proud Norman', though that last bit sat slightly uneasily in this Welsh setting.

The society had already lined up John Spiers to come and talk about Chaucer, giving us advance warning so that we could read Spiers' *Chaucer the Maker* beforehand. So it must have been the Philosophical Society – Politics not being taught as such – that had brought Geoffrey Hamm to Lampeter. Gilbert Ryle had already been, and had given a tough talk on 'Memory', easing up only at question time when he condescended to make the odd joke at Bertrand Russell's expense – once when someone asked about Russell's 'popular' books on social issues, and again when prodded about the 'famous incident' with the poker at Cambridge, in 1946, when Wittgenstein and Karl Popper came to blows in the presence of a gathering of philosophers, with Russell asleep in the chair. (Everyone except me seemed to know about 'the famous incident'; but never mind, there were still nearly two years to go. And Popper *was* common currency: we were all halfway through *The Open Society and Its Enemies* for a philosophy seminar, fascinated to discover that Plato was a fascist.)

Russell, though, was a favourite at the time; I would have preferred him to Ryle; but Russell was said to be too old to travel, except on Committee of 100 business, and similar anti-bomb campaigns – though we thought there might be a chance of his coming to Lampeter, as he lived in Wales.

At the end of the lecture I put up my hand, but wasn't called; and was relieved, in a way, because I hadn't worked out which of the jumble of questions in my head I would eventually ask Geoffrey Hamm.

Then I was enraged that I should be put in the position of having to question Geoffrey Hamm, *in my place*, in a room reserved for the Gilbert Ryles talking about 'Memory' and the John Spierses talking about Chaucer.

Though I did want him to acknowledge me: would he *in this setting* recognize me as a member of the family who lived next door to him in Ladbroke Grove, whom he met sometimes more than once a day and, on occasion, nodded a greeting to? One wasn't fooled by politeness – the English were, on the whole, polite – Mosley, Geoffrey Hamm's boss, when he came to our house that afternoon, a few years back, was polite to my mother.

That was during the 1959 General Election campaign. (Remember Macmillan's 'You've never had it so good!') It was probably the conjunction of Geoffrey Hamm living next door, the 'useful' symbol of my mother owning the house in which we lived, and attracting black visitors; and the fact that because of the public loos in the road – under the road in front of our house; that bit of street being unusually wide – everything came together for the fascist statement. Mosley had proved surprising and obvious in equal measure. Surprising in his courtesy – but that was only showing his *class* – and disappointing in the shabbiness of his message. We were, he said, standing on a podium which brought him level with my mother who was sitting at her first-floor window, looking out – we were misled in having been brought to this country and sold the lie that the streets of London were paved with gold: now we were here we knew that this was not the case. We were hard done by because we had been encouraged to leave our countries where the sun shone, where we were warm, and brought to this country where we were cold and unhappy: surely the best thing all round was to admit the mistake, and to return us to our own countries, where the sun was still shining, and where we would be happy. Before his speech, and again at the end, he tipped his hat to my mother, who had effectively attended the meeting.

One had no idea what was going on in my mother's mind as she sat there listening to the polite insults; but there had been a conscious decision among us, children, not to be intimidated. That's why I put aside what I was doing – reading up on the history of the Roman world, to see if that would help me with the Latin – and joined my mother at the window. My brother, who was older, went further: not only did he get up – he worked nights – and go downstairs and out the front door and saunter past the gathering a couple of times, getting small things from the shops, he also encouraged a cousin in the army, who was visiting, and wearing his army uniform ('Better than cleaning train engines at Paddington in the middle of the night') – urged him to go down and stand, casually, among the crowd. When I reflect on this the balance seemed right: members of the family calmly looking out of their window on a late Saturday afternoon; and down among the 'crowd' a representative of the family in uniform.

The uniform was important to us, for we encouraged, I suspect, the suspicion of being 'soft'; and it was increasingly clear that 'softness' wasn't going to be enough to keep you secure in this country; so one had to draw reassurance from the other strand of family history – the strand represented by my father's war experience in Europe in the last war and, before him, by my great-uncle, Cousin Reggie who, aged fifteen, signed on to fight in the Great War. My (later) going to university to read English and philosophy had to be balanced by all this.

So, to return to the question: after leaving Ladbroke Grove which you thought of as an accident you could walk away from – a scene where a man touting for bets on the horses claimed our pavement, a scene with the rag and bone people occupying your large room downstairs – above all a scene with a declared fascist living next door: after moving from that accident to the safety of Socrates and Plato, and Anglo-Saxon and Chaucer, so far from the scene, what malign prankster would see fit to stage a similar mishap in your new place – and bring the barely literate Geoffrey Hamm into the room where you attended philosophy lectures!

Nothing was spelt out in our family concerning why we were here in England. (Did other migrant families sit down and talk about these things?) And I suspect this was partly because we never quite saw ourselves as a migrant family.

The feeling, hinted at, and sometimes articulated, though with growing lack of certainty, was that we were a special case. We were a special case because we were, 'at home', a middle-class family expected to set (or maintain) standards on the island; and that it was important to have this status recognized in England. A special case because unlike many others from the Caribbean and the sub-continent – and certainly those from Eastern Europe, fleeing persecution; and maybe even some from Ireland seeking a better life – we didn't *have* to come to England. Canada had been an option for years; my father lived in Canada, a prominent clergyman; a citizen of that country.

A special case, too, because we were from St Caesare, and St Caesare was a colony: we had no other citizenship but British. And then there was the family history of travel (different, in our mind, from *migration*) where members – some of whom my generation didn't know – went to Panama (to work on the canal), or to Cuba and Haiti (for years and years, later to return), to America to settle and, like my father, to Canada. Coming to England, then, meant rejecting other options; and coming to England was, in a sense, coming home to the place that one's father and great-uncle had gone to war to keep free. That was the family's version of 'Mother Country'.

We were different, then, from the university students from the West Indies who visited our house in Ladbroke Grove at weekends: they were all here for a few years to further their education, and then to return home, hopefully, to play a part in their country's development – in reality, to pick up the plum jobs. The question of ownership of England wasn't one they were concerned with. This was *our* challenge when we went to the shops, when *we* ventured out after dark, when we opened our mouths to lay claim to the language.

So everything was awkward in those days: my mother's

assumption of being 'in place' sometimes embarrassed us. When, on the train, on the tube, she would frankly gaze at the next passenger's newspaper and comment on the contents ('It's shocking, shocking') we tried to distance ourselves; when, at the greengrocer's on Chesterton Road (who were these Chestertons?), she tried to educate the owners on the poor quality of their fruit, we had to apologize. But we were conscious that we were making similar howlers in *our* efforts to be 'in place'. I remember having an in-between-school job on Mortimer Street in the West End of London, making ladies' belts; and people in the factory got curious about me ('You don't sound West Indian', etc.) and I admitted that my mother had bought a house in Ladbroke Grove and would have bought a house somewhere further upmarket but that there were sitting tenants in the house, English people, and that we didn't know if we could get them out so that we could move in. And one man listening was fairly abusive at the idea of our buying a house with sitting tenants and expecting them to move out. ('You're all the same,' he said; 'all the bloody same.') And even though I could see the tactlessness of my admission, I wondered why he thought we were seeking to buy the house: we weren't buying it to *let*.

*

So there I was at Lampeter, in 1963, maybe, with my hand up, pondering which question I would ask Geoffrey Hamm.

The man was unprepossessing in every way, the university setting, in a sense, bringing out the worst in him. Even the organizers deplored his lack of grace when, in the middle of a question from the floor – a rather long and involved one that he didn't much like – he unfolded his newspaper, the *Daily Mirror*, I think, or the *Daily Sketch*, and pointedly appeared to read. In my jumble of questions not asked I was determined to plump for the *lightest* I could manage, being already irritated that, not only on the street but also in the academy, Caribbean people, Asian people – black people, generally – were already falling into the trap of accepting that there were 'black' subjects, different from other subjects, that had been earmarked for them. I'd like to think that my eventual question might have been prompted as much by the man's lack of good manners, as by his offensive politics. For now that he was in my place – the university – he should be held to a minimum standard of good manners. Just as he would be if he were to enter our house in Ladbroke Grove, by invitation, and be introduced, formally, to my mother.

In our house at that time the debate spluttered on about who was civilizing whom in this encounter between ourselves and the English of Ladbroke Grove. The danger here – as my brothers, who were older and more experienced than I, pointed out – was not to define ourselves too narrowly. There were others, from the Caribbean, from India – indeed, from England – who were of a different class, if you like; but who now had to be roped in as allies: I might be doing philosophy and Anglo-Saxon at university, but alone on a bus or on foot in London at night, or on the train to Wales, no one wishing me ill was going to ask my position on Wittgenstein before rearranging my features. (I recall on television the face of Dr Banda, Dr Hastings Banda, 'firebrand' from Nyasaland, coming on to demand 'Independence Now' for Nyasaland. A fairly unprepossessing man, Banda. ('I have come to take what is mine by conquest': was he a military man, then?) But on investigation you discovered that he had got himself a degree in philosophy at an American university, and after that had qualified as a medical doctor. More to my point he had practised for years and years as a doctor in Kilburn, where my mother had now moved the family from Ladbroke Grove. So I had an image of Banda going home at night on the 31 bus, or the 28 bus along Kilburn High Road – and being confronted by the night-prowling friends of Geoffrey Hamm: *Psssh Dr Banda. Now tell me: Is Aristotle's Theory of Knowledge a priori or tautologous?* Or *Is the Hippocratic oath really good poetry?*

I would have to find ways of converting the (largely symbolic) security of my-cousin-in-the-army at Mosley's 1959 meeting, for protection. Negotiating a safe place in England, drawing on my father's role in the relief of the Port of Antwerp in 1944, was tenuous. As was that of Great-uncle Reggie doing whatever he did in Palestine in the Great War. So we had to find allies here and now who would help us protect our space in England; in Britain. In that sense this family was no different from any other unwelcome immigrant.

The sense of looking over your shoulder was persistent; it wasn't just a question of safety, it was a question of ease. You had a feeling of ease only when you weren't being looked at. So anything distinctive or extravagant was out: a brightly painted front door in Notting Hill signalling West Indian ownership was out; an African with face-markings and traditional dress was – a target, at least, for comment. Even history graduates researching slavery rather than rewriting Tudor history were falling into an 'ethnic' trap, etc. But yet, you were defined everywhere by that most distinctive feature, your colour. It must be strange for an African, in Africa, say, on coming to England sud-denly to find himself *black* (a point that Jomo Kenyatta, on visiting, made on television one night – 'You make me black' – to the bafflement of the BBC interviewer). This re-labelling wasn't entirely new to a West Indian, but it was irritating none the less. Shouldn't this be discussed in the philosophy tutorial alongside Kant's *Critique of Pure Reason* and Aristotle's *Laws of Thought*? But the philosophers were not helpful. Locke was, disappointingly, a man of his time, in favour of slavery; and even exemplary Bertrand Russell, in one of his 'popular' books, made a vulgar assumption of black people, acknowledging them to be loud. My mother would have been amazed at this: loudness had never been allowed in our house – in any of our houses. That's why I put in my mother's head one of those familiar warnings:

[She's looking down on the Mosley meeting] *Don't put yourself in the position of being accused of 'desecrating' their country houses (by ownership). Or to be accused of 'over-running' their medical and legal professions, etc. Don't get into politics and expose yourself, to be accused of 'running' the parties; don't be successful in business and be a target.*

Lady Polonius, my mother.

Preparing yourself for the task of settling in, colonizing your own space, was not just a migrant fixation. I remember, in an early history tutorial, a lad in my year, Dave Weatherby, from somewhere in middle England, expressing surprise – and some consternation – that he had come up to university firm in the belief that the English were always top dog and had set about civilizing the rest of the world. History being one of his subjects at university, he now had to get used to the fact that the Romans and the papacy had played a hand; and the Franks and the Ottos of tenth-century Germany. (What were the dates of that beautiful woman, Abigail: was she German or Italian?) And before the Romans, the Greeks and Egyptians . . . I had suffered a similar sense of bafflement when, after the stage reading of *Murder in the Cathedral* (great title!), I reread the text that night and was both impressed and disconcerted by the Archbishop's Christmas morning sermon (which was the interlude between the acts). Noting that it was delivered in 1170 was slightly unsettling. The fact that Weatherby would have connected with this in a way I didn't, rankled. I was brought further down to earth by Utchay, a man from Nigeria in his third year, reading English. Utchay, who had been at the play, was less than impressed with all this stuff at the end equating Englishmen with fair play, with sympathy with the underdog, etc. Utchay said, dryly, that Eliot couldn't have read very much colonial history. (This caught me off-guard. I had been prepared, to date, to credit the English with these virtues: I had been subjecting English texts to *new* readings, but there was a way to go.)

It was going to be hard work getting yourself prepared to take on the likes of Mosley – who were educated and well-connected – even if you could trust those other (unseen) allies to deal with the threat from the Geoffrey Hamms of the street. Even in an area that I thought I knew – Shakespeare – I had to admit my ignorance (to a superior boy, Lyle, reading Honours Latin, who casually put me to shame on the staircase outside his room, in Old Building, on the Shakespeare plays *seen* as well as read). I still had ringing in my ears my brothers' grammar school talk of Bolingbroke here, of Longfellow's *Hiawatha* there as if they were contemporaries; and had come armed with new interpretations of my favourite texts; and here was this *Latin* scholar with the genealogy of the House of Lancaster off pat: I had read history in the first year, and was still hazy about all this history. I had a nightmare, which has stayed with me: maybe my debate wouldn't be with Mosley, after all, but with Geoffrey Hamm, who was, perhaps, closer to my intellectual level – or my *knowledge* level. Or maybe, I tried to convince myself, there wasn't a difference to be made between Geoffrey Hamm and Oswald Mosley.

II

When my mother had her stroke and was in St Charles' hospital we asked her to compare hospitals (as I was later to compare universities) as she had had a spell in St Mary's in Paddington and we thought, I thought, that comparing hospitals was not just a way of distinguishing between good and bad – but signalling a preference for some things over other things, that was to be part of our living experience in this country.

The question to emerge, during my mother's hospitalization, was where would one bury a member of the family who had died. If it was true that your home is where your family are buried, this was our biggest decision yet. (We had already had one family member, an unlucky cousin, buried in England, but that had been an accident.) My father had fought in Europe and had managed not to get killed; therefore we had no claim on Belgium. But my mother – we hoped she would get better, and she did get better – would be buried somewhere and that would be our home. (Five houses in the West Indies still somehow failed to make the West Indies secure. *Houses, servants, land, a groom: don't think about it!*)

There was a character in an Italian film, a lad of no particular merit, saying that he thought his family home consisted of 300 rooms. This fellow could be dismissed as unreliable. But then there was Marlborough House, the 200-room mansion in the Mall – a Christopher Wren building – that the queen had given to the Commonwealth for its meetings. Macmillan had reported this 'imaginative gesture' to the Commons, and also the fact that the Commonwealth premiers (*Roy Welensky? Archbishop*

Makarios? . . .) had welcomed the gesture. There'd be a reference library attached to it, etc. (I had fleeting images of my mother looking out of her window of Marlborough House – her status the same as the original owners rather than the new tenants – looking down from there rather than from a house on Bevington Road. But then the image proved stronger than my fantasy, for if it relocated my mother's residence to the Mall it also rerouted Mosley's rally to the same place.)

If a house with so many rooms attracted attention to us, maybe we should start at the other end of the process and investigate the burying ground. Do some research. Through no fault of her own my mother lived next to a fascist; we probably couldn't have prevented that. But could we avoid burying her next to a fascist? We would have to do a study of the likely burial grounds of West London. What discipline did this entail: sociology? Philosophy? Ethics? *Geography.* My personal cosmology was getting complicated.

Fortunately my mother recovered and we didn't have to think about this for quite a few years.

III

So I said to him; I said to Geoffrey Hamm: Were you present at Mosley's Albert Hall speech on 28 October 1934 – were you present at that BUF rally when Mosley finally admitted his hatred of Jews and affirmed his solidarity with Nazi Germany? And did you also arrange attacks on tailors and shoemakers in the East End of London – old Russian migrants, you know – in Bethnal Green, in Shoreditch, in Stepney; and have you now moved on to Ladbroke Grove thinking that cane-cutters and serving women, and bus conductors and nurses and students and wideboys from the Caribbean living here are not going to defend their right to live here? Do you deny, little ill-dressed man, being an emotional voyeur, driven by feelings of sex-envy and fear of the black-skinned woman next door who might introduce you to the use of cake-forks should you come to dinner?

I said, of course, none of this, not having been called, not having the information to hand at the time: I may have been doing a quick compare/contrast of the weakness of the monarchy in France at the start of 911 with the new German monarchy and the succession of Conrad, elected to the post after the death of Louis the Child, the last Carolingian. And then how would one link the 1832 Reform Act to . . . to the fact that now in the 1960s there were only 7 per cent of the people of this country who made it to university; and I would have conceded that keeping his friends out of the university and on the street hadn't worked; keeping his friends in ignorance hadn't worked. But was Mosley ignorant? *But wasn't Mosley ignorant?* I had been abused, casually, by a woman in Bayswater, as I joined the cinema queue: why ask an Anglo-Saxon education for her? She already sounded word-perfect in *Beowulf*. But you would still have said to Geoffrey Hamm: I, too, want to do something about your situation, for, apart from anything else, I can't be sure how many of you are out there looking in on us in envy and resentment.

So I said to Geoffrey Hamm, long after the event: *Here's what my mother thinks of all this* . . .

*

A friend of ours was at Bristol University, reading English. He was from Mauritius, and through Mauritian friends at Lampeter we got together in Bristol, Clifton, a bit of big-city relief from Lampeter. And just for the hell of it we accompanied him to a lecture, a lecture by the legendary

L. C. Knights, who was professor there; and whose austere book *Drama and Society in the Age of Jonson* we were expected to stumble through.

There was a bit of daring going into this huge hall with what must have been a hundred people – Lampeter lectures averaging about twenty or so – and listening to this dressed-any-old-how man talk on some seventeenth-century subject. Though the lecture was undoubtedly brilliant, what stuck with me was less the clever tying of Wilmot and company to some concept or other of 'plain dealing', than something said almost in passing – that the characteristic spirit of the age is best captured or communicated not by the major talents of that age but by the lesser, the second division so to speak, artists, thinkers, architects, etc. And of course I missed the burden of the rest of the lecture wondering whether I was first or second division material. (Was James Baldwin first division or was he forced into being a black man commentating on racist America?) First division I would be dealing with Mosley, but fate had set me down next to Geoffrey Hamm.

It was all right for some – the sons of bankers with Morrison-Welles-type names, and white-skinned, non-Jewish features – to say that Mosley had passed his hour, was a throwback, and a serial fornicator into the bargain; and that it was Macmillan and 'You've never had it so good' who was a threat to civilized values. And it was Kennedy and Khrushchev who were the real threat to our life; so maybe Mosley's 1,900-odd votes in the North Kensington constituency in the 1959 election didn't matter too much.

I was reading English; and was pleased that going to university hadn't constrained my education. I had been struggling to write plays all during the GCE years and was frustrated by the mounting rejection slips; but there seemed a possibility of a play of mine being broadcast on BBC Radio Wales. There was a sense of occasion in being invited down to Cardiff to talk to the putative director, Frank Davies, about it. (The play was never broadcast but it gave me a sense of self – as a writer – which made me see university work essentially as identifying source material for the writing.) So it was the odd, the offbeat, the strange that attracted my attention during those years. It was Frank, the urbane Nigerian in his final year, who was about to go up to Cambridge to take another (I think, first) degree who intrigued. This very handsome man in a spotless blazer, after talking Plato with me in the quad one evening, declared that he intended to marry an ugly woman, as she would be grateful to him for having married her, and being ugly, she wouldn't be attractive to other men; so he would have no cause for jealousy. This observation seemed to me to come not out of Africanness, or out of Lampeter, but out of Plato. I had written a 'Platonic' play, *The Masterpiece*, which was going to be produced by Dramsoc: I was intrigued by Frank.

But it was from Utchay, the other Nigerian reading English, that I learned to gauge my responses. He, also, was in his third year when I was in my first; and he took, I fancy, a protective interest in me. It was after the remark about Eliot that I marked him out for special notice; and, in fact, submitted the manuscript of my play to him for an opinion. I remembered him earlier as setting the tone in the Junior Common Room one night, when other people laughed at a sketch that was, at best, dodgy. It was one of those *That Was The Week That Was* sorts of sketches where two nineteenth-century Englishmen, made up to look more than usually comic – travellers in long shorts, pith helmet – go out to Africa, meet the 'natives' and run into a spot of bother. One of them eventually takes his pogo stick and beats off the African, beats him. When his fellow

Englishman, apprehensive, remonstrates and says, in a somewhat high-pitched voice: 'You hit him,' our man, in an equally clipped, high-pitched voice, responds. 'That's all right: they like violence.' Utchay's tut-tut dampened the splattering of laughter in the Common Room.

And Utchay didn't disappoint. He patronized me slightly by praising my accent: I patronized him slightly by apologizing for it. But we weren't yet even. I didn't know what he felt about Fidel Castro or about West Indies cricket – about the *aesthetics* of those late cuts by Frank Worrell, late in the afternoon, at Old Trafford, in the first Test. Still less, what he thought about Bob Dylan and Françoise Hardy. So we talked aimlessly about Eng Lit matters, while Utchay seemed to concede to me all sorts of advantages: they seemed to have something to do with my knowing England. (Yes, I now lived in Kilburn and my friend Chinque lived in Hendon, and after visiting his place in the evening I would then walk back to Kilburn late at night, through dodgy Cricklewood, and feel as if I were a character in Dickens, the old man in *The Old Curiosity Shop*, reclaiming the city.) Utchay praised me for this or that (Did I really appreciate English humour?) till I realized that he wasn't really praising me. Suddenly, my West Indianness seemed in need of explanation. (*Did I appreciate English humour? I didn't appreciate the comedians' joke about Nasser back in the 'Suez Crisis' days, when they talked about Nasser's dismay when he went to an English tailor to be measured for a suit, only to find that he didn't need as much cloth as he usually did in Egypt; for though Nasser was a physically big man, he was a much smaller man in England than he was in Egypt.*) So we agreed it was time to talk about my play. Utchay had only one objection, it seems, though he framed it as a question: he wanted me to expand on my use of a word in the 80-plus page text. The word was 'atavistic'.

Now, back in GCE days in Kilburn I was proud of my (large and expanding) vocabulary; and would have been praised for the use of words like 'atavistic'. So in Utchay's room in Old Building we looked it up in the dictionary:

Atavism. *From* atavus. *Great-grandfather*; *grandfather*. *Resemblance to more remote ancestors rather than to parents*, etc.

This related to not parents but grandparents, great-grandparents. What did a West Indian mean by that term, if not reference to Africa? And why, if Africa, was the term used negatively in my play? (The flashing lights in my mind brought up the Congo, the rape of nuns, the murder of Lumumba, the 'shame' of Sharpesville but also the dignified Chief Albert Luthuli, President whatever, of the ANC, African Nobel Peace Prize winner; and, indeed, my shaking hands with an 'African' in the street in West-bourne Park the afternoon in 1957 when Ghana secured its independence.)

My eventual response to Utchay was to say that in my use of the term my impulse wasn't to distance myself from Dr Nkrumah, say, but rather to engage in a literary conceit that might have amused Dr Johnson, compiler of the *Dictionary*. Utchay was a man of grace and civility – so we agreed to disagree. But he taught me there were other constituencies for my writing than a West London Evening Institute (which had agreed to stage one of my plays) or a university audience in Wales.

IV

Of course, I remember what I was doing the day J. F. Kennedy died. It was evening, actually, when we heard, and we had just come out of a philosophy seminar (unusual to have one put on so late in the day), and it was on Aristotle; or maybe it was on Ethics, and the examples I recall were from Aristotle. So I remember that. But I also remember other things, too, the day when – the first time, actually, that I was moved on by the police. I was sitting, with two friends, on my mother's front step in Kilburn, early evening; and a couple of policemen walking up the street stopped and came over and asked if we knew the owner of the house, on whose steps we were sitting. My two friends were Mark, who was half-Indian, and Bill, who was half-Chinese. The moment of confusion on our part was working out whether the police were, unwittingly, performing a service for my mother, who was inside the house. But of course it was clear that we, three non-white boys sitting on a step in West London, created suspicion. And when I owned up to being related to the owner of the house the policemen's easy acceptance of that again gave the wrong signal. Was my mother's safety in her house of so little regard that they could just take our word for it, and move on; was it of so little regard because they suspected her of being a black woman?

I remember where I was – in Ladbroke Grove – when a visitor to the house (not to us – we had let the upstairs flat, temporarily) – a young man leaving the house one winter's night came back very agitated claiming to have been shot at in the street. We didn't know whether to believe him, but then a few days later – this was at the tail end of the Notting Hill riots in 1958; a few months after the riots – a 32-year-old carpenter from Antigua, Kelso Cochrane, *was* stabbed to death on leaving his girlfriend's place in our street, Bevington Road. The murder took place two streets away, by the 'Keep Britain White' brigade, the 'Teddy Boys supporting Mosley'. So my allies weren't doing a good job at keeping the streets safe from Geoffrey Hamm while I tried to find the means – through Bishop Berkeley and Kant and Russell – to prepare for Mosley. *So I put new words into my mother's mouth . . .*

*

Just recently, sitting in the refectory of another university – one in which I work – a colleague relayed a question for us, one asked by her four-year-old son. Why, he asked, are there good things and bad things in the world? And we couldn't answer that. Maybe I was making up all this philosophy and stuff.

9

Thompson in the GCE Class

Thompson had returned to his island. I'd met the 'returnees' in island after island, men and women who had
spent a working life in Canada or England: the women
had had lives you'd more or less expect, as factory
workers and nurses (a few had been maids in Toronto),
but mostly as teachers and people who worked for the
local authority in Britain, as well as the odd local councillor
and community lawyer. The men, though, had prospered
differently. They had been the head of this, the head of
that; they had had so many men working under them; they
sometimes had photos of themselves with people in the
news whom we all know, or ought to know. I had a friend
who wrote a play about the 'returnees'. It was based on a
Molière play: the subtitle was *A School for Liars*. And
there's a line in the play when the cynical tutor explains
that if you said 'liars' in a certain way, everyone would
think you were saying 'lawyers'. Initially, I thought of
Thompson going to that school, prior to returning to his
island. Then I thought better. Thompson, surely, would
have played the game differently, forty years on.

In 1958 we were in the same class at Kilburn Polytechnic
studying for our O Levels. I remember Thompson taking
the teacher on over the question of Macbeth, who, apparently, had reigned for, what, seventeen years and, contrary

to Shakespeare, was a relatively good king: could it be that Shakespeare was anti-Scottish?

This was a new one to me, having always made a clear distinction between the English and the Irish (tending more to the English), but with no particular feeling about (or for) the Scottish, except for their somewhat strange accent – though there was a very clear, English-sounding, middle-class woman on the radio (often on a Sunday), who always claimed to be Scottish. But the point was: in this O-Level GCE class in Kilburn, how did Thompson know so much about English – about Scottish history?

Thompson was famously a slow – I will say 'reader' rather than learner; because I didn't like the implication of calling a fellow student from the West Indies mentally slow. But he himself made the point of not being able to get through *The Old Curiosity Shop*, which was another of our texts – though there, again, he knew something about Dickens' world. (He pointed out once, in class, that Dickens was from Portsmouth and was, in that sense, no more of a Londoner than we were, coming from the West Indies. This embarrassed me, for I felt that a claim could legitimately be made – and was silently being made by both class and teacher – for someone white-skinned from Portsmouth to be closer to London than someone from Jamaica was. Or from St Caesare, for that matter.)

I found the presence of Thompson useful, nevertheless. I was old for the class, eighteen, having taken three years out to work in the rag trade in the West End of London, and Thompson, at twenty-eight, was ten years older. So though it gave me some slight, if you like, degree of 'shelter' in having someone older than me in the GCE class, for him to be that much older was in a way drawing special attention to ourselves, to the fact that we were the only two West Indians in the class, where nearly everyone else was sixteen or seventeen. That made my identification with Thomson slightly troubling. There were two other non-white pupils in the class – another worry was that word, 'pupil': at our ages Thompson and I should be *students*, not pupils. The other two non-white pupils in the GCE class were a couple of sisters from India, who wore traditional dress, and were depressingly fluent at Chaucer, sailing through their section of 'The Nun's Priest's Tale' in less than half the time it took me to stumble through mine. *And I was supposed to be a good student.* Indeed, I regularly topped the class in English, particularly in the essay or short story slot.

So that was another source of puzzlement: there was I, sitting usually in the second row, expected to do well; and Thompson on the back seat – bigger, though not taller than others – wearing a suit and a tie. He was critical of me, once telling me that I was not a good speaker; and I took some secret pride in not returning the compliment. By 'good' he meant fluent, he conceded later: he was not referring to my accent, which he put down to my having come to England earlier in life than himself.

So, soon, it was not the teacher, Miss Jameson and later, Geoffrey Stone, whom I spent hours in Ladbroke Grove Public Library and at home trying to outdo, it was Thompson; supplementing my notes from our Verity text with Introductions from the university editions with quotes from Holinshed, etc. And then looking up stuff on Scottish history. And this was reflected in my mark: I maintained my position at or near the top of the class while Thompson maintained his towards the bottom. It puzzled me how so much knowledge failed to translate into being able to answer the essay question. True, Thompson's attendance was erratic – he did have a full-time job – but then he seemed to be so cavalier with Shakespeare's text, we didn't know whether we should be impressed or not. Anyway, Thompson affected not to worry about any of this, about his mark; something that would have caused me – and, indeed, my mother – the deepest shame.

I was reminded of Thompson maybe about a year or so ago, first night in my Portuguese class, in Sheffield, at a community college on the other side of town. And last weekend in London an incident concentrated my mind further. Of the Portuguese I was certainly the worst in the class and, if not the oldest, the oldest one who had come in for the language rather than the convenience. (Not so much the old cliché, to keep warm, but for the company: an older man who had a house in Portugal accompanied his son to the class – and was asleep after ten minutes of *chamo-me* Steve Earnshaw; *como se chame? Chamo-me* Lisa Hopkins. *Obrigado. Obrigada.* Observing my fellow *velho – reformado?* – I made a mental note not to look too tramp-like in future.)

This was in Sheffield forty years on. I had joined the class late and there was no real opportunity for introductions; which relieved me, as I hadn't made up my mind what to say about myself. The class was taught by a friendly young woman in a short skirt which seemed to embarrass the men there: she must have been in her early twenties, and was somewhat pleased and relieved when I responded to my own name, in English; and confirmed that this was the right class. She then pointedly said – taking care of my feelings now I was in her class – that she wouldn't ask my age. (The game old man ventured that he considered himself an older man than me; so I had, ritually, to deny it.)

I had come prepared to explain my interest in Portuguese this 'late in life', but nobody asked; and I learned, during the break, that a couple of others in the class had holiday homes on the Algarve, that one woman had a Portuguese boyfriend, who was a waiter in Huddersfield, that the dignified middle-class couple in the corner were parents of a young man who had a Brazilian girlfriend to whom he was about to get married; so the parents had come to bone up on their Portuguese. (Later, I wondered why I didn't reveal my interest in Mozambique: did I suspect that with everyone else having a connection to Portugal or Brazil, my Mozambique interest would make me seem *ethnic*? But then I thought of Thompson and how he had helped me once, all those years ago, and that made it easy to reclaim Mozambique with pride.)

Thompson had eventually dropped out of the class, and I, in time, went on to university. But not before getting to know more about my fellow 'pupil', who, subsequently, supplied me with the idea for a play.

We knew that he worked for British Rail in a clerical position, at Paddington Station, near Royal Oak; that he had bought a house in Queen's Park and that he was married to a woman who worked at Harrods. Queen's Park seemed an OK place to live, and Harrods seemed a glamorous place for one's wife to work. And on the two or three occasions I visited Thompson (who introduced me to his wife – or whoever happened to be in the house – as 'my intellectual friend', something I could live with) I was treated to the best of the Harrods food store. By then, of course, the mystery of Thompson was cleared up. He had been, in a sense, slumming it at Kilburn. Talk at the house in Queen's Park was about food, yes, dishes with names that Thompson knew how to pronounce; but also about, oh, technical stuff about accounting, casual references to 'back-to-back credit' and 'distributable profits' and 'distributable reserves' and all sorts of acronyms to do with business and finance that Thompson was keen to explain.

*

After last weekend in London, paying a visit to the house after maybe twenty years and not finding Thompson, I couldn't altogether banish an uncomfortable feeling, a low rolling sense of anxiety. The house now belonged to a stranger; the stranger (fixing me with the eye of suspicion), not of course inviting me in, and claiming to have no knowledge of anyone called Thompson. So, as I apologized and walked hesitantly away, with the man standing at the door as if to see me clear of the street, I had feelings of rebellion. (The synagogue at the end of the road had become a mosque; but this man wasn't Asian.)

The last time I saw Thompson I remember him making fun of his growing deafness; the wife, too, made a joke about his refusing to wear a hearing aid. And, in truth, there was a solidity about the man, in his home, which made you almost think that deafness in his case was an oddity (he was still in his fifties then) rather than an affliction; so you could make a joke about it.

*

Among the returnees Thompson would be saying that his wife worked at Harrods, and everyone would say, yes, that was good; but he would not be believed. He would say that after doing his Higher National at Regent's Street, he was made head of his section at British Rail (and don't forget the racism of the time, not like these days when these fellows don't know what racism is) – he was made head of his section in the Paddington office, but that he still maintained his interest in Shakespeare and Dickens, which he had studied over at the polytechnic in Kilburn. As this account of himself wouldn't draw the expected approval he would have to go on to say that he had done the polytechnic thing as something of a political statement, just to show that, with his experience of the world, he could teach these young innocents – including the teacher – a thing or two. And, warming to his brief, he would go on to confide – like a character in the *Returnees* play now – that he had come within an inch of being knighted by John Major, except that a short-arsed boy from one of the small islands had badmouthed him to the authorities. (This everyone would understand; this was what we did to one another, not like the Indians and Chinese; we were our own worst enemy.)

But Thompson was relaxed about all of that because the thing is, the thing is – and people who knew him knew that something important was coming, the way he adjusted his hearing aid: the thing is, what people didn't know, at the time he was having a little thing going with Norma Major, who was John Major's wife; and the award would have just drawn attention to things, caused suspicion. And, anyway, none of this affected the good relationship he still had with the queen. And after that he'd be accepted as a genuine 'Returnee'.

So I felt I had to rescue Thompson from that play.

*

And then I was thinking of my friend Lewis, who was planning to return to Jamaica. Lewis ran a minicab firm in Stoke Newington at the bottom of the street where a close friend of mine lived. So, over the years we got to talking about things – on the way to this or that station, to St Pancras, to Waterloo. Lewis hadn't been 'home' in nearly fifty years, and was apprehensive but claiming, in a hesitant way, to be excited. I had made the mistake of thinking that he was apprehensive of what he would find in Jamaica and how he would cope there. (You couldn't inflate a couple of run-down vehicles that I couldn't identify, into a *fleet* of the latest, whatever, models from

Japan or Italy. Not unless you had the funds to play the Big Man at home, which Lewis clearly didn't.) But it turned out that what was bothering Lewis was his inheritance in England, the fact that his children – his son, his children – had no interest in taking over the 'business' he had built up; that the name 'Lewis', amateurishly etched over the shop in Evering Road, would never grow and be transformed into something like *John Lewis & Co*, his namesake on the high street; and that his name would disappear.

What Lewis said, however quaint-sounding, had a certain resonance for me. I remembered leafing through a book on Britain's Great Houses, the main characteristic of which was not the architecture but (apart from the intervention of the odd pop-singer or footballer) that they had all been in the same family for generations; centuries, without changing name; and I'd been thinking of my own situation of having had a dozen addresses in under fifty years of living in England. Should I retrace my steps to places I had lived, I would not be recognized, or, indeed, welcomed in most of them; I felt I could relate in some way to Lewis of Stoke Newington. So I did him a favour. I'd been wrong about his concern, so I did him a favour.

But, to Thompson. The idea he gave me for the play – indirectly; his pointing out how reckless Shakespeare had been with *his* sources – was this: the idea was a character called the Bank Manager. The bank was located in Maida Vale and the manager was black. At parties I was told this wouldn't do because there were no black bank managers in Britain in 1962, or whenever. And although *Front Line* was turned down by all the major theatres, it eventually got put on at a university.

*

As I was turned away from the house in Queen's Park I was tempted to shout:

Do you know that Macbeth was a relatively good king; indeed, a very good and compassionate king (it was Duncan who was the ineffectual bastard) and that Macbeth had reigned for, whatever, seventeen years and went on a pilgrimage to Rome, etc? And did you know that Dickens was born in Portsmouth and not in London and got to know London the way the boys from home got to know London in the 1950s; colonizing the Edgware Road late at night, from Marble Arch all the way to Colindale, dropping in on friends in Kilburn and Cricklewood: remember the old man in *The Old Curiosity Shop* tramping through London at night? I would have recalled that memory with Thompson.

But the people in Thompson's house were *foreign.* You'd have to tell them about milk bottles delivered on the doorstep, in the old days, sun or rain; and the trolley-buses along the Harrow Road, down past the little cinema before the bridge, before Royal Oak; and the trolley-buses linked up to the electric cables running high above the street, and the cables sending out sparks in the night, so that you had to take an interest in science to make sure you were safe passing by – or sitting on the bus! And that was only one thing that newcomers to this House of Thompson needed to know. Don't forget, too, we were boys at Kilburn: down at Kilburn there was the cinema on the High Road that changed its name to the Grange, where one night, the great Ella Fitzgerald, visiting from America, did the twist. That must have been 1960 or 1962. Not many people know that. On the 31 bus from Westbourne Park to Kilburn, to the High Road, a boy at school claimed that the conductor gave him a hard time, and that incident, twenty or thirty years later, found itself into a *play.* So you never know what will come in handy. And it's true that on a wet morning in West London – did I tell you about this? – standing outside that very bus stop,

I had to get used to the sudden news of Buddy Holly's death in a plane crash somewhere in America, and somehow had to continue my journey to Burton's on the Harrow Road to be measured up for a suit; and I remember the 'debate' inside the shop when I had to protest to the man measuring me that I shouldn't have to pay the same as a man twice my size who would need twice the amount of cloth for his suit. And as Thompson's 'intellectual friend' I would have to introduce – back at the house still – something that showed wider reading, something like the 1832 Reform Bill; or about women chaining themselves to Parliament gates in order to gain the vote, etc. All that. Then to ask – this was the 'intellectual' bit – what we could do, with our degrees and diplomas, to earn our place.

I had given Lewis a Master's gown. I was an academic, I gave out degrees. I literally gave out degrees not only by teaching a subject and assessing it, but by being on the Honorary Awards Committee. And that was Lewis's request to me, one morning as he was driving me to Waterloo to pick up Eurostar to Paris. He had a wedding coming up, of a niece in Jamaica; he had been a student way back, you know, in the 1950s, but had never completed; and it would be nice now to go back and wear a gown at the ceremony – something he'd like to do for his niece.

Some jokes cease to be amusing, others grow on you. But your protective interests come to the fore; in this case to protect your profession, your university. Then one day I happened to be drifting in the area where the *other* university was located and walked into what had always seemed to me to be the most elegant of street theatre, people, young and not so young, gliding through the traffic and past others going about their business, decked out in their graduation kit (spotless, elegant gowns, creased in the right places), the bits, the hoods wonderfully colour-coded, the mortar boards – all dressed in the past tense, accompanied by parents and friends in present-day costume. Initially, I thought of making Lewis a Doctor, replete in billowing gown – two glorious shades of red. But that seemed a trifle obtrusive, a bit cardinal-like: for some reason I thought of Cardinal Mazarin; of all those medieval popes; painted by whoever. But, so attired, Lewis might be invited to field questions he might not have prepared himself for. So, in the end I made him a Master of Science (MSc): the green and pale yellow colour scheme seemed understated enough to suit a man who, as far as I know, lived a low-profile life in Stoke Newington.

(Getting the gown was easy. I put on my suit, donned one of the gowns from my own university, approached the Porters' Lodge at the other place, and suggested I'd taken the wrong gown by mistake, for the Conferment; and I initialled a form and made the change.)

Last night I had an unpleasant dream which, if I were younger, I'd call a nightmare. In it I was explaining to someone the background to the Scottish play; that first there was King Malcolm, the Second – fifth century, don't you know? – derived from a fellow called MacAlpine, a name still in use in Scotland today. After a bit of rough stuff with Malcolm, then came the appalling Duncan, unrecognizable in Shakespeare; and then came Macbeth.

And what about old Thorfinn? Thompson wanted to know. For Thorfinn, remember, who was the Earl of Orkney, was the cousin of Macbeth or the brother of Macbeth or the same man as Macbeth, who ruled Scotland for all those years.

But then that's how it is: you can't argue with a man grown deaf.

So things in the dream didn't come together. And today? Well, got to think of something.

Part Two

The Mozambique Connection

10

The Dakota Club

1

Pewter Stapleton wasn't working today – or as he would have occasion to clarify several times, wasn't *at work* today, because of his cataract operation – but he came into the office early to print out some bits 'n' pieces because his printer at home wasn't working. Before that he had a quick check of his email: a new one from his friend in Mozambique which wasn't strenuous. He really must eliminate all this stuff clogging up the system, his old hoarding habits extending to the screen; must do something about it. As he scrolled down the messages even the unopened ones were guaranteed to tell him things he didn't need to know: news of meetings, reports back on past meetings, other memos from office potentates, junk junk junk, students demanding tutorials, references. But back to that new message:

cretford@hoteltivoli.org.mz

Auntieman to Battyman,

Nice one: Dakota seems as good a name as any. Can't let the new Americans appropriate all our names. So get in there. And remember the words of our national poet: Wipe feet on mat before entering house.

Rendezvous Cambridge. Eat good. Walk upright.

A luta (as they say) continua. CR.

The fool, Pewter thought. Yet, he was quite looking forward to seeing Mr Cretford. Say what you like, the fellow delivered. He must somehow have delivered his granddaughter to Cambridge. Retford was a rich man who played the rich man: he gave away money.

Which means he probably wasn't a rich man; or would very soon not be. But meanwhile, he made things possible for the rest of them; he was the only one they knew who went to Africa to make his fortune. Pewter quite warmed to the fraud.

But he had to get on; get something printed off the disc, and some stuff from the net, before people started drifting into the building and the phone started to ring, and he would have to explain again about being not at work, officially, and bore the arse off everyone with the explanations. So he busied himself, put the disc in the machine: if they saw all this material about Dakota (he thought it important to fix in his mind whether he meant North or South), they would think he was already demob happy, and be resentful at *their* continued drudgery in the department. As he was leaving to go to the English office where the printer was, the phone started to ring. He hesitated but ignored it and proceeded to retrieve the information he was printing off.

Back in his room Pewter wondered for a moment if he should make the calls from there. Too early; and to hang on would be to get caught up in work: couldn't be doing with that. At this hour the calls would have an unwarranted sense of urgency, anyway. So – it was still before nine o'clock – he turned off the computer and the lights, locked his door, and left for home.

*

In Maputo Colin Retford was sitting in a shaded outdoor café a couple of hundred yards down from the hotel on September the 25th Avenue, talking to a friend. They were facing the street. The other man spoke first.

'Then what?' He was foreign, and spoke with a Scandinavian accent.

Retford toyed with his pear-flavoured drink, half taking an interest in the already busy street.

'What are your plans?' the other man prompted.

'For the woman or the world?' They acknowledged the joke. Then: 'Might give England a miss, though . . . Need to put a little girl through university. That, and to bail an old man out of his . . . predicament.'

'Ah, business!'

'Business. Pleasure. Friend in need, that's all. Desperate to get out of his . . . ghetto. University ghetto. Borghetto, as they say.' Then, taking a good sip from his drink, Retford said lightly, 'Pewter's a man grown . . . short in the service of the university.'

'I think I get your meaning.'

'A friend you wouldn't mind rescuing from the hardship post in an English university.'

'What's he teach?'

'Got ideas he can't afford. Some of them not bad.'

'And he teaches what?'

'Oh, who knows what Pewter teaches? Tells them jokes, by all accounts. Tries not to be too tempted by twenty-year-old cleavage. And wants credit for that. Apparently, the government demands they give all the students degrees at the end.'

'That's the same in my country.'

'Keeps them off the dole.'

'The same in my country.'

'I like it. Look, Jens, I gotta go; gotta get to Marracuene; got to see a man about . . . some sand.'

'Marracuene. If you run into, er . . . Sander. Laetitia and Sander . . .' He raised his glass.

Retford nodded and half-waved, before leaving.

*

In Sheffield the day was going and Pewter's thoughts returned to Colin Retford, particularly as he was going to London and he would visit the club. Also it would be good to see the old boy when he came over. Retford had been unexpectedly civil last time round. Pewter remembered with some satisfaction that on their trip to Lisbon Retford's Portuguese was shown up to be shaky: Retford's picking up the tabs for everything didn't disguise that. And, in the end, Pewter minded less being patronized by Colin Retford than by some of these jackarses at work who actually thought that to teach in a university was the high point of their family's fortunes. At least, Retford wasn't vulgar. Or didn't make vulgar assumptions about him. Not those sorts of vulgar assumptions.

Through Retford – he preferred to think of him by his email name of Cretford – Pewter was shamed into opening up his own life to risk, not the sort of thing he was always urging his students to do with their poems and stories, but to a sort of risk which made you think that a bodyguard wasn't an absurd idea: the sort of thing you must do to match a man who, never having spent a day of his life at architectural college, was now putting up high buildings in Mozambique.

So, why are you ripping off Africa?

I'm not ripping off Africa, Professor.

How come you manage to stay out of gaol in Africa?

Lots of people stay out of gaol in Africa. Our favourite uncles in Zimbabwe; they're not in gaol in Africa.

Both men tried to belittle the other, it was an old routine; damning the other with faint praise. Retford told the story of Pewter being ripped off at the Tanzanian High Commission. This was back in the 1970s. Pewter had come back from France where he had been living in a commune – building houses, for Christ sake – and had come away after three years with a certificate confirming him to be a Master *maçon*. And he had the certificate *stolen* at the Tanzania High Commission. Pewter had panicked in case some wideboy from Tanzania had got hold of his certificate and was already putting up high buildings in Dar es Salaam *in his name*: what if the buildings fell down! Now it was Retford who was putting up buildings in Africa; while Pewter was teaching people to write poems in Sheffield.

*

Their joint business in England was the upstairs of a house off Tottenham Lane in Crouch End, which would be turned into a club: the downstairs was full of crates and whatnot to be shipped out to Mozambique, presided over by Bob, an ex-bouncer. It was largely up to Pewter, the man on the spot (so to speak) to decide what the 'club', eventually, would turn out to be: they were 'visionaries', these boys, out to impress each other. The club wouldn't be too literary as that would typecast Pewter, the literary man. But then it wouldn't be aggressively money-making, to save Retford from parody. So no museum, no library, no Literary Institute. And on the same calculation, no front for betting and speculation activity.

So, meanwhile, Pewter arranged to let out space in the flat for rehearsals and lectures; they sometimes showed an African film – nothing remotely cultural was ruled out. Pewter (bad habit) started using it as a storage space for his books. Retford, from afar, was relaxed about this, even as he called it Pewter's drawing room. They had a little naming competition – the Chip Shop, the AuntyMosque, the UncleCathedral, etc. – to show that everything was kept playful. Recent email exchanges suggested names like the Gomes & Logie House. Or the Da Firenze Club. And now, of course, Dakota. (Gomes and Logie were West Indian cricketers of the 1970s and 1980s and da Firenze was a painter. There was no particular reason for Dakota.)

A couple of days later Retford is one of the passengers getting off an SAA flight somewhere in the middle of Mozambique. The terminal building says WELCOME TO QUELIMANE. He takes a short taxi ride to the town, conscious again at its flatness; and stops in a wide, quiet street in front of a medium-sized house with iron railings and a gate. A stocky young man emerges and quietens the dogs and the two men have an exchange in Portuguese (Retford's efforts seem to employ mouth-burning phrases consisting mainly of the sound 'vez/vezes'), as the other man starts unlocking the gate from the inside. At the front door, which is round the side of the building, Retford greets the lady of the house.

'Faye, my princess.' Retford is welcomed like a partner. Faye is fair-skinned and petite.

'How did you come; did you get a taxi?'

'I didn't want to call you out.'

'Thought you'd catch me out, did you?'

'Don't mind your toyboys about. As long as they stay out of my way. Anyone who gets in my way here is a dead man.'

'I'm impressed. So what brings you to Quelimane?'

'The tattoos. Tattoos on the stomach of . . .' he whips up her top to expose the tattoos on her stomach; she slaps his hand, but indulgently '. . . the lady of the house.' They go inside. 'Actually, my plane was diverted from Tete. So I thought I'd get off. I *had* to get off.'

'You're staying the night?'

Later, at dinner (joined by another couple; she Portuguesey, he Indianish), served by a young man (different from the one at the gate) from the kitchen, the conversation turned to Retford's impending trip to Europe.

'You're not going to Portugal?'

'Probably not this time. England. France.'

'So you're not going to Portugal!' This, from the other woman, and in Portuguese.

Retford explained that though Portugal was properly recognized as the centre of the universe – Vasco da Gama, and all that – *nevertheless*, this time he'd have to give Portugal a miss, and head instead for the offshore island where the natives still spoke English.

Would the English let him in? They didn't like asylum seekers in England.

Faye said that Retford was going to see a woman in England.

Retford said that was true. Two women in fact. A granddaughter and a . . . well, her mother with an unforgiving temper.

'What d'you expect; beating up her boyfriend?'

'Never touched the throwback.'

'You're such a warlord.'

'And a grand-daddy, too!' That was the other woman.

Retford said he was only a businessman who paid his taxes. And yes, turning to the other woman; he admitted to having married young.

And the married-partner – ex-partner – was she in England?

There was, indeed, a beautiful woman to whom he had been willingly married. She lived in Cyprus, her country of origin. He would not be going to Cyprus. When he was a young serviceman in the late 1950s, doing the British state some service, he had been to Cyprus. True, he didn't have any quarrel with the Cypriot people, that he could see, but it was so damn hard to convince old Harold Mac-the-Knife Macmillan of that fact. Anyway, his reward (apart from an engineering degree, more-or-less), was a wonderful woman with . . . remarkable assets, who, *in addition*, had taught her child how to use a knife and fork, and to chew her food with her mouth closed – bourgeois habits that the child subsequently punished the parents for. Then, at some point, the discussion turned to Retford's friend Pewter Stapleton in Sheffield, who was, it seems, a bit of a standing joke.

Apparently Pewter was in some financial difficulty because he had miscalculated his assets. Remember, this was a man who, apart from university business, had been all over the world. British Council, you name it – Malaysia, New Guinea, the lot. Flat in Sheffield full of artefacts – a real son of Lord Elgin of the Marbles fame, with other people's artwork. Anyway, all these fancy drums and things that he had collected abroad, when he sent them off to be valued, to auction, or whatever, they turned out to be junk – though poor people's artwork shouldn't be so described, as all it meant was that they weren't currently fashionable to the international money launderers who controlled the art market. So Pewter had had the stuff valued at Sotheby's and Christie's and some other place. And you could work out the rest.

'Junk?' Faye helped out.

'You're so damn sexy when you talk dirty.'

At which point Faye mouthed something really dirty.

'How can a man not learn the language with this kind of incentive?' he confided to the others. And then, picking up his story: 'No, sir, what Pewter Stapleton brought back from New Guinea was junk. It was like the reverse of Columbus and our friend, da Gama. This time, the beads and bits of glass were passing from the hands of the natives to the visiting professor.

Faye, who had studied in England, and met many odd people there, but not Pewter, said that the duped professor sounded rather sweet.

The Pitt Rivers Museum in Oxford. That's another place that had confirmed the professor's junk.

*

Pewter came back to the office, really, to check the post. Had to be careful; couldn't give the impression of prowling round the place as if he didn't have a home to be ill in. And on top of that there was no second post worth talking about: no motivation now, even, to tidy up. Couldn't cope with responding to student requests. Why were problems with his eyes draining him of *body* energy? He forced himself to deal with some emails, to eliminate some more emails while he was about it.

In this state of not quite knowing what you were doing, things were easier to wipe off the screen. He must have got rid of 300 (of the 836) messages in under a minute; and suddenly saw how not difficult it was to get rid of more stuff.

But no, you couldn't really change the habits of a lifetime in a few seconds of tiredness; so he stopped – reprieving all that communication from the union reps and . . . odd things he really *might* want to look at before wiping. Inevitably, Mr Cretford came into that category. An old one, this.

cretford@hoteltivoli.org.mz

Aunty Tank to Uncle Aircraft,

I axing a favour, Sah. When you go Cambridge, check out Trinity for central heating.

Report back whether safe for grand girl-child. You his her ahaparejos, yu hear.

> And remember, Professor, no man is a philosopher at
> the dentist's. Or, as the Austrian Uncleman him say:
> 'Don't try shit above your arse.' Clearly some man you
> and me does know doan learn that yet.

Pewter had already reported back that Trinity now had central heating, no problem, and the worst the poor girl-student might have to endure would be to go to breakfast first thing and have to suffer the superior gaze of an indifferently painted Earl of Essex and his mates peering down at her over her cornflakes – the mates being the likes of Byron and Tennyson and Rupert Brooke. In order to enter into the spirit of the thing Pewter had sent young Isabel a little Cambridge publication: *Lady Margaret Beaufort and her Professors of Divinity at Cambridge*, with the dates (he couldn't remember now: sixteenth century? Seventeenth century?). Duty duly discharged; but he didn't wipe the message. The nonsense about Wittgenstein he might be able to use somewhere. He continued to check the (already dealt with) Retford correspondence.

cretford@hoteltivoli.org.mz

Gay to Updike,

You're right. Must make streets of Hackney safe for beautiful and beddable.

Like those under 25ers in Seattle. PS: any chance for an Hon. D.Litt. for Bob, the Caretaker? (Would a little donation help the cause?)

And remember, Professor: 'Don't cook your horse in enemy territory if you want to ride him home.' More wisdom. So – wish you long lines of verse with feminine endings. Nuf Respect.

A luta continua. CR.

The fool. Bob was a Jamaican ex-bouncer in a casino on Kilburn High Road who Retford employed in London to protect his daughter (Isabel's mother), without her knowledge. Pewter felt slightly contaminated in not having erased this earlier; and got rid of more messages, when he remembered something and reached for the phone; and dialled a London number.

'Hi. Hi. Oh, I'm in Sheffield. But I'm coming down, I'm getting . . . I'll try to get the . . . 2.27, so I'll be in London at five. Quarter to. Must get to West Hampstead to . . . Oh no.'

He listened for a bit. 'Damn. I was hoping we could go out and have a bite later. Yeah . . . Oh, OK. Only I read like an illiterate, now; one line at a time. Ummm. Expect so.'

He listened for a bit and made the appropriate noises.

'Yeah, we have to, y'know . . . organize it better next time . . . Yeah, next time.' He put down the phone.

The call somehow interrupted the drive to erase more emails, and he was thinking of shutting down the system when there was a knock at the door; and even though he said, 'Come', he was preparing to tell the unwelcome student that he was ill and not at work. But the door was pushed open; and Helen from linguistics hung in the doorway.

'Helen.' (From linguistics, he said in his mind.)

'Ready? I . . . I said I'd come to –'

'Ah, Helen! Yes, of course. Come in, come in . . . Sorry about the . . .'

He cleared papers from his visitor chair and stacked them on other stacks of paper.

'Really good of you to –' (He wondered what the linguistics penalty was for not finishing your sentences.) 'Really good of you to *come*.'

'No no no, I don't mind. I can't think of anything worse than not being able to read.'

'I mean, it's not as bad as . . . Y'know, I can read – I read like an illiterate, one line at a time, but . . .'

'Oh, that's terrible, Pewter. *Terrible*. I really don't mind reading to you, I can . . . manage an hour most days.'

(*Most days!*) 'No no, and I . . . can still look at the old screen, eh?'

'Well, I'm not sure: are you sure that's wise? When my mother had her cataracts removed, she was advised not to expose them to too much light. She went around in dark glasses all the time.'

I'm opting for the fishnet tights. But what he said was: 'Fortunately, we live in Sheffield, so we're not going to be challenged by too much light.'

As that drew an uncertain response he said quickly, 'I'll get myself some dark glasses.'

'Oh yes, right; I see what you mean.'

(And that, too, seemed a joke too far.)

'Anyway, I listen to the radio, a lot. World Service through the night. Obsessively.'

'Well, the radio is very good.'

'So . . . where are we?'

He was busying himself, maybe trying to find something from which Helen could read to him. Not now, of course, but just buying time. He couldn't help thinking of the examination questions she set her students: *Is the distinction between creative metaphors and dead metaphors clearcut?* Finally, he seized a small book. But found himself asking a question someone, a young musician, had asked him.

'What're your favourite eight records? Your eight favourite records?'

'My eight favourite records!' She gave a nervous laugh. 'Like on *Desert Island Discs*?'

'Yeah, that's it. Jazz records.'

'*Jazz*. Oh, I'm not well up on . . . You should ask Dave about jazz.'

'Nah, it was just . . . nothing.' *If you look for recurrent structures and intertextual forms, making these the objects of your study, then at best you miss the point of literature and at worst you betray its spirit. Discuss.*

And holding up the book in mild triumph, he asked: 'How about a bit of Balzac? Big man. Fat man.'

'Yes, right. As long as it's in English.'

'Rodin painted him in the nude.'

'What?'

'Well, one of them was in the nude, I forget which.'

At which Helen squealed; and then immediately became wary: 'I won't trust my French to read Balzac aloud.'

'But when we get to Proust it's got to be in French.'

And at this she laughed more easily, then coyly played with the top button of her blouse.

After Helen had gone, Pewter was soon describing to someone on the phone that on top of everything Helen from linguistics was threatening to read to him for an hour a day. He went on to describe Helen coming into his room and demanding a tough, scholarly text to read from, and psyching him out by talking dirty about Balzac and undoing her blouse and getting out her left tit just to check how much the cataract operation had affected his eyesight.

*

In London Pewter eventually got to the club, just to check on things and to pick up a couple of canvases that had been left there after a function, and return them to the owners in West Hampstead: he had a mini-cab waiting. The club was open but Bob wasn't around, though a young lad whom he knew (and whose mother he knew) was toying with the piano, waiting for his friends, for some sort of practice session.

Was Bob around?

Bob had got into a fight and was laid up somewhere.

What sort of fight. Who with?

The boy didn't know but he thought it had to do with drugs.

Drugs!

Bob trying to prevent a couple of lads bringing drugs into the building.

After enquiring where Bob was now Pewter calmly let it drop. The lad had merely come to play his music; he was, in a way, responsible for the lad, because he knew the boy's mother; so they talked for a bit about normal things; jazz musicians of the past, mainly. Pewter knew that the boy was indulging him, but he didn't mind. Then one of the musician's friends arrived and Pewter left them to it, remembering to send his greetings to the lad's mother; and he went to collect the pictures; the taxi was waiting.

He approved of jazz, of course, at the club, and was a bit anxious that the notion of drugs seemed still to go with that of jazz; and was (absurdly) relieved that the club was to be called Dakota rather than New Orleans. (He still had to check up on details of the Dakotas that he had downloaded from the internet this morning.) Of course the suggestion of Dakota had had nothing to do with America, in that sense; it was from Longfellow's *Hiawatha*:

> *From the land of the Ojibways*
> *From the land of the Dacotahs*

A boyhood dream, a private joke, shared (he didn't think) by Colin Retford. All their attempts at naming had had that degree of finesse about them. Even the earlier cricketing reference had that. Gomes & Logie. They weren't *great* cricketers, in a sense; but that was the point, to choose them rather than the superstars of the world-beating 1970s and 1980s sides. Not Greenwich & Haynes opening the innings. Not Holding & Marshall bowling out the opposition. With menace. And, please, not the great Viv Richards coming in at number three to pulverize England. Coming in at number three or four. No, this support act of Gomes & Logie showed strength in *depth*, people you could rely on when the stars occasionally failed, to reveal a *structure* you could have confidence in. Something like that.

He preferred to see his association with Retford as something buttressing in this way. If he objected to Retford's political ideas on capital punishment, say, and was in the 'don't know' camp concerning nuclear weapons for Iran and South Africa, he didn't necessarily object to Retford's determination, through whatever paid thug, to convince another thug who had beaten up his daughter that you didn't do that and get away with it, or get away with it with a slap on the wrist from the courts. But that you would live for ever with the evidence that *This is what happens to scum like you when you lay hand on the man's daughter.* And to have, from afar, the ability to enforce that message was something like the art of government. It was appalling, humiliating and something he would never admit to in public, but he had a sneaking liking for Retford and shared, in a small way, Retford's contempt for people like himself who had played it the other way all their lives, and would seem to have lost.

It was the damn London traffic jam that was getting him mired into these thoughts.

*

In Mozambique, in Matola, a suburb of Maputo, now restored and tranquil, Retford is being entertained by a beautiful woman and her daughters. Having had a splendid dinner and accepting as a gift an artefact hanging on the wall, Retford decides to regale his hosts with table talk, over coffee. Having earlier espoused rage at the treatment of Matola by apartheid South Africa, he now settles down as the perfect, genial guest. He is telling a story about a friend in England, Pewter Stapleton. His friend was visiting Paris, where he had a cousin living. Now, this cousin lived somewhere near the Eiffel Tower in south-west Paris. Her metro station was Emile Zola. But Pewter is a writer, a scholar, a man of the university. And as he sets out for his cousin's place he remembers that she lives near a metro named after a great French writer. He thinks no more about it as he makes for his destination; and when he gets out of the metro he is lost; not an area he recognizes. Different part of town. For the great French writer he has in mind is not Emile Zola of *The Earth* but Victor Hugo of *Les Misérables*, a metro map away. So, Retford asks his hosts in Matola – mother and daughters looking like a picture an Impressionist should paint, though not that fraud Gauguin – 'What do you say to a man of Pewter Stapleton's age and distinction, a man who doesn't know his Victor Hugo from his Emile Zola?'

11

On the Game

I

I picked up a few books – nothing special, the usual nonsense, stuff I'm unlikely to read – at the university book sale, and thought, how pathetic. Not the old cliché that now I'm having problems with my eyes I'm becoming more of a book junkie; no – more that here was I, with all sorts of things on my mind, choosing a book on archaeology to impress an eighteen-year-old, whom I had no particular personal desire to impress. Before I paid the derisory sum for the half-dozen books, I knew I wouldn't get around to the archaeology, even though it was one of those *A Very Short Introduction* jobs: I would not be manipulated by this child; or by a man smirking on the other side of the world.

Nevertheless, I had agreed to do the fathering thing for a week; and I would no doubt be monitored from afar: Isabel, I'm sure, would have gone along with her grandfather's scheme, with a grown-up disdain. She was, by all accounts, not naïve.

'Remember, she's not very bright,' Retford had said. 'We could only get her into Cambridge. And you know what these places are like nowadays. You, better than others.' Retford was the grandfather; it was his tiresome way of boasting. Colin Retford and I went back a long way, as they say; all the old jokes ('Mick Jagger and his child-bearing lips', etc.) shared. I knew his style: he would no doubt have said to the girl, 'Old Pewter is OK; he teaches at one of those pretend places north of Watford. Makes up for it by telling jokes to the students in Latin. If you don't laugh at his jokes he'll think you don't know your Latin. So try and laugh at the good professor's jokes.'

Retford was supposed to be back here in England doing his own dirty work; but something had 'come up' and the great man was delayed, en route, in South Africa; therefore I was standing in to be the cultural guide for a week to someone who, very properly, might have preferred to be spending the time with people her own age.

This wasn't as straightforward an assignment as it might seem, because I was, in effect, acting as a stand-in for the grandfather; his programme for the girl more or less set out. The Retford Programme: visits to radical theatre, an alternative book fair and, it seems, a decaying country house somewhere in Lincolnshire – all had the vaguely packaged feel to it, though there was only one tourist involved. I may have been guilty of sending it up a little, suggesting that I introduce the grand-daughter to a feminist architect in Sheffield (*Excuse me, madam: are you the feminist architect in Sheffield?*) – a clumsy attempt to shift the joke in my direction, I suppose. I lived in Sheffield; I knew, by reputation, the other university's architectural department; but I had no knowledge of whether they – or some of them – were feminist *architects*. (Certainly, the high-rise building at the top of which the architects did their thing was as shameless an example of the 'erect penis' as you could find, nineteen embarrassing storeys long. This was just to prevent Retford trying to wrong-foot me, as he liked to give the impression, from the vastness of Mozambique, that he, Colin Retford, knew better than me what was going on in my own backyard.) He would have heard *from me* that the young – not so young, now – doctors who made up my GP practice here used to refer to themselves as 'radical' or 'preventive' or 'alternative'; and he liked to refer to the place as 'your old socialist town'.

So, no feminist architects' introduction for young Isabel. But I *would* take her to the theatre in London, to see a play I wanted to see, anyway; and to a couple of art galleries that I hadn't visited for a long while. And, of course, up to the Edinburgh Book Fair where I would be making a tiny appearance. I was, in a sense, pleased to be involved in the *Radical Book Fair* having, in the past, done the Other Thing, in Edinburgh. Linton Kwesi Johnson would be at the fair. And James Kelman. And the usual Scottish suspects. Tariq Ali, too, plugging his new book on western and eastern fundamentalisms. So there'd be people for Isabel to meet. As it turned out there was a man called Greg Palast, a whistle-blower, exposing the dirty tricks of big business, globally, and the press; and the American government and the CIA and their client states round the world. I had duly bought his book, *The Best Democracy Money Can Buy*, got him to sign it, and asked Isabel to take it with her as a present to Retford, as she'd be visiting Mozambique before the start of term. I hadn't put myself through reading it, my excuse being that the print was small.

II

But I'm running ahead of myself. With my newly acquired second-hand books from the sale I was thinking not archaeology but – what? Something else: if only the Caribbean constituted itself a museum – a museum archipelago – and appointed an intelligent curator; one part of the museum presenting West Indies to the world, another part presenting the world to the West Indies – then what? A stray thought going nowhere, prompted, maybe, by leafing through the book on archaeology. What I had to admit was how the Isabel effect was already beginning to work on me: here was I jotting down the odd note as I glanced through these books, as if I was preparing for a class.

A week ago, before all this Isabel business, I had a lunch date with an old friend, a doctor recently retired from general practice (from her Preventive Medicine practice), but still working elsewhere in the NHS. Over the years we had the odd meal together, visited the theatre, that sort of thing. She came, as usual, to the flat to pick me up and, as usual, forgot which bell to ring. So she (for some reason) drove out of our parking space at the back and round the block, and phoned. When I went downstairs to make sure that the front door was open, another resident, a woman maybe in her mid-eighties, appeared and asked if there was a visitor for me.

I explained the situation.

'Was the lady in the red car for you, then?' she asked.

Possible, though I wasn't sure of the car.

'An old lady with white hair.'

My friend, the doctor, would have been in her early sixties; I didn't recognize the description. I said I wasn't sure; I didn't know what car my friend was driving now. I thought back to that humiliating moment, what, twenty or so years ago, when, after delivering my 'visiting' lecture, at Toronto University, I paid a visit to one of the halls of residence, only to be met by a couple anxious to help: did I have a *daughter* staying in hall? Now, a friend, not very much older than me, is neutered as 'an old lady with white hair'. I would have to clean up my image as a functioning male; I would have to insist on having other female guests who couldn't be so desexed; I would have to introduce in this plot to unman me by proxy, the young, long-bodied, smooth-chested Isabel. I would emphasize the point by taking her on a tour of the university, the department, making sure that the secretaries (who saw all evil, heard all evil, spoke all evil) had a good look at her.

I had played this game of male escort before; and was relaxed about it. I had a friend in London, French, who had been married to a man from the Caribbean; and the marriage hadn't worked out. I was a friend of the wife, and she was very concerned that the children have a role model in lieu of the absent father. And from time to time – over two decades or more – I would be wheeled out to accompany mother and children to public cultural events. The arrangement wasn't onerous, and the relationship wasn't sexual, a factor, perhaps, in why it was unstressful and lasted so long. But now the children had long grown up and their mother and I had drifted somewhat apart. Friends still, but not conspiratorially close. This business with Isabel was beginning to make me revisit that earlier period of my life, asking the sorts of questions of myself I usually reserved for other people.

III

As you would expect everything seems more interesting when you get to know something about it. (*So why doesn't it work with Film and Media Studies in the department?*) I was beginning to be interested in archaeology and was surprised that the Tutankhamen exhibition way back at the British Museum hadn't made a bigger impact on me at the time. And what with flitting from one thing to another, I began – for some reason – to imagine the mindset of a prisoner in a South African gaol; a man whose first act on being sentenced to life was to enrol for a university course in archaeology. It was by accident that I flicked through the book, again, the early pages of *Burger's Daughter* by Nadine Gordimer; and realized it was *anthropology* and not archaeology that Lionel Burger had plumped for. That registered the usual sort of letdown: would I have to reread this book, too, to defend my memory? But that was a sort of diversion one would pursue with Grandfather Retford, not with young Isabel.

When I picked up the paper one morning I turned as usual to the sports pages to see how the West Indies were doing against India, in Jamaica: it seemed, at last, that we would get away without being defeated in a series, first time for a couple of years; but still one wouldn't bet against West Indies blowing it even from this winning position – as they had done earlier in Trinidad. (Most of the sports pages were given over, of course, to comment on the football – the World Cup.)

Flicking through the paper to the European news, I paused at the feature on Turkey, showing a cabinet meeting: this happened to be set up in a hospital, where the prime minister was, apparently, not dying. And he did look like any other prime minister dressed for work, sitting at the head of the cabinet table, surrounded by his ministers. The surprise was that the man at the head of the table with the moustache was a familiar figure: surely Bülent Ecevit couldn't *still* be prime minister of Turkey – in 2002! He had been prime minister ever since I was aware of Turkey, alternating with the other fellow – Demirel – for thirty years or more. (This put me in mind of the old Italian political soap opera, with – what was the fellow called? – Fanfani, bobbing up as prime minister every few years, going back to the time when I was doing GCEs.) Here, the evergreen Turkish prime minister not dying in hospital might prompt me to exchange Turkish recipes with old Retford in Maputo. I was daydreaming as I flicked through the *Independent* and came across the obit pages and a tribute to Stephen Jay Gould.

I knew who Gould was: this was a subject more fitting for conversation with my young charge next week. Gould was, like Isabel, the scientist. Gould was, according to Melvyn Bragg of *Start the Week* and *In Our Time* fame, the man currently with the biggest brain. Until a few days ago, that was.

Now, as a thinking person in the society *ha ha*, I should be lamenting the loss of Gould. Stephen Jay Gould – who in his obituary photograph looks somewhat like a street-trader hawking a giant, plastic dinosaur – is the evolutionary biologist we should have read. The long obit sketches out his career: popularizer of evolutionary science; sometimes careless of his facts in the broad sweep of theorizing; scourge of the loopy scientific creationists. Or, unwittingly, their ally. And what exactly – I ask myself – was the meaning of all these terms attached to him that I didn't know how to relate to biology? Even the more familiar 'palaeontologist' manages to put me vaguely in mind of 'palaeography' which was a course on handwriting I took at some long-forgotten period at university, in the 1960s, when I was trying, among other diversions, to decipher Ralph Crane's handwriting, in an effort to authenticate a Shakespeare text. Isabel, the scientist, would have a sort of clarity about the issues that Gould confronts, even about the *terms* that Gould uses that would consign me, in her eyes, to the status of an anti-scientific creationist. *Was this, perhaps, Retford's point?* Of course he wouldn't have known of Gould's impending death at an early age. So, get on with the agenda. It was only for the duration of a week; discharge it with grace and don't let it complicate your life.

This is what I normally did; prepare myself for the student; certainly, the graduate student. So why not prepare for *this* tutorial? First, I must read Stephen Jay Gould before next week. Archaeology. Stephen Jay Gould. Remember to distinguish your Monets from your Manets, etc. Archaeology. King Tut. Harold Carter. 1922. 1922. *Ulysses*. 1922: *The Waste Land* . . .

On the tour, we visited Somerset House and – why not? – the Courtauld. Somerset House we know about but who was Courtauld? (And, incidentally, have you dipped into the little novels of that quintessentially Courtauld person, Anita Brookner – worked here for years – lot of art criticism in the novels; won a prize for a rather slim effort, *Hotel du Lac*. Booker.) It was at the Courtauld that I pointed out the Tiepolos on the top floor. Not that I find Tiepolo particularly interesting, but as a background to Walcott. Isabel must be one new scientist at Cambridge who would be knowledgeable about Walcott from day one. (Derek Walcott. My Gift to a young lady with the name of a Spanish queen.) I would urge Isabel to read *Tiepolo's Hound* (*See the little dog in the bottom right-hand corner, there!*), a triumph of versification that all the supposed professional poets claim not to be able to get through. (I will get you through *Tiepolo's Hound,* my young, long-bodied, small-girl-chested charge.) I told her about Anthony Blunt, his notoriety, and his connection with this place. I bought some postcards in the shop downstairs for her to send to her friends.

And then next stop, Scotland. Before that, remember, all this – as my women friends would again point out – was about Isabel, not about me. She was the scientist: I didn't really know what a scientist was; I must do her the courtesy to try to think into the eighteen-year-old scientist mind. So, at the Courtauld as we moved – past a some-what disagreeable official; boorish, even, who refused to lend me a pencil, so that I had to issue a vague threat before going down to the shop to buy pen and pad – at the gallery, as we moved from the Manets (she preferred *A Bar at the Folies-Bergère* to *Le Déjeuner sur l'herbe*) and the always good-value Cézannes (*The Card Players,* etc.), we talked of things nearer to her interest and experience, *trainers* (for shoes) for instance; things everyone young (though, happily, not Isabel) wore on their feet these days; we talked of how the advent of trainers had led to the demise of the shoemakers, the shoe-repairer's trade; and of whether, on balance, having the whole world properly shod (democratic) in shoes that more or less fitted (a statement against class?) and did less damage to the feet and to public buildings (we are conservationists) than before – how all this clearly minimized the cultivation of leather, with half of Argentina given over to the cow. Surely, must be a good thing. Or, conversely, whether the chemicals for the production of trainers weren't condoning the use of Third World land as arid deserts rather than restoring them to the production of biblical-type food. (Yes, good great-uncley talk.) So, it was the scientists' fault, after all, to have fitted the world's feet into trainers: what would Isabel, about to go up to Trinity, do about all this? Meanwhile, let's read the biography of our hosts: *Samuel Courtauld (1876–1947) was descended from a Huguenot family which first settled in London and the south-east of England in the late seventeenth century.* Ah, asylum seeker. Send him home.

IV

She came to Sheffield. Luckily, Isabel was pleased with herself, having found a music CD in town, for her grandfather (it was Van Morrison's *Cleaning Windows*), and was having a cursory look at the books in my room (at the university) while I checked the emails, keeping an eye out for anything from Retford. (I'd been down to the library to check on some terms used to describe Stephen Jay Gould, but couldn't find a proper biological dictionary; I came away with a couple of books on biology instead.) It was good that Isabel wasn't looking at the screen; and so missed the grandfather's latest idiocy. It began, in schoolboy fashion:

cretford@hotelrevuma.org.mz

Breast & legs man to Englishman with different orientation

And the message was a rather stupid one about buying up land cheaply in pauperized Argentina and restoring the place to Indian rule. Plus the PS about his new address, where you had to endure a better class of revolutionary.

But Isabel had sprung (if that's the word) a surprise. She had brought a manuscript which she wanted me to read. It was her mother's, and her mother didn't know that Isabel was showing it to me. It was a family saga; full of anger, and she urged an honest opinion on me. In the manuscript her grandfather came over as a monster. Isabel herself felt the old man was a monster for the way he had treated her mother and even her grandmother. Naturally, her mother was bitter. Isabel felt a bit guilty thinking this way about her mother, even more so being indulgent to the old rogue in Mozambique. Anyway yes, yes, she was enjoying the trip to Sheffield; enjoyed meeting everybody; she wished she was coming to this university rather than going to Cambridge. Did I really think she *had* to go up to Lincolnshire to look at some boring old . . . whatever it was? (Of course not; whoever thought of going to Lincolnshire?) Anyway, she was looking forward to Edinburgh: would I meet her at the airport in Edinburgh on Friday; she had the details stored in her mobile. Then her taxi came to take her to the station; and I asked her to give her mother, in London, my best.

*

At the packed meeting on the Saturday I couldn't avoid the feeling that Retford's man Greg Palast was enjoying himself; rather, was so full of himself we didn't even have to read between the lines to know that here was a man heroically, single-handedly preserving our freedoms: I had had the same feeling of something slightly bogus which – not a million miles away from here at the official festival two or three years ago – I felt when a preening government minister promoting his book, *How to be a Success in Government*, or something, embarrassed us all with his sense of self-importance ('The Prime Minister asked to see me'). Back here, Palast seemed to have rumbled so many bad guys, so many lethal organizations, found out so much about the thugs in power – in half a dozen countries: how come he was allowed to *live, and* continue to write for the *Observer*? When I asked him about this at the end of the lecture he made a joke; gauging its effect on Isabel; but I was prepared to believe what he said about dirty deeds in high places – and the way in which those in real power, behind the politicians, bought the media.

I kept my reservations to myself and asked Isabel's opinion.

'He fancies himself,' was all she said, and turned away to inspect the books laid out on the stalls.

I (the great-uncle) was reassured. She wasn't going to be a pushover at Cambridge. I – and her tutors – would have to cut through Palast-type PR to get to the core of the argument. (Core of the argument?) I was pleased I hadn't done the Retford-like thing by pretending to be knowing about Cambridge, reminding her, say, she was travelling in the wake of Byron and Tennyson and folk who went to Trinity – no mention of the scientists, whom I'd looked up. I bought, as I said, a copy of *The Best Democracy Money Can Buy*, and was relaxed about sending it off to Retford, unread. Isabel dipped in and out of the stalls, a mix of alternative and small-press reading as well as the big-name familiars (John Pilger, etc.); and eventually she bought herself a book called *Our Scots Noble Families*, with chapters on our friends the Campbells of Cawdor – one of four lots of Campbells; one bloodline of Stuarts, another of Stewarts; the Homes. (Now, how do you pronounce this one? There was a funny man who had briefly succeeded Harold Macmillan as prime minister, when I was at university. His name was Home, and he pronounced Hume. Class.)

So, was she looking forward to Mozambique?

Yes. Sort of. She was going with a girlfriend. Friend from Mozambique studying in Canada.

Had her mother been to Mozambique?

To that she pulled a face. Then she smiled sweetly.

I apologized for the indiscretion.

Isabel wanted to know if I had had time to look at her mother's manuscript. I apologized. (The old eyes, y'know.) I suspected the mother rather disapproved of me. She didn't think much of the academy, and would probably assume I was wrong on the big issues – racism, New Labour betrayals, globalization. She saw me as an ally of her father, a man whom she had apparently always dismissed as deranged. Retford's early decision to transfer his patronage to Isabel would, of course, be seen as blackmail. And I did, as they say, go back a long way, with Colin Retford.

*

So, it was done, leaving a certain flatness. Lots to do, but lots of time on my hands. I should go down to the library (now called a Resource Centre). I should have a closer look at some of those new books I'd acquired. My first eye operation wouldn't be for ten days. Not clashing with the World Cup. There were no particular do's and don'ts in preparing for the operation. There was a slight hesitation, though, when the nurse requested details of my next of kin. At that time I thought of Colin Retford. Lucky bastard. Genially dismissive grand-daughter. Caring-enough-to-be-angry daughter. Two pretty women as next of kin. I should go to the library. Look up those terms: *Ontogeny. Allometry. Phylogeny.* Reading was still possible. I would have to read Mr Palast's book some time, if only to keep up with Retford's emails.

Such a lot of time: where to start? OK, might as well take a look at this, ah, manuscript of Isabel's mother.

12

Notes at Maputo Airport

I

Kennedy was late and I delayed him further by insisting on posting my cards. The detour to the main post office would cost us no more than ten or fifteen minutes. But the service was slow and I had to take responsibility for possibly missing the plane. Of course we got to the airport in what would seem plenty of time, close to an hour before take-off, and having confirmed the flight, I thought we would be OK. But there you go. Over-booking.

Somewhat self-consciously, almost pulling rank, I assured Kennedy that I would somehow get on the plane, urging him not to wait: it was a working day and although he seemed to have flexible hours, I didn't want him to cut corners at work on my behalf. I didn't want to patronize him by seeming to take on responsibility for his actions; but people in Mozambique went out of their way to accommodate you, to welcome you as a guest, and you didn't quite know what it cost them. Eventually I convinced him I'd be all right.

It was a slightly flat feeling, leaving. Normally, abroad, I get restless after a week or so, itching to get home to the post, to watching something familiar on the television, to getting back into your own rhythm; but after a month in Mozambique I felt I was just beginning to get my bearings;

every contact, every trip through this large country seemed to promise revelation, surprise, a new way of thinking about Africa; indeed, of thinking of myself in relation to Africa. Of course there was ambivalence, because I was going away feeling that I had got the best of the bargain; people I had in mind seemed to be on the point of being let down by my departure: it seemed too unfussy. Everyone had been generous and open, helping me to understand something of the country, inviting me into their homes; and it was as if I was walking away with their secrets, giving nothing back. So I would eventually write a book: that was for *me*, that was my project; that had nothing to do with people in Mozambique.

Already – as I tried to talk myself onto the plane – I was reflecting on Kennedy and his proud, new car and wondering how he could afford it: he worked in the IT building in the middle of town and, certainly, had a position where he could take time off when he wanted; but I didn't know what wages were like in this country; the Japanese weren't going to lower car prices in response to the GDP of Mozambique. But even then I was thinking, frivolously, beyond that, to Kennedy's name. He was the elder son; they named him after the American president. Nothing unusual there. But then his younger brother was called Arafat. What do you make of that? Hedging their bets? A sort of calculating African balance; or people with a mature sense of humour? I had hoped to meet Kennedy's father, but they were from Tete province, up in the north, close to Zambia and Malawi, so the father will remain for ever in my mind, an African sage, sitting in his back yard in the shade, under a tree, surveying the comedy of geopolitics, and giving a verdict in the naming of his sons.

No, I wasn't going to get on this plane. When a man, a steward from the airline, agrees that, yes, your ticket is in order, you've confirmed the flight to Johannesburg but the plane is full, there is no argument. He is trying to help: even though the plane is full, he will see what he can do, as some cases have priority. I don't quite like the sound of this, as trying to prove any sort of priority other than first come, first served would be problematic for me. Lots of people in the 'queue' are similarly disappointed: I wouldn't want to be forced to argue my priority against theirs. I regret having spent so much time at the post office, first waiting to buy the stamps, then having to get the pot of glue to stick them on, a slow and messy business; only to be reprimanded by Kennedy when I got back to the car for buying stamps in the first place. For, apparently, all you needed to do was to hand the cards over the counter, pay the required amount, and the attendant would do the rest. In any case, cards didn't need a stamp.

This was new to me.

No, the stamp was only for letters.

I was prepared to accept that a franking machine might be used for postcards while stamps were put on letters, and that the young woman behind the counter could be relied on to sort the cards according to destination and put the right amount on; but when Kennedy insisted that in no country are stamps put on postcards, only on letters, I had to argue my corner. Though I suspect his irritation that I had used up maybe fifteen minutes of time that we clearly couldn't afford was not unrelated to the fact that he had been a little late coming to the university to pick me up. So I let it go. Also, I didn't want to admit that I somehow felt more comfortable posting the cards myself rather than handing the money over to someone behind the counter and trusting to that person's honesty. Or efficiency. This was not, I hope, a crude response to Africa, for I had had a similar sensation at Charles de Gaulle Airport some time back, when I had come through to embarkation with my postcards (stamps already on) only to find there was no postbox in that part of the building. When the surly man observing the X-raying of your hand luggage said he would post the cards, I didn't altogether trust him. (I recalled visiting Guyana in the early 1970s, spending some time in a suburb of Georgetown and – a weakness of mine – avid for letters. And being dismayed to read in the newspaper that a postman, in our area, was taken to court and fined for dumping his sack of mail in a field, and, in one case, setting the contents alight, because he couldn't be bothered with the hassle of delivering them. The thing that rankled, as I remember, about the incident in Guyana, was the extreme lightness of the fine that the judge had handed down; little more than a smack on the wrist: my letters and rejection slips, I concluded, would now end up, embarrassingly, in the cane field.) But this was all my own mental baggage; I shouldn't have made the detour to the post office on September the 25th Avenue; Kennedy was right.

But now, how to play this scene at the SAA counter? Also among the disappointed was a couple, expatriate, who seemed to know me. As I tried to work out who they were the woman reminded me that they taught at the International School in Maputo where I had given a writing workshop a few weeks previously. The woman knowingly shrugged off her disappointment at not being able to get to Johannesburg, as this was the way things were.

I was pleased, now, that I hadn't made a fuss about not getting on the plane because at the school, giving the writing workshop, I had said all the usual things about people like us, like myself, Africans from the diaspora, setting some sort of example to Africans both out there and at home. Also, Kennedy and his friend, still in concerned attendance at that point, couldn't be made embarrassed by my behaviour.

But the woman brought me back to what had generated the real interest during my visit to the school. It was my search for Colin Retford, a man who had ended up in this country, and whose whereabouts I was tracking; and the pupils had been full of suggestions of where I might look.

He would be lying low, a gangster, creeping out to rob and steal, to keep himself alive.

He might be a spy.

If he didn't speak Portuguese he would have to pretend to be dumb.

He would be in a refuge, in a coma, looked after by one of the aid agencies.

He might be teaching in one of the international schools. Then he could speak only English, and not be thought suspicious.

To recap: Colin Retford was a character created by me, and first appeared in a short story, set mainly in England and France. When he walked out of the story he ended up in Mozambique. As I had no direct knowledge of Mozambique, of Africa, I was fascinated at how a man, who was 'British West Indian', a man of mature years – though with no history you could trace, as his narrative was lacking a 'back story' – how he would survive in present-day Mozambique. And yes, this Retford character spoke none of Mozambique's languages, no Portuguese, no other language of *place*, of clan. My curiosity about him had led me to Mozambique – twice in one year – and I hadn't yet decided what had come of it. Newfound friends and acquaintances in Maputo, in Beira in the centre of the country, in Quelimane in the north had played along with the idea. The pupils at the International School in Maputo had more or less sorted it.

'I hope you'll put this in your book,' the woman in the queue said. 'How're you getting along? Y'know, tracking your fugitive?'

(This is the problem when you tell people about your projects: they hold you to them.) She had sat in on my workshop at the school, where I had taken some pleasure in demonstrating the . . . ah! – the tangle of thought and whim; of coupling people through past history *and* accident; of chance; of the unstable chemistry of truth telling and lying – which formed the basis of the simplest line of dialogue. And here was I at the airport privately going through the same process with her: *How was I getting along with tracking down Colin Retford?* I had tried to sneak him into Fr Andreas' refuge outside Maputo; then to the centre of the country, to Beira (too potholed and exposed and in need of refurbishment for this potentially fastidious man). From there, further north, to Quelimane – only to rethink and start again. I couldn't, on second thoughts, bury him in Fr Andreas' refuge because it was for women and children; boys over sixteen had to be moved on elsewhere: the morning I visited I was so taken by the easy intimacy and sense of family, which extended to the visitors, that I couldn't implant Mr Retford here. (The communal body would reject him.) Also, it would be like playing a trick on Fr Andreas. The night before I visited there had been a rape at the refuge. Someone had scaled the walls and abused one of the young women. Everyone was devastated. And, whatever I thought of him, I didn't want Retford to be a rapist. Other locations had seemed equally problematic. Beira was parched as well; you couldn't hide anything there. Also, Beira was in the hands of the opposition, the political opposition to the government. Well, you couldn't set your man down there and not delve into decades of local (and national) politics: I wasn't ready for that. In Quelimane I had a different problem. In Quelimane, north of Beira, I had been treated graciously by a woman, a scientist, of outstanding grace and beauty – part of the Portuguese contingent who threw in their lot with Frelimo at independence. Before independence. Retford could certainly hang out there, hide, construct a new identity in this faded, elegant provincial town. But I didn't want to set him down too near to the delightful Faye, my host and contact in that town. Retford was not a man whom I would trust, so early in his construction, with women I respected. So, as they say, it was back to the drawing board.

Naturally, I said nothing of this to the teacher at the airport. I suspected she saw *me* as something of the Colin Retford figure, without legitimacy in this society. In my own (British) society? Or she might be thinking along practical lines, telling herself that Retford, being a construct, being in the making, would naturally have difficulty boarding a plane to South Africa. But then, she was in the same predicament; with her partner. (It is true that in an early – abandoned – scene I had had Retford holed up in a cheap hotel room in Maputo, perfecting his signature, like a schoolboy; or like an illegal immigrant, fleshing out a history behind the new name.) How had he come into possession of someone else's documents?

The couple needed to get to Johannesburg for two p.m. to attend a wedding (it was eleven thirty now), and the next plane out after this was at two p.m. There was additional urgency for them as the man, the partner, was going to be the best man at the wedding. (Do they hold up weddings if the best man is late?) So the representative of the airline said that the plane was full but as a wedding was a priority, particularly when you were best man, he would see what he could do. I ceded my right in the priority queue as I was not scheduled to be best man at a wedding. (I privately questioned whether he really was going to be best man at a wedding, but decided to be generous.)

My case was patently not urgent. I was on my way back home to England via South Africa. I had friends in

Johannesburg with whom I'd planned to spend the day, flying out early next morning. In Johannesburg Laurence and Phyllis (the people who changed, for the better, my view of Johannesburg) would be about to set out to the airport to meet me: I would have to ring them any time now to catch them at home. (It would be tacky to get them on the mobile after they had set out.) The official who was trying to allocate priority agreed with me that as I had this 'window' in South Africa, I wasn't, really, a priority. So, I might as well retrieve my case and go back out to phone Laurence and Phyllis, while Kennedy and his friend were still here to watch the bags. As I was heading for the phone, the couple from the school were allotted a place on the twelve o'clock plane to Johannesburg, in time for their wedding.

I was pleased for them, gave them the thumbs-up. But one thing left a question mark in my mind. Earlier, when the woman had talked, in a fairly amused way, of the frustration in not being able to get to the wedding, I had reassured her that it was OK to miss the wedding; OK for her partner and herself to continue to live in sin. And it was with a straight face that she put me right: the wedding in question wasn't their own but another couple's, friends of theirs. Imagine someone with so little humour travelling all that way to teach in Mozambique!

Before heading back into Maputo, Kennedy and his friend helped me up the stairs – with the heavy bag and heavier case, out along the wide platform overlooking the runway – to the canteen. They didn't want to have lunch, so we had a drink and said our goodbyes, promising to keep in touch. I wasn't *guaranteed* a seat on the two p.m. flight, but I was pretty near the top of the standby list; so I had told Phyllis (in Johannesburg) that unless she heard from me in the next hour or so, I'd be on it. (I'd gone to the loo on my way up to the restaurant. It was spotlessly clean; but the water was off. Enter an attendant with a ewer of water. A middle-aged man of some grace. I made a mental note that service needn't be demeaning.)

In the restaurant, out of habit, I took out my notebook and started jotting down my impressions. I deliberately didn't pursue the first thing that came to mind which was that in the confusion downstairs, in all the wrangling over 'priority', no money had changed hands and there was no hint that cash would have been a factor in rearranging the queue. This immediately and with some relief put in context that poor woman at customs in Quelimane who opened my little travelling bag and, smiling bashfully, suggested change for 'one coffee', before checking me through. I could live with a 'one coffee' airport tax at the world's airports, as long as it went to the industrious poor: in the scale of corruption I call that the sanitized end of 'finesse', of 'wit'.

But sitting upstairs what I was contemplating, again, was the business of leaving new friends behind. There was Kennedy, of course, and his friend João, whose flat I had ended up staying in at the university. I was a bit miffed that João had presented himself as a junior lecturer in the social studies department, and had invited me to make use of his university flat as he was away doing fieldwork for the next month or so. The offer had seemed genuine; I liked the ambiance at the university, the radicalism: they, at least, hadn't sold out to the IMF and other international bandits. Moving to the flat was convenient as I used the Centre of African Studies library every morning when I was in Maputo. (It closed at lunchtime, and that helped you structure your day.) What unsettled me, somewhat, was to find out, after I had moved into the flat, that João was a very political figure: Number Two Man, it seemed, in the opposition party. He had revealed nothing of this.

He knew that I was close to the family of one member of the government, someone in the cabinet; he knew that I supported the Frelimo revolution, and had spoken of my admiration for the two great leaders (assassinated) of that revolution: I didn't like to get myself into situations the implications of which I couldn't fathom. I was still uneasy about this as I prepared to leave Mozambique.

So I put that aside, and focused on other things unresolved, acquaintances that had provided, what shall we say, a certain emotional ballast anchoring me to Mozambique: Patricia at the British Council (so English in this setting, and so not out of place) and her husband, Paul; Wim, married into a delightful Portuguese-Mozambican family, generous and uncynical, despite his own rough treatment by the university bureaucracy. Then, there was the lovely Faye in Quelimane. I was trying to sort out my feelings of mild depression. What had all those mornings in the library doing 'research' added up to? Did I say goodbye properly to Amelia and her staff for allowing me free use of the resources? And how did I dare walk away so lightly from the place where Ruth First – ah, the inestimable Ruth First, but who am I to . . . – was assassinated; blown up by a letter bomb by agents of the South African apartheid regime? There was a little statue to her in the university garden. I had copied down the inscription somewhere.

I decided to have lunch in the canteen, in case I was delayed again; and the waitress moved me to a bigger, more central table.

All the waitresses seemed to be mixed race, smooth-skinned and striking: did this mean that waitressing here was a prestige job, a bit like air-hostessing used to be? This is the vulgar assumption that South Asians and Caribbean people, wedded to the hierarchy of pigment, instinctively make of situations like this. But João, the opposition poli-tician, once said to me, casually, that he wouldn't get to the top in politics because he was mixed race. That would also be unacceptable, if true; but it would seem, at least, that Africans did not instinctively feel the need to apolo-gize for the colour black. How, I wonder, would people here relate to those fraught debates we used to have in the 1970s about the coded, loaded nature of our inherited lan-guage: a black man or woman or *child* having to endure on a daily basis the implied insult emanating from the terms 'blackmail', 'blackball', 'blaggard', and other meta-phors still current, for disappointment and defeat – 'a black day', 'a dark cloud', etc. The only compensating virtue seemed to be that relating to your finances; being in the black. But that oversight was soon edited out by the banks.

The downside of moving table was that I came face to face with a rumpled, middle-aged man, overweight; who was tucking into his something or other and chips. He was white, bearded, and seemed to have no teeth whatever; and he was smoking a cigarette as he ate. You couldn't imagine a woman, anywhere in the world, waiting for this man to get off a plane. (Of course you could, and that's what was depressing.) But here was something so lacking in grace and sex appeal that it seemed made up, almost an affront in the people's refectory. Next to him Colin Retford would look OK. Initially, I was irritated that so many 'characters' that I came across seemed so much less worthy of the 'label' than the sorts of people that writers of the past – Somerset Maugham, say, at Raffles Hotel in Singapore – had run into. Even the Naipaul brothers had met better on their various tours of character assassination.

So it was a sort of welcome diversion when I looked straight up and noticed, hanging from the ceiling above the table, a giant art object, a sort of futuristic (or more accurately pre-modern) globe of planet earth. Severely reductive, it reduced the land-mass of the world largely to its continents: the only islands represented – apart from a necessary Antarctica to hold the structure together – are Madagascar and New Zealand, the North Island being the tiniest geographical expression admitted. Where is Indonesia? The Philippines? No Borneo. No New Guinea. The Caribbean, of course, is see-through space. (Granted they may have got this last one right. How could they, dwellers in the developing world, be so cavalier with that worldview? Africa is, of course, secure. Mozambique is part of the acknowledged map of the world that da Gama might have recognized.)

II

I had been reluctant to come to Africa but not for the usual – what I call, tacky – reasons.

People at home talk of unpredictable politics, civil/ethnic/ religious wars, corruption and inefficiency, the perception (and reality) of Aids limiting one's choice of sexual part- ner. Even having to be inoculated for medieval diseases such as dengue fever didn't appeal to those living in the security of the NHS. And, in fact, some or all of these things weighed with me to a greater or lesser extent. But since I'd been to Papua New Guinea and to many 'medi- cally suspect' parts of the 'developing world', my reluc- tance to go to Africa wasn't designed to keep bugs away from the body.

I felt I wasn't ready. I'd visited, indeed worked, in the other four continents and felt I hadn't really got that much to show for it. To have done the run of all five, you really had to come up with something special, for you would by then have travelled more widely than those fellows of legend, all of those people encountered in Hakluyt – Columbus, Drake, Hawkins. Or, since we're talking about Mozambique, than Vasco da Gama himself. It was no longer interesting to come back with new maps; but the feeling was that, having touched down on your fifth and final continent, you had to come back with *something*.

I was pretty certain that what I was looking for wasn't *root*. I wasn't with the African-Americans and West Indian intellectuals on that quest, which seemed to me to play largely into the hands of the white-skinned ethnics at home who liked to pretend that we didn't belong here. So no tracing of West African slave routes for me. That was one of the reasons that Mozambique appealed. It appealed, too, because of its revolutionary politics and the heroism of Mondlane and Machel, whom I would place with Nyerere and Mandela as the best that Africa had produced. Mozambique appealed, too, on aesthetic grounds, the name seeming to be one of the most pleasing concatenation of sounds you could utter. But I mustn't get ahead of myself. This isn't about me: this is a literary challenge, this is a self-imposed task, to track down the whereabouts and the survival potential of Mr Colin Retford.

I didn't send him off defenceless, of course. He was a man of mature years, he was witty and resourceful; he had survived life in a succession of First World countries; he had had a family, families; and he spoke the English language. In Maputo he would at some point find his way to the Centro de Estudos Africanos at the Universidade Eduardo Mondlane. He was a poseur, he would use the Portuguese version whenever possible. He would quote the speeches of Samora Machel in the original. He would sign off his letters and emails: 'A luta contínua', like the president. But this is later; he has yet to get to this point.

He will wheedle his way into the British Council on Rua John Issa, middle of town, but how is he to get past

Patricia, the press officer to the director; and do I want
him to get past Patricia? If this was a play, I would put him
through three gruelling acts, at the end of which, only,
would he get past Patricia. (He would be found out at Fr
Andreas' refuge, found out living under a false name when
he turned up for a job in a school. He would have access
to a computer – everyone has access to a computer – and
would try to impersonate someone, maybe this author. He
would get an aid agency to pay his bills at the Tivoli Hotel
on September the 25th Avenue, pending posting to his
station. On the down side he would be suspected of
playing off both sides of the political argument and suffer
the consequences (how severe we haven't yet decided). In
Quelimane he would fail to get past the lovely Faye for she
was a woman of fine perception, a scientist, had studied in
England, and seen off one (fairly benign) husband. So
before he finds his feet (and comes to the International
School to explain his Houdini act) Mr Colin Retford must
be made credible. And here is the scene, written on the
plane to South Africa, where the process starts.

SCENE ONE

Night: Two men bring in RETFORD, *dead or injured. They
lay him on the floor, gently. (Not dead, then.) One man,
the younger, is a* BOY SOLDIER.

*They exit; sounds of key turning in the door; fade. Lights
up on* RETFORD *checking the extent of the injury, trying
to lift, to stretch one leg, then the other, then the arms;
problems, clearly with the right arm. Key in lock.*
RETFORD *pretends to be asleep.* OLDER MAN *enters.*

OLDER MAN (*starts saying something in Portuguese and
stops*): Ah! I forget, you are English. And, like the
English you like to play the trick of being asleep when
you are awake.

RETFORD *opens his eyes.*

We, in Mozambique, should learn from you English.
Too much of the time, we stay with the eyes closed
when we should have them open. It is the old, how is it,
saying, about the missionaries and the Bible.

RETFORD *nods and grunts.*

You know it?

RETFORD(*carefully*): When they came . . . when the
missionaries came, they had the Bible . . . Bible and we
had the land. (*pause*) And they said. The missionaries
said, 'Close your eyes, let us . . . let us pray . . .'

OLDER MAN *nods encouragement.*

'Let us pray . . .' And when we opened our eyes, we had
the Bible and they had the land.

OLDER MAN: I thought that was a Mozambique story. So
it must be a story shared by others. But which others?
You are possibly a mistaken identity. Not one of those
come to attack and burn down villages, steal the
villagers' food and livestock (*beginning to recite*)

burn down schools

murder teachers and kidnap pupils

destroy hospitals and murder the medical staff

attack and burn down shops

blow up railways and mine roads

attack passenger trains and buses

destroy fuel tanks and sabotage power lines

destroy tractors, lorries and other means of production

attack economic projects and kidnap foreign teachers

kidnap, rape and kill the wives and daughters of the
peasants

kidnap nuns and missionaries

spread terror among the people, cutting off ears, tongues, arms and breasts.

(*Slight pause*) We don't believe you did that . . . (*pause*) Nevertheless, you are obviously not Mozambican. (*pause*) Some thought you were South African. Or Rhodesian. Malawian, even. From the days when these countries were not friendly to Mozambique. We cannot forget our southern neighbour's gift to us during those years of struggle, that Total Strategy, that . . . holocaust – on the hospitals, the schools, the railway line – the Beira–Umtali railroad; and of course, Maputo. The repeated attacks on Matola, attacks designed to miss the target, to maximize what you call, euphemistically, collateral damage. (*pause*) But you do not speak with a South African accent; and even when caught off-guard, you do not slip into that . . . error of pronunciation.

Pause.

You do not even speak the language of the present South Africa. When Thabo Mbeki says, 'I am an African', I believe him. When he describes his more than physical relationship with the landscape, the hills and valleys and wildlife of his country, I – I might not see the exact same shapes of Drakensberg or the sands of Kgalagadi. I might not even include the springbok in my selected bestiary – but I know Mbeki and I share an experience that makes us African.

P*ause; more businesslike, brisker*.

We accept that you are not Mozambican and that your . . . organization (*He extracts a folded paper from his pocket, but doesn't consult it.*) isn't on our list of terrorist, bandit gangs hostile to the independent and democratic state of Mozambique. We will, of course, investigate the nature of your recent . . . encounter with . . . person or persons unknown. As far as we are concerned, we are satisfied that you have no connection with (*and here he consults the paper*) R.E.T.F. we don't know F.O.R.D. we don't know. But no connection with (*reads from paper*) the pretend Lisbon journal, *O Dia,* with the so-called Voice of Free Africa, the multinational First Church of Christ, Scientist, based in Cincinnati, (*speeding up*) with the Conservative Action Federation from you know where; the Free the Eagle Foundation, the Heritage Foundation, (*draws breath*) the Hanns Seidel Foundation, the Konrad Adenauer Foundation, the Franz Josef Strauss Foundation and the London BBC.

Pause.

So as far as we're concerned you're free to go in search of your . . . memory. Or free to stay in Mozambique. As you are, clearly, a man in a somewhat traumatized state, we can give you access to services devoted to the care of such persons: you will be eligible for treatment at no cost to your sponsors. Er . . . to yourself.

About to go.

Incidentally, where are you staying in Mozambique?

RETFORD: Ah!

OLDER MAN: Oh, I forget. Memory loss. Well, we'll check among the hotels.

Pause.

Problem is. No name. Papers . . . acquired, shall we say, in error. Well. Until then, we'll see what we can do (*indicates room*) in the nature of furnishing.

About to go.

RETFORD: Can I ask a question?

OLDER MAN *stops*.

I . . . just wanted to compliment you on your English.
I hope that doesn't sound too . . . patronizing. I . . .
Where did you learn your English?

OLDER MAN: Here. And at Cambridge. Which is a
university in England. You can certainly patronize me
with compliments. The English way, I think. Have a
nice cup of tea.

He leaves. RETFORD *returns his attention to his right
arm, which looks in a bad way. Fade.*

III

Where to place this scene? Obviously, this is late on in the
story. Much of the play would have to precede this. By this
scene our man has been rumbled. (How long did it take?)
He would have been fished out of his hiding place (among
the 'flood' refugees?) and deemed not to be a provincial
hardship case come to town, not one of the displaced and
traumatized, his memory loss suspect. That cover for his
lack of Portuguese (or any Mozambique language) again,
would have limited duration. Who rumbled him?

If he was in a refuge, less well run than Fr Andreas', say,
one run by the myriad of aid agencies – and, statistically,
Mozambique heads the list of these – he could exploit that
confusion. (There was grumbling at the university that the
country was being ruled, if not governed, by these agencies.)
The ideal would be one run by high-minded, non-English-
speaking volunteers. Maybe Swiss or Scandinavian; someone who would put down Retford's laughable Portuguese,
which he would be furiously, secretly learning, to the suspicion that he was fleeing from some neighbouring English-
speaking country (Zimbabwe, maybe) and just wanted to
lie low for a while. (In the film of the play the young woman

doctor from the aid agency and Retford would be lined up to walk out into the sunset, together.)

Here he's been rumbled, and brought in front of our OLDER MAN. Yet, this is a very sophisticated encounter. (The preceding scene was obviously less pretty.) But by now the authorities have accepted that he is not a spy. The very urbane OLDER MAN is, in a way, an advert for Frelimo. We've moved from the rapid response of the War of Liberation and the Civil War days (what the administration calls the War of Destabilization) into a world of diplomatic and verbal finesse. The revolution has matured and is now a million miles away from barbarities practised in places such as Liberia and Sierra Leone and Angola and Sudan and the Congo and, alas, Zimbabwe. The OLDER MAN is heir to the civilizing ethic of Samora Machel. One story of Machel, the humanitarian, was told to me several times. We are in the middle of the Civil War (the War of Destabilization). The bandits are everywhere, burning, killing, kidnapping. Roaming through this province, that province. The security forces can't keep up. Everyone is frantic. In this particular village, the same. Unspeakable atrocity. There are seven bandits. But by the time the security forces catch up with them, they've disappeared, vanished, merged into the village population. There are forty people in the village and, whether through terror or collusion, the villagers refuse to identify the bandits. So what have we here? Forty villagers and seven bandits. Or forty-seven bandits. The debate goes this way and that. No one can decide. The war is going badly. A decision has to be made. Then someone has a bright idea. Call up Comrade Moises. This is a decision for the head of the army, Samora Machel. They explain their dilemma to him and ask the question: are there forty-seven bandits in the village? Or, despite everything, forty villagers and seven bandits?

And without the least hesitation Commander Machel says, 'There are only seven bandits in the village.'

The OLDER MAN is of that tradition. We can almost believe that at some point he will call on RETFORD at the Tivoli Hotel on September the 25th Avenue, and have a drink together in the bar. But not yet; Retford hasn't done nearly enough to get out of this one. Language must be one key to it. He must acquire that in order to survive, to scrounge, to earn some money. (At some point he will end up starting a business in Maputo, he will manufacture post-cards. For that, he would need allies. As an entrepreneur, he doesn't need to take the pictures himself or to develop them; just to convince the odd street trader here, the odd photo-developing agency there, to do the business; and then get the hotels to stock his cards.) He must have enough Portuguese to get by, but it would be an asset being foreign. For his credibility and capital would be presumed to come from abroad. As Portugal is too easily checked out, South Africa a bit suspect, England would be perfect. Neverthe-less, we'll see him in the British Council library on Rua John Issa flicking through books on photography: it is possible to imagine Mr Branson, say, of Virgin fame, idly flicking through colour displays of trains and aeroplanes. Maybe, in the interest of irony, we'll find Retford, instead, at the American Information Center, on Avenue Mao Tse Tung. But first, we've found him a refuge out of town, at Marracuene, twenty or so kilometres from Maputo.

Laetitia and Sander used to be the volunteers in charge of the Marracuene agricultural station; and one day they ran into Retford in Maputo; he ended up bunking down in their spare room, helping out, holding the fort for two weeks when Laetitia and Sander had to fly back to Holland, and is now in the running to replace them when their time runs out. (He won't, of course, settle for that; this is only to buy him breathing space.)

I wake on the long journey back to England, thinking of this and that, wriggle my toes and flex my feet and ankles against the dreaded deep vein thrombosis thing. I think of the good times recently had in Johannesburg with Phyllis and Laurence; and feel less nervous for South Africa because of them, of people like them; and my thoughts, unstable, shuffle like a pack of cards. Talking of cards, how careless to have posted them only yesterday, so that I would, as always, arrive back before them. And of course the mind flicks back to that residual fear: crash, hijack, engine failure. I'm thinking of the Arthur Miller play, *All My Sons*, corruption where business rules. And then the rough joke about Kennedy, the president. People in the White House failing to turn off his signature machine after he'd been shot, so that the dead man continued to sign letters with the official White House stamp for, apparently, hours. And then, as in a surreal state, my thoughts turn back to Retford.

He'd end up in the construction industry in Mozambique, postcards being only a trial run. He will improve his Portuguese and acquire useless information on precolonial Africa which will impress his listeners; he will conduct email correspondence with persons in England and elsewhere with whom he claims to go back a long way; he will admit to having an ex-wife and grown-up children. So, that's all in the past. Now, in the present, on a business trip north to Zambesia province, he will head for Quelimane, and call on Faye, and be admitted.

13

Colin Retford:
a Progress Report

I

He put aside his papers, quite a thick sheaf, as if a new thought had struck him. He's forgotten his signature; how pathetic. He hadn't forgotten as such, but . . . well, he wasn't happy with the way you linked the 'n' and the 'r' – the capital R. It was still a bit clumsy, needed work: there was a double movement there, an unnecessary stroke that had to be ironed out. So he grabbed the newspaper and signed *Colin Retford. Colin Retford.*

Obviously, not satisfactory. A man of his age would have smoothed this out decades ago, simplified to the point that the letters would glide into one another and be, yes, more or less undecipherable. That was the problem, the signature was too damn *clear,* as if he were a schoolboy signing for his first post office account. Thing is, he had already put the signature on a couple of documents – a good feeling, that; another little bit of evidence that you existed. But what the hell, better to make the break now than be stuck with something that made you uneasy: you weren't, after all, in a bad marriage that had to be kept going at all costs. And his name, after all, *was* Colin Retford. Colin Retford. (*Were you in a bad marriage that had to be kept going?* That wasn't his thinking, he had his own thought processes, he was Colin Retford.)

He was happy with the name; he could have been called something less easy to live with. He was, indeed, called something else at the start, a name that even the Little Brother had thought better of. Stuck with one of those early names, he would not have been so malleable.

Though, coming back to the business of the signature: it would have been better with an *initial* thrown in. Initial of his middle name. An initial added class. Colin *T.* Retford (T for Tyrannosaurus; Colin W for Wicked Retford, Colin *J.* Retford, etc.). Any of those large, strong letters would make a big statement in the middle of the signature. Others had it. Bringing them closer to the Monarchs of the Realm in their plenitude of middle names than to the deprived of this world, like yours truly. The Little Brother signed himself P. C. Stapleton. (A policeman or a police joke.) He would find out more, that was a condition for his own survival. But he was making progress. Again, he reached for the sheaf of papers and made as if to read, but changed his mind, turned the pile over; and on a clear, blank page signed his name. Worryingly, the thought crossed his mind that he didn't know if he smoked. It wasn't a physical, all-craving need, just a passing, idle thought. So, obviously, he didn't smoke. Not seriously.

It seemed logical to write to the Little Brother whose address is stamped all over these papers. He must hit back, at least *write* back. The energy's been flowing too much one way. Why did this malignant Little Brother give him the wrong language to start with? What would it cost him to have sent Retford to night school, twenty years ago, thirty years ago to sort out his Portuguese? Or sent him to Portugal on holiday and falling in love with the language; or with a woman and learning the language on her account?

That would give him the ability, the option to challenge the supremacy of Little Brother. OK, he'll start by writing a letter, a letter of complaint.

*

Rua John Issa, 226, PO Box 4178, Maputo, Mozambique.
  This isn't my address, of course, it's the British Council's; but it says here that I have initiative, so I will come up with some excuse before I have to deal with the question of picking up the reply. Fact is, I haven't got an address. The information on my desk is confusing. I'm not a thief, therefore I'll steal no more documents, but work with what I have. Two identities and a Mastercard. I won't take the identity of the owner of the Mastercard, which I recovered from a malfunctioning machine at the airport (too complicated to go into the details), because I'm not that type of character, but I'll work out what's possible from the other notes. One has me in Maputo, the other up country: why would you go up country when you can be in the capital? Only the rich and satisfied move out of the capital. I don't know for sure, but I've read that some-where; and I'm not rich and satisfied. (What would it be like to be rich and satisfied?) At the moment I'm a man with memory loss trying to remember his skills, his pro-fession. It would be good to know if I've been to agricul-tural college with a background of farming. Good to know lots of things: my eventual address, the date when all this is happening, the time of day. The clues are, presumably, all here. Am I in a hurry to find out? Who knows?

Dear Little Brother,

(Retford glanced at the questions scribbled on the back of the 'briefing notes'.)

– How long have I been here?

– Finances. Can I use the Mastercard without comeback?

– Family in England: what's going on there?

– Are the women in my life pretty?

So, to the letter:

Hello Little Brother, you Bastard,

You haven't thought this through, old man. Is it deliberate, etc.?

II

In Sheffield, Pewter Stapleton was in a mood to confound his critics; he was out of sorts, though he denied being out of sorts. He resisted the notion that things were falling apart; and yet, and yet. He had thought of going south. To France. But hadn't booked. And now the price was prohibitive, as he knew it would be; yet he hadn't pre-booked. He trotted out the excuse of a cataract operation, after which he wasn't allowed to fly for six weeks. Well, this was long past six weeks. So he had to look for another excuse. He had read somewhere of a poet, an English poet, offered a position in Australia, who felt he couldn't go to Australia, though he was tempted to; for what would happen to the country, to England, if he went to Australia? However comic, it had the right sort of ring of madness. Like those characters who get out of the house at five o'clock in the morning and head for some strategic place, a hill above the town, say, and then conduct all sorts of rituals, the better to make the world safe for mere mortals who expect cause and effect to proceed along the lines of traditional logic. There's a man in Dr Johnson like this. *Rasselas*. So Pewter Stapleton would press on regardless, through the problem with his eye, the new problem with his teeth, the problems with friends, the new two-year-old in the news, tortured and murdered by her parents, through the prospect of war with Iraq that nobody wanted; and Terry Venables having a hard time at Leeds and Man United closing the gap on Arsenal. So fast forward to Retford and Mozambique and a partnership of the Brothers.

*

No time to waste. By now the Brothers had opened a bookspace on September the 25th Avenue, and everyone thought the name *Brothers* was both self-deprecating and resonant. As a name it was less empire-building and family-obsessed than Stapleton (drawing comparison with Waterstone?), and suggesting that his relationship to Africa was not colonizing: And who was his brother, who were his brothers? That was the open, generous question.

Who was at the opening of the bookspace?

The people from the British Council were there.

He was sitting, admiring the crisp, laundered cloth spread over the table before him, the way Albie Sachs observes (in *The Soft Vengeance of a Freedom Fighter*) that the Mozambicans do this sort of thing; that and a bunch of fresh flowers in a vase.

The bookspace was neither a bookshop nor a library. These were not just his books, but books that colleagues and friends had tired of: this was a gentle way to anglicize a space on September the 25th Avenue. Careful. Colonialism.

Also present would be people, invited by the Council, who wrote in English.

And that woman doctor, a volunteer, who hailed from Bedford. With her friend.

In his address, from behind the table, with its crisply laundered cloth and vase of fresh flowers, our man gives an address full of references to librarians of the past (Mao, Borges, Larkin – Crates of Pergamum . . .), and to brothers who shared the same name, like the Humboldts of Berlin, and others like the Plinys of Ancient Rome – great man and his nephew – all the way down to Pewter Stapleton and Colin Retford, who would in the end convince you that Stapleton and Retford were the same name. Throughout this address Pewter was striving to impress the woman doctor from Bedford.

He may have overdone it slightly when, conscious that he was in Africa, he invited discussion on the published exchange of letters between the Nobel laureates, Nadine Gordimer of South Africa and Kenzaburo Oe of Japan on the ills afflicting people trying to survive in the world today, and our responsibility for rehumanizing . . . ah! But this is being done clumsily; he is coming over as something of a show off. He has lost the woman doctor from Bedford and has attracted the attention of her male partner. Damn.

He would have to go back to the drawing board, as they say; work out more clearly just what the 'bookspace' was, and why the bookspace scene had to be rewritten.

He was working at it, was Mr Retford; in Maputo he went to sleep and was conscious of having had his first dream. Waking in excitement he was trying to pin it down. Pen and paper. Quick. A first dream. So yes, he's in flight, and that must have come about by accident because he can't remember the occasion for the flight; but he remembers going through a secret passage, through hundreds and hundreds of doors climbing up, each door fastened on the outside with a little bracket you lift up and you're through to the next room along the passage; and after some time he's passing through Romania, which is the only country mentioned. And he remembers he's the only black person he meets on the trail; and before that he wasn't conscious of his colour. And eventually they get to a point where they've reached the end and they could look out on a wooded area, look down on what seems trees and a trim, square lawn, where there are puppies playing with car tyres. And he suddenly realizes that there aren't only puppies but children with old tyres. And the lawn isn't a lawn but a huge open-backed truck or lorry disguised as a lawn; and the tyres are what the children use to get across from the high place to the lorry; and it's a dangerous operation because there is a wide street in between, a street patrolled by the army. And although he is bigger than all the others, he curls himself inside the tyre and bounces across and safely lands into the lorry. And there is one further disguise. After all the child-escapees, mini-elephants are brought across into the lorry, as cover for the children; and the elephants are carved objects, brightly coloured. And even though the army turn up towards the end they don't recognize the children under the carved elephants. And they actually escort the lorry (two lorries now, for the next lawn is a lorry), first through one gate, then through another, and they're on their way. There are other difficulties that he can't quite recall, there is a space, like a room, with the stub of a pencil, but no paper he can remember, where you can write your name; and where they said you could phone your family; but there is no phone, just two bare wires that you use to start a car without a key; and two girls come in and say their names, and he says his name, but no one uses the wire-phone; and before he knows it they are beginning to drop people off (grown to adulthood now, and throughout they haven't had a single meal or a single drink, or a trip to the loo); and all the houses of people returning to their families seem hidden in trees or tall grass and one thing he notices throughout is how silent the lorry is, how smooth the ride, as if it's floating above its tyres; and the driver is never seen; and now it's his turn to be let off; and they follow this tree-lined lane round the bend and there is the house, a cottage, with his father at the gate, leaning on the gate, looking out; and he recognizes his father instantly, but his father doesn't recognize him; and he goes round the side of the house and there is his mother sitting in a chair, young and beautifully dressed in a casual sort of way and in another chair is his sister proudly wearing her girl guide scarf. This is the sitting room, the drawing room, and he enters through another door and recognizes them instantly but none of them recognizes him because he's been away, lost, for twenty years; and they don't even react to his coming into the room; and before anyone says anything he wakes up.

This gives him a huge surge of energy; he's on a roll. Suddenly, he's like a man possessed.

III

I know a thousand things.

Retford is beginning to fill in the blanks, like a series of mini-jigsaws, piece after piece gradually revealing the pattern. A mistake, then, to be hung up on the big things – of where the condoms in the luggage came from, for instance, and the equally big ones of when and how often he'd have occasion to use them: these things will be solved when the . . . pieces fit. If, as he remembers, from something he has read, a man has a daughter and she knows a thousand things, and that is the beginning of the world; and if he is older than his daughter, as you would expect a man to be, he must get to the point that he knows at least a thousand and *one* things, to be beyond his daughter, particularly if she is very young. But must he know the exact thousand things his daughter knows, plus one? Or could his thousand things be different? So, first, he must find out his daughter's thousand things.

So tell us some of your thousand things. A thousand and one *things.*

(Ah, he knew it.) But he was the father to the daughter. He had to encourage her to get even further ahead of him.

A thousand and one; *that's even better than a thousand things. A thousand and* two *things.*

At this stage Retford must learn from his young daughter and begin to stock his mind with things: I am the father (one) not the young daughter (two) this is a good thing (three) for I can acquire an adult's things quickly (four) maybe overnight (five) like last night's dream (six) if it was last night (seven) and I'm Colin T. Retford (eight) or Colin J. Retford (ten). Already ten things and no effort at all. Ten things in no time at all. Little Daughter, look out. Little Brother, take good care.

IV

Before he brings him into the bookspace, Pewter, in Sheffield, must keep pace with the man from Mozambique. This is easy; he's got the data; as is expected he's boned up on the recent political history of Mozambique.

16 JUNE 1960: *Portuguese authorities open fire on black Mozambicans calling for independence during the visit of the provincial governor at Mueda in Cabo Delgado province. There are believed to have been several hundred casualties.*

23–25 JUNE 1962: *The Frente de Libertação de Moçambique is founded in Dar es Salaam, Tanzania. (Dr Eduardo Mondlane elected president.)*

25 SEPTEMBER 1964: *The Frelimo movement initiates its armed struggle against the Portuguese state with guerrilla actions in Mueda district (Cabo Delgado province).*

3 FEBRUARY 1969: *Frelimo party president Eduardo Mondlane assassinated in Dar es Salaam.*

9–14 MAY 1970: *The fourth session of the Frelimo central committee elects Samora Machel as the new Frelimo president.*

1971: *In his 1971 anniversary message Samora Machel states, 'The seventh year of war was the point of departure for the conscious evolution of the nature of our organization, its evolution towards becoming a vanguard party of the working masses of our country, a vanguard party with a vanguard ideology.'*

25 APRIL 1974: *A coup d'etat in Portugal led by officers of the Movimento das Forças Armadas (MFA) overthrows the regime of Marcello Caetano.*

7 SEPTEMBER 1974: The Lusaka Agreement. *Portugal and Frelimo outline the unconditional transfer of political power to Frelimo. (This provokes some Mozambicans in Lourenço Marques to attempt to seize power.)*

25 JUNE 1975: *Mozambique becomes independent as a Marixst–Leninist state. Samora Moises Machel is appointed Mozambique's first president.*

3 FEBRUARY 1976: *The capital of Mozambique, previously known as Lourenço Marques, is renamed Maputo.*

5 JULY 1976: *The* Voz da Africa Livre *commences political broadcasts by Mozambicans opposed to the Frelimo government, an opposition made up of former members of Frelimo's military and political wings, and Mozambican nationalists, which would subsequently form itself into the* Resistência Nacional Moçambicana (Renamo). *This draws support and direction from Rhodesia, apartheid South Africa and other international right-wing forces.*

17 AUGUST 1982: *Ruth First, research director of Eduardo Mondlane University's Centre of African*

Studies and prominent South African ANC/SACP
member, is assassinated by a letter bomb.

16 MARCH 1984: The Nkomati Accord. *The 'good-*
neighbourliness and non-aggression' pact between
Mozambique and South Africa, signed by Samora
Machel and P. W. Botha.

19 OCTOBER 1986: *President Samora Machel 'dies'*
(along with thirty-four others) in an unexplained plane
crash at Mbuzini in South Africa's Transvaal Province.

He has given his man in Mozambique enough 'things' to
be getting on with. These are among the two hundred and
fifty or so 'things' about the history of the Mozambican
revolution he has released in one go. In time, we would,
perhaps, find out something of our man in Maputo when
we discover which of these 'things' he chooses to remember.

Meanwhile, this is no one-dimensional creation, not a
West Indian or a black Englishman tendency; our man
must have more than a political culture. There will be an
artistic dimension. Starting with the literature: what does
he read? To make this easy, give him a weakness for quoting favourite authors. So who are the authors? Before the
authors, something of the folk culture. Quotations from
the market, the street, from the café – the agricultural
station. (African proverbs: must go to the library.) After
that, the authors. Five, ten bits of literature that constitute
his artistic security. He's not, of course, a literary graduate. (Is he a graduate? Yes, maybe something low-level like
sociology or media studies. From where? Leicester, maybe.
Or Nottingham. Wherever.) So he makes a fool of himself
when he pretends to be literary. Does he know Kipling's
'If' or Tennyson's 'The Charge of the Light Brigade'?

This still doesn't tell Pewter Stapleton enough about our
man in Mozambique. Nothing to tell the tone of voice in
which he would intone 'Cannon to the right of them, /

Cannon to the left of them', etc. The rest of his reading matter would help. How about Conrad's *Heart of Darkness?* Is he pro or anti-Conrad on this one?

While Pewter tries to make up his mind, a new strand of thinking has to be sorted out for our man: how much of an asset is he to Africa? When he hears Africa insulted by reference to the crocodiles who have feasted on Africa, when the media, the dentist, the man in the pub puts him down with a joke about Idi Amin and Bokassa and Sani Abacha, and the fellow in the Congo, and those in Rwanda and Sierra Leone and Liberia, is he able to defend Africa more convincingly than Stapleton in Sheffield has been able to? If not he's no use to anyone. This realization – that our man has a role – makes it easier for Pewter to lighten the literary section with a bit of ridicule.

So Retford, being a chauvinist man, would be aware of up-to-date feminine literature, and would feel able to quote from, say, Dylan Thomas's, the Reverend Eli Jenkins' send-up prayer in *Under Milk Wood*, and that joke poem that Tennessee Williams gives poor old Nono in *The Night of the Iguana*: 'How calmly does the orange branch/Observe the sky begin to blanch', etc. That'll do for now; that, and maybe the second verse of the English National Anthem.

> O Lord our God arise,
> Scatter our enemies,
> And make them fall:
> Confound their politics;
> Frustrate their knavish tricks;
> On Thee our hopes we fix;
> God save us all.

Pewter had had in mind for Colin Retford to start a church in Mozambique, to tide him over, so to speak, until he got his act together, the First Church of Christ, Biologist, after that fellow in America. Maybe that won't now be necessary. But it would be a pity to waste the little scene he had written to that effect, set in the Tivoli Hotel in Maputo, on September the 25th Avenue. But he had to move on, become more ambitious. Who knows, he may have created, in Colin Retford, an insatiable self-improver. Here is Retford, late on in the proceedings, setting out to fly to the northern province of Quelimane (home of the lovely Faye, who will become his partner) to visit the International School there. He is, of course, revised into being word-perfect. He's still at the Tivoli Hotel on September the 25th Avenue.

ACT TWO, SCENE ONE

Room at the Tivoli Hotel, Maputo. Day. Language tape on. Portuguese. RETFORD *repeating phrases as he lifts weights. Problem, clearly, with right arm. Half-packed bags on floor. Piles of books, papers, laptop, camera, a newspaper (*Noticias*) on table. Television turned off. Telephone rings.*

RETFORD (*answers phone*): Ola? Ah. Amelia. Hang on a sec.

Goes and turns off tape; comes back.

Right, how're we doing? . . . Next week. Yeah. Fine, next week is fine, I'm going . . . I'm heading for Quelimane this afternoon, I'm told . . . I'm told there's, there's a rather good English library up there . . . No, not really, going to the school. International School . . . Yes, had a great time in Beira last week, spent, what, three, four days. Yes, fantastic, well, yes and no . . . *etc.*

Fade out; puts down phone, looks at watch, goes to desk and picks up laptop and camera; picks up newspaper and reads headline aloud: 'Chissano visita Inhambane', *etc.; puts down newspaper, picks up towel and starts going OFF; stops, comes back; lifts receiver, dials.*

Yes, er . . . *Ola. Boa tarde.* Urrr. Colin Retford. Room 310. *Queria* . . . Sorry. *Presso de um taxi. Por favor.* Ask for Jorge. To the airport. Yes. *(puts down phone)* Obrigado.

Goes out to bathroom; phone rings while he's in bathroom; he doesn't hear it; fade.

Lights up in hotel foyer. Desk ATTENDANT *with phone, listens, shrugs, puts down phone.* TWO WOMEN VISITORS *talk to each other in local language, hand over small, square package to* ATTENDANT, *and leave. Little Richard's 'Good Golly Miss Molly' coming through the loudspeaker system.* RETFORD *enters foyer, dressed for travel, with bag; goes to desk. No one.* ATTENDANT *comes.*

ATTENDANT: Ah!

RETFORD suddenly sings along with Little Richard, with great energy. ATTENDANT *looks out of front door but* TWO WOMEN *have gone.*

Something for you, Dr Retford.

RETFORD: For me?

She hands over the little package. RETFORD *puts his key on the counter, takes package, reads the card on the outside of the package.*

Colin Retford, Associates. Ah, brilliant.

Opens packet.

Take a card. Take a card. *(pause)* These are the cards that are going to put all of Mozambique on the tourist map. See? Xai Xai's never looked like that. Well, Xai Xai *does* look like that but you don't make it look like that on your cards. (*Gestures at some tired-looking hotel postcards, and back to his.*) Now, even you would want to buy this card. Last week we did Beira. We'll market the potholes as 'local colour'. The Americans will love it. This week, Quelimane. (*Pointing finger.*) The hotels will have to play their part in this. But I'll talk to you when I get back from the north.

BOY SOLDIER *appears.*

Taxi?

(*To* ATTENDANT.) See you in four days. I've still got something on account, right?

She indicates yes; he starts to leave; stops.

I'm expecting a message from the British Council. Tell them I'll get on to them on Thursday. Friday.

He goes; fade.

(*To be continued.*)

14

The Muse from Home

I

Isent him this instruction:

<u>cretford@hoteltivoli.org.mz</u>

Mr Architect, Sir,

Here are your instructions.

And I emailed him the entire short story.

II

I hadn't taught him to read because that wasn't my function, but the extent to which he could read the signs would determine whether I'd done a good job on him. I didn't want him to be massively dysfunctional, what's the point of that; you meet dysfunctional people all the time. I have a colleague at work who teaches a course called 'Making Monsters', which we took to be a Renaissance conceit gone wrong, you trip over from Hamlet into Frankenstein, sort of thing. Till we realized that we had among our number a couple who actually *were* monsters. No point in going through the hassle of *making* something you've already got. But, to the project. I didn't want Mr Retford to supplant me in the area of normalness. (I know, since when have I been accused of being normal?) So he had to be slightly strange. Stranger, let's say: I would expect him to be intelligent; and then we would see where to go.

So what are the things to be picked out in this story of his? We are rivals, of course, but in a civilized sort of way, so civilized that I let him win the girl in the end. Twice. First, she is a girl from Cyprus, generously endowed. I push this back to the tail end of the 1950s, before the PC thing became a problem; and I take credit for introducing him to her – her to him. One up to Mr Retford, then, for getting the girl from Cyprus. One up to me for the introduction. No mistaking, she was desirable, the elder of two sisters. 'My breasts would be down to here,' she said to me, 'if I didn't wear a bra.' So she wore a bra throughout the braless 1960s. And why did she fall to Retford? Ah, who knows? But I like to think it was because I had to go off to university to read Plato and transliterate *Beowulf*. Plato and *Beowulf* were no match for the more direct philosophy and Old English of Mr Retford. 'I only sleep with stupid men,' a friend says to me, now, almost in triumph. And after a lifetime of pretending not to be stupid, you can't suddenly do a *volte face*, and claim stupidity. So the world – and the women of the world – must be ceded to stupid men. I wish that Colin Retford were stupid. I fear that he is not stupid. So it must be the women of the world, then, who are, ah, duped, doubly. That Retford and his lady from Cyprus are no longer together is no consolation. None of us, whose fate is similar, can take solace in that. So back to the text, his map of recognition.

I am in the South of France with friends and he is visiting. I have some grounding in that place, despite Monsieur Le Pen and the Front National, despite my very accommodating neighbour, who takes me to lunch – and votes Front National. I've known the region for over thirty years.

Friends, the children of friends, are part of my extended family. So, out of good manners, if nothing else, I must make Mr Retford welcome there.

I make him welcome; I meet him at the airport in Nice, and drive him north into the Var, forty minutes or so on the autoroute to the turn-off (Les Adrets), past the Lac St Cassien and straight ahead to Montauroux where we've rented a house. Over the next few days he meets my friends, visiting. I introduce him, also, to friends I've known for thirty-odd years since I was here, in the early 1970s, as a member of a building cooperative, building and restoring houses. I introduce him to the architect, a special friend, who was a member of that cooperative, and ended up writing the history of the movement. I take Retford into the Alpes Maritimes, into Spéracedes and Cabris, little villages I used to know, now gentrified; and I take him down to the coast, to Cannes, which as a first-time visitor he wouldn't want to miss out on. In the same spirit, on the return trip to the airport, we pop into the Negresco at Nice for the souvenir as much as for the drink. All this is in the story emailed to him.

Other things there might be more coded: the details of his life as seen by me, are open to debate. (I tell people that, like the famous prisoner and author, Jeffrey Archer, I have difficulty being clear about some details of my own life, so how can I be certain that I will get Retford's right? This is just a biased version, after all.) That he is a man from the Caribbean is certain; but from what island, what territory, is unclear. He is not either small enough (good) or honest enough (bad) to claim any one Caribbean camp-site to the exclusion of all others. So far so good. He is a man who needs the *geography* of a Mozambique to thrive in. Or to survive. He has been married. His ex-wife, from Cyprus, provided me with a difficulty, as I saw her first; but that's my problem, not his. He has a daughter in

England who hates him. That's better. He has a grand-daughter called Isabel. Will he be happy with this? I won't negotiate changes to his biography until I need to. That's why I'm not bringing him to London on business; because the business would be something tacky, and the company dubious; that would be for a later stage. That would be Plan B, should he fail Plan A. (In Plan A Isabel, the grand-daughter, is about to go up to university. In Plan B Isabel works on the checkout at Tesco's. No big social point, just getting the feel of things. Until then I wouldn't know whether Retford, at dinner, is likely to talk sense of clearing landmines in Mozambique: why must it take four hundred years if the world really wanted to clear landmines in Mozambique? Or whether at dinner he might be regaling us about the challenge of hosting the next Miss World contest in Maputo?

I've held out the carrot of sharp dialogue for him; *with* him. Of his increased living space (Mozambique for the Caribbean; for England), he can already say that this new setting allows him to make his mistakes and not blame the world. Some wit at table would then have a go at me, as they do, for being still here in England, imprisoned –

Worrying the carcass of an old tale.

And I would apologize, yes, for measuring out my life with coffee spoons.

And someone would observe, lightly, that I didn't drink coffee.

And for that I would credit Retford with a hit, a hit, a very palpable hit.

This conversation takes place in England some time in the future.

*

About this estranged daughter, then; she is living in Stoke Newington, something of an activist. Just as in the old days in the good old US of A a lot of black people pretended to be white, now here, in Europe, a lot of people with white parents are pretending to be black. Ah, well, fashions change. Many of them would plead mitigating circumstances – one parent the wrong colour. Retford would have occasion to wonder aloud why his daughter had to pretend to be black to be taken seriously as a radical since most demonstrably black people in the world were so touchingly of the conservative tendency. But what did he know? He was only a man who couldn't get his story straight in any language.

The detail about his first wife couldn't divert him. If she was so good looking why did Pewter Stapleton hand her over? And how come he knew so much about her physical make-up? He'd better not get into this; an obvious wind-up. Nevertheless, Stapleton was playing a dangerous game; he had given Retford military training. In Cyprus. Late 1950s. Though Retford reputedly met his Cypriot lady in London. Nice detail. (In a ladies' belt factory in the West End of London.) That further hint of detail, never fleshed out, was maybe a trap to divert Retford's attention from the main thing, which was Plan A.

Concentrate on the case in hand, that first visit to the South of France. So Retford is left alone in this house in Montauroux while everyone is out. As he is to meet the architect friend of Pewter's, he is probably glancing over his proposal for the renovation of the town in central Mozambique. He's certainly not sitting around on the terrace reading Dickens. Or Balzac, for that matter. (He will not succumb to Mr Stapleton's tastes.) He is surprised that they have central heating in the house, which signals that the South of France isn't all it was cracked up to be, climate-wise. Central heating *and* a fireplace. Wood all round the place, a forest, so firewood not a problem. Pewter says it's oak and pine, as if he is the god of forests, naming the trees. He says, too, that the new-cut house keys don't fit, so you have to jiggle them. Pewter is, also, the god of entering houses.

Anyway, a knock on the door cuts all this short. It's the *pompiers*, dressed like firemen.

It has to be a set-up. Why would they just come when everyone else, those claiming to know the lingo, have gone out shopping?

This was a test. *Think.* The pompiers brought their calendars. They were collecting for their calendars. Was it one-off or annual, he didn't know. If annual what did the good host give in exchange? (Not, surely, the wife, the daughter of the house?) In the end it says that Retford gave fifty francs and collected not one but two calendars. One for the house, one for his own verification of the event. (He would put one of those calendars in his bag so he could study it when he got back home. Then he thought: a *clue.* So he took it out and sat down.)

Two things about the region he took in for further reference. One was the trip to Cannes. It's December. The Croisette is windy and cold (though the light isn't bad), and the palm trees outside the Film Festival building are described as being a bit conscious of being in the wrong place. Interesting that he is denied a sight of Cannes in summer when the stars are out. There is, too, dog shit on the streets. Why weren't First World dogs taught any better? (Retford will have to study the email further; he can't remember if that last observation was in the text. Or if he's making it up.)

But first, something more important for passing the test; the meeting with the architect, who, like Pewter, had been a member of a house-building, house-restoring cooperative in the early 1970s. Retford had tried to get hold of the book about the cooperative but had drawn a blank. But he'd tracked down someone who had a copy, and got them to photocopy the Contents page, and *that* he had off by heart. There were fourteen chapters. Pewter's favourites were Two and Nine. This was Chapter Nine.

Coopérative Ouvrière du Bâtimant
Cooperative of Building Workers

PART ONE

Chapter One Work as an Alternative

a On the petty inconveniences/discomforts, the more generalized disenchantment that a person accumulates on his way to the cooperative.

b A *professional* alternative for those who do not change profession, only the mode of organization.

c An *intellectual* alternative for those who've (in some cases) failed elsewhere (teachers, artists, etc.).

d COB's openness to all (how the implications of this gradually come to be understood – reunions).

e Importance of weekly reunion of all members, reviewing the week's work, planning the next week's work; a get-together, fostering group identity.

f Biographical notes of members.

Sorry, this was Chapter One.

The two 'biographical notes' he paid most attention to were those of the architect and, of course, Pewter Stapleton. He'd make those work for him. But let him run through the other thirteen chapters quickly.

*

He knows that this is Plan A. Plan B is worse. Plan B would involve murder. That's his incentive for making a fist of Plan A. Plan B would be to enrol him as the avenging arm for the hurts, accumulated and festering, in the breast of Pewter Stapleton. Apparently, this man's partner had been abused in England, on a train from Hebden Bridge to somewhere and Pewter had done nothing about it at the time. Now, this is to be avenged. Vengeance, also, must fall on the literary establishment that has ignored and marginalized him over the years. Colin Retford is now being brought in to lay waste the Arts Council of Great Britain and other guilty bodies. He must also take out two or three talentless prats who pick up the literary prizes. Then there's the outer ring of resentment and rage; of the violent murderers and rapists banged up and pampered in the gaols. Seventy-four women murdered by their partners in London in the last two years. Something must be done about it. Plan B would have Retford taking out the murderers, wife-batterers and child-abusers before he could be written back into the story.

Of course he has the military training, has Retford; he was in Cyprus tracking Grivas in the 1950s.

*

From the thriving village of Fayance (familiar; the cross-roads; there's a story of someone crashing into that café on the right), he heads straight on for the next village, Seillans. The turn left into the village after the supermarket (*Huit à Huit*), careful, careful through this olde-worlde hill village; and then out again. Then another turn-off. The left fork; the narrow beautifully kept lane (why are the rumours of this road so wrong?). Drainage bump at the bottom and, yes, the big – surprisingly big – old property coming up on the right.

*

p.c.stapleton@scu.ac.uk

My Professor,

Good news from France. Friends here remember you. Will I come to England to celebrate? Or will you come to France? My father always promised us ... that we would live in Fraaaance!

PS Remember change francs for euros.

They're odd about these details here. Francs run out in about five days.

C.W. Retford / C. J. Retford / C.T. Retford?

15

The Mozambique Connection

I

C. J. Harris had fallen asleep, in bed, in the middle of dictating the letter. The boy at the computer had saved the letter, and was tracking down some other subject on the machine. Then, after some time, CJ started talking as if they had never been interrupted. The boy had to make a decision whether this was to be part of the letter.

'I remember it used to have a jackarse over there in Africa, called Idi Amin. And he did one thing that I approve of. Amin made a donation to England when England was in trouble. That was in the '70s, the 1970s. That's the only thing the fella did I approve of. At the time it had a man in England named Edward Heath, used to be prime minister, I don't know if he still alive. And Amin said to the Prime Minister of England: "I see your people having a hard time of it, what with the three-day week, and all that." So he send them some shillings. Send them shillings from the Ugandan people to the English people. I like that. I call that, that's what I call *style*, no question about it. That's something that's maybe going out of fashion these days . . . Because when you come to think of it the shillings he offer to England only make sense as a gesture: those shillings, however many, aren't going to be enough to do the trick; they not going to turn a three-day week into a four-day week. And looking at it the other way, forget those fellas who say: "Uganda is a poor country out there in the middle of Africa. They should spend the shillings on themselves, you know, on the poor people of Uganda who need it more than the poor people in England." And you think, maybe they got a point. Sound all right in theory. But when you look at this thing closely, you're not talking about such a vast amount of money. The money is all right for a gesture, not the same thing as money that could turn your economy round. That money not going to make a big difference to the people of Uganda, whereas it enough to make the English people feel *shame*. Even if you could, what you call it, distribute that money in Uganda, it not going to make the people in Uganda any richer, not that they'd notice. You get my meaning?'

'Yes, CJ.'

By now the boy had turned his attention back to the letter, but he still wasn't typing. He asked CJ a question.

'So what sort of time was it back then, CJ?'

'I remember passing through England . . .'

'I don't understand when you say three-day week, you know.'

'You work for three days, not five days or what have you, six days of the week, and then . . .'

'And you don't do nothing the rest of the week?'

'Well, not in the factories and thing, if you don't have any light or . . . And if the lights go off you can't cook and that sort of thing because there's no power for the gas and electricity, they not using coal fire and coalpot to cook on, you know; you talking bout England. They not teaching you this sort of thing in school?'

'We doing the EC and trade and how it affecting all the small country in Africa and the banana trade in St Vincent and St Lucia.'

'I like it when you say "small" countries in Africa.

Maybe they not teaching you the size of some of them countries over there.' And with no switch of tone, he continued. 'Is a lot better to be one of them communist places, what used to be communist countries coming into the EC from what they used to call Eastern Europe. If I were people in St Vincent I'd just get up and go and live in Poland and Lithuania. But I forget what we were saying.'

'Three-day week. Idi Amin sending shillings to England.'

'Look it up, man; look it up on your machine there. So that you know what happening in the world. No sense in pretending that you living in the world if you don't know how things come to be as they be. Even in the rum shop in the old days people knew about things like the Vietnam War and Solidarity in Poland. If I was in Poland at that time, I would have joined Solidarity. Yes man. You might walk along the road there in Barville, going through the village; and maybe you think them fellas you see there in Mr Lee rum shop, you think they just scratching theirself and talking nonsense, full of rum. But when you listen to what they saying they actually talking strategy about which way Lech Walesa going move next. Or that fella before him, fella in the place they used to call Czechoslovakia, Dubček. Alexander Dubček. Fighting the Russians. Fighting the Russian bear.'

'It don't have any rum shop any more, CJ; not since the volcano.'

'They there, they still there. Only you don't see them. The fellas doing they drinking inside the buildings they used to use as churches.'

'I going quote you, CJ.'

'Quote me. Quote me, I ain't mind. Then there's the Mozambique War of Independence; they teach you about that?'

'No, CJ.'

'I didn't think so. So that's why they send you here. That's why they send you fellas up here. So you can get an education. Without an education, boy, how you going stand up to them people in England and America who think you're from a little backward place where everybody ignorant and don't know anything? They think everybody back here sitting down under breadfruit tree wondering if is time to milk the goat again.'

'People not eating so much breadfruit now, CJ. We have a dietician at school. A German lady. And nobody milking goat here any more. Hey, CJ, I didn't realize they speaking Portuguese over there.'

'What? Over there in Portugal?'

'No man. In Mozambique.'

'Mozambique is this place on the far side of Africa, you know that?'

'It have a map of the place here. The continent.'

'On the other side of South Africa and them places. Samora Machel, you know about Samora Machel? So what was I saying about Mozambique? The Cubans, of course, help to liberate that country. Did I tell you about the Cubans? Helping to liberate Africa?'

'Yes, CJ, that time when we talk about chess.'

'Ah! Our old friend, Capablanca. The ignorant people here only talk about Cuba when they want to say stupidness bout cutting cane; cutting sugar-cane. You can play chess, now?'

'No, CJ.'

'So what is it you asking me, boy?'

'I was just saying, CJ, I didn't know they speak Portuguese over there in Mozambique.'

'Well, you don't have to know everything. And let's put it this way. You're not the only ignoramus on this island. Or, in the world, for that matter. You nearly make me forget: I was writing a letter to our friend, to see if we could help him out. Maas Pewter Stapleton in England; in Sheffield. Now, Maas Pewter manage to live his life without having a home. You have to admire him. Like what they used to say about Italy in the old days. Governing itself without a government. And no worse governed than any other place for that. The Wandering Jew, that's Maas Pewter. I remember Pewter writing to me from London; that was in the '60s, the 1960s, long before you born. And over the years we keep in touch: we always arrange to see each other when I was in England. Unless he was someplace else. On the continent: I don't believe he speak those languages. France and Germany. You never know what address he going write you from, even in England. Ireland. Wales. Manchester, all them places. I used to ask him: what driving a man that he want to outdo Drake and Hawkins and Columbus and – if you asking me bout Mozambique – the fella they used to call Vasco da Gama? You know about Vasco da Gama?'

'No, CJ.'

'Boy, I too old to take on you education. You have Maas Pewter's address in Sheffield, yes?'

'Yes, CJ.'

'I think if I don't write to him the poor fella won't know which place he is, any more. So what were we saying to Maas Pewter?'

In Sheffield, Pewter was missing the letters he used to get from CJ: he wished he could turn the clock back.

*

Pewter and CJ had exchanged gifts of a kind over the years; though a degree of self-consciousness only began to creep into the exchanges maybe after the 1989 hurricane, Hurricane Hugo, when Pewter had visited the island and found CJ in better shape than people had prepared him for. Pewter noted at the time how untouched the man had seemed in contrast to the devastation of the island. (A bit like those boys – and women, too – on the street wearing the I WENT TEN ROUNDS WITH HUGO AND WON T-shirts.) Anyway, Pewter and CJ had had several long talks about how best to represent the latest disaster; and the result was a coffee-table book, glossy and expensive, an upmarket calling card rather than the usual begging bowl. Both Pewter and CJ were wary of the way the Third World, in the wake of its disasters, tended to present itself to the rest of the world as penitent, reinforcing the haves' notion of themselves as protected people: orderly, long-lived, smooth-skinned and lucky in their god. Therefore able to be generous. They were secure in the view that they occupied the high ground while the poor bastards in Bangladesh or wherever were created to remain like people in a disaster movie, to be flooded from time to time, for the big scenes. The point is: the Americans in Florida or wherever had all these thousands of miles of hinterland to retreat to – to give up to their hurricane to exhaust itself in that sort of sexual frenzy that these big storms have. Of course a small island couldn't match that: if you gave more than a few miles to the thing, you were back there into the sea, my friend. Only these poet fellows like to romanticize that sort of thing, but other people have to be serious.

In their discussions about not wanting to present them-selves as 'disaster people' Pewter and CJ were following a personal agenda. Pewter didn't want to give the impres-sion that he had distanced himself from 'home', and was just jetting in when disaster struck, as an old-fashioned donor come to relieve himself of a bit of guilt and collect the praise, and then going back to his safe place in Europe. Till the next island disaster struck. CJ's ideas concerning Pewter were perhaps less precious.

CJ had always joked that Pewter was his favourite black Englishman; liking status, minor status in England. It was a favourite charge of CJ's – levelled against those who had left the island and done well for themselves, including one of his own sons. But he liked to get a rise out of Pewter over that.

CJ used his own patchy experience of England to illustrate what the likes of Pewter who lived in that place most of their adult life were prepared to put up with. CJ would tell the stories – the same stories over and over again, but then he had nothing else to do; he'd long given up writing and he couldn't see to read; he had to distract visitors to the Home – this was his excuse – to prevent them going all foolish when they dropped by and felt they had to pray to him: CJ used to talk of visiting his friend, Ransley, in England. (Ransley was a man from Guyana, a teacher in a school somewhere in London, in Ealing, a place with lots of people from India. That was sometime in the '70s, the 1970s, and there was a little bookshop, a Guyanese-run bookshop in Ealing, that the racists used to attack at night, breaking the glass and doing pee pee and sometimes even worse. Some say the police, even, used to be doing it.) Anyway, Ransley: CJ was meeting Ransley in this pub for a drink, and there was this other man and his slightly anxious girlfriend in the pub: the man taught in the same place as Ransley, the same school; and they spent half the evening, these two English people, praising Ransley for knowing his subject so well. Ransley's subject was English. Shakespeare. And Ransley admitted to knowing things such as the genealogy of the Houses of Shakespeare's monarchs, York and Lancaster and all that, as background, you know, for *Richard III*. And throughout the evening no one said to this other fella – who taught something they call General Studies, a little bit of this and that – no one said to him: Is really impressive, Manheim, that you doing so well with your General Studies. Granted the subject is such an anything-you-want-to-make-it sort of thing; but seeing that your father was only a farm worker in some country place that didn't have running water till you were whatever age; and after all that, here you are up here in London as if you born in the place, putting up your population statistics on the blackboard, dividing up the country this way and that as if your name is King Lear; and having a girlfriend sitting here to admire you: I surprise you not calling her something like Miss Cordelia, if you get my meaning. And CJ sat there in the pub and thought: how does his friend, Ransley, a man he'd known a long time; how does Ransley, who was not an easy-going man normally, how does he put up with this treatment day in day out and not turn round and kill somebody, despite the smile on his face? And CJ just concluded that that was the sort of thing that England made these black Englishmen put up with; and he was glad that he was just visiting.

Pewter had always tried to convince CJ that he, Pewter, could play the host in England to friends visiting from abroad; but CJ didn't believe it. For what he saw was that all the Pewters of this world were merely tolerated as guests, however long it was they lived in that place; and this was borne out the last time he was in England. He had gone up to Leicester to see a fella who used to work in Public Works in St Caesare and Montserrat. Nice enough fella. No playing the big man, and all that, when he came back to visit. Nice wife, too. English. So, after the visit, CJ has to get a train back to London; and his friend couldn't drive him to the station because of the state of his eyes; and the wife maybe doesn't drive, or had something else to do. So he gets a taxi to the station, no big thing. Nice enough fella, taxi driver. Indian. The door to the taxi doesn't shut first time round because CJ doesn't slam it, as some of these ignorant fellas at home used to do, fellas not used to cars. And as he's about to shut the door – open it again and shut it properly – the Indian turns to him and says: 'The door ain't shut.' Now C. J. Harris, by then, is a man into his seventies, who's been, y'know, to four of the five continents of the world, and had been in and out of more cars than you can name; and some brown-skinned jackarse of an Englishman in Leicester turns round and tells him, as if he couldn't see it with his own eyes, that the car door ain't shut.

'You can see it, can't you, why in countries like England and America, with all this sort of thing going on, with everybody treating you like you're an idiot who don't know anything and never been anyplace – you could see how people just sometimes get up out of the blue, and lash out and kill people as if they're acting out the characters in one of our friend Carrington's plays. Ah, but didn't the man tell us: "Obedience, Struggle and Revolt". You have to choose. And there's no point choosing Obedience and Revolt? So, you're only left with the Struggle.'

'Who say that, CJ?'

'You got me there, boy; can't remember. Look it up; look it up on your machine.'

II

Pewter was half-expecting the call; the maths were against them, the *math* was against them, Ohio was moving the wrong way; Bush would be re-elected by breakfast time.

'I thought you'd be up,' the Reverend Carrington said, from, presumably, near to where it was all happening.

'Michael! Where are you?' Maybe he was going to counsel prayer, for the night's disaster.

'Oh, my friend, I'm somewhere in the sanctity of empire,' Michael said. 'What does it matter where? Remember at the start of that early Edward Bond play, when Gladstone and Disraeli come on to the stage at Windsor Castle, and look around furtively, and one of them says to the other: "Are we safe?"'

'Like when Laurence Olivier, the Nazi whatsit, playing the dentist, says to Dustin Hoffman: "Is it safe?"'

'Exactly.'

'And Queen Victoria and Florence Nightingale are having their same-sex thing.'

'Wouldn't be allowed in Wyoming.'

'Oh, God. They even say that David Mamet's gone into hiding. Warrant out for his arrest after all that *Sexual Perversity in Chicago* thing. What's a good Jewish boy like you doing turning your back on the Bearded One: you think your name's Philip Roth?' At least the man could laugh about it, Pewter thought.

'Well, that'll teach them to cross the fundamentalists,' he said. 'So where are you?'

Michael Carrington and Pewter Stapleton had had their gradual falling out over . . . over something that was perhaps too nebulous to name so they both settled, in the end, to agree that it was over Mozambique. That sounded less petty. That sounded more grown up; that might make others think that the disagreement was over ideology. Neither man, it seems, could back down now, so each kept his distance (no email jokes about West Indies cricket performance), which wasn't so bad now that Michael was living in America. Pewter had somehow linked it all to the break-up of Michael's marriage, but that thought, too, he was uneasy in pursuing, as that could be interpreted as one man emphasizing the misfortune of the other. So both men – they were old friends, collaborators; one had written a book about the other – both men grasped at things that were, in a sense, less important to them than their professional disagreement over whatever it was, Mozambique, providential things like the American presidential election. And now they were playing that safer game.

To the question of where he was ringing from, Carrington replied: 'Good question,' making Pewter feel that it was Carrington, now, who was in need of the lifeline. 'I feel like waking up to find myself a black man . . .'

That set Pewter thinking about Coleman Silk, a Philip Roth character in an American university pretending to be white.

'Coleman Silk in *The Human Stain*,' he said.

'Got it,' Carrington said. 'Great book. No, a black man in a sea of . . . Republicans!'

One to the Reverend, he was ahead of Pewter there. He imagined his friend, Carrington, in middle America, somewhere in that swathe of red on his TV screen. And yes, he had the image of the man down and bleeding; in his preacherly robes, the church empty and burning; the 1960s back. And Pewter very quickly revised the image and thought of Dick Cheney, Bush's vice-president, humiliatingly, a man younger than Pewter – he imagined Dick Cheney making his pig joke about John Kerry – who was, clearly, losing the election – making his pig joke at an election rally, a joke which instantly transmogrified Cheney, who anyway looked pig-like, into a pig; and Pewter thought of all those Scandinavian farming women in the unforgiving Midwest states, and the fat black men and frenzied black women in the churches, with their god, making a caricature of themselves. And through all this the Reverend Carrington was saying something, having shed his preacherly voice – was saying something about Don King of the big hair getting a post in the new Bush administration and the prospect of Schwarzenegger, the Terminator, Arnie Schwarzenegger, the Governor of California, and Iron Mike Tyson, the man who bites off ears, when the mood takes him – those two American superstars being lined up as slugging it out for the Republican nomination next time round, in 2008. Facing our friend Gerry Springer, on the other side; Springer having disposed of the Lady Hillary Clinton in the meantime.

'So, where are you, Michael?' (He had done enough tonight – this morning – to kick the Reverend label.)

'I'm thinking of a place that . . .'

Pewter tried to help him out. 'I know. Not easy to trace, phone not tapped, no sharp-shooters in the upstairs windows at the ready. Remember that film with Donald Sutherland, insider job, wants to get rid of the president and bring in a fascist state, and this little guy and the woman, nice-looking woman, on the run in the little van?'

'*Shadow Conspiracy*.'

'Was that it?'

'Well, give it time; give it a week or two. I guess I just need to think . . .'

'I *guess* . . .'

'. . . of myself in a place where . . . like mentally buying a bit of time before going home to face the music. Like one of those, y'know, Wealdstone or Ruislip sorts of mock-Tudor places outside London.' And putting on a mock-English accent, he said: 'I'm phoning you, my friend, for your protection as well as mine. I'm phoning from, ah, let's just say . . . Budleigh Salterton.' (And Pewter was thinking: *home*? What's home to a man who's lost his family? Or did he mean 'home' to England and out of America; so he went with the flow of it.)

'Oh, you're safe with Budleigh Salterton. West Country somewhere.'

'Man's gotta cover his tracks.' The accent was now mock-rural England.

'Cornwall or Devon or . . . maybe Somerset.'

'Let's drink to that.'

*

Afterwards the irrelevant thought occurred to Pewter that his friend, Carrington, like himself, was on a restricted diet – including the wine – and he wondered if Carrington, from Budleigh Salterton, Pennsylvania or Budleigh Salterton, Washington State, which had come through for Kerry, or wherever, had had that extra glass of wine at what, for him, would be the middle of the night. For Carrington could ease up on himself now that he had lost his family and his church: you could at least joke about a man losing out on his venture, a church that tempted the Fates, a storefront church in middle America calling itself the First Church of Christ, Biologist, when you couldn't joke about a man losing his family; for even if the atheistic Reverend had got it together and thrived among the church-going elect, he would certainly have been swept away this night on the tide of Republicans. And Pewter thought of the promised toast of wine and decided he'd ease up on himself, too, and not take his own dieting too seriously. Though he never had his first glass before lunch-time; unless there was champagne in the fridge and the work was going well. Or perhaps if there was champagne in the fridge and the work wasn't going so well. Anyway, there was no champagne in the fridge.

On the phone they had talked about Kerry's good joke about Massachusetts, his home state, where he was the junior senator, over-shadowed by the other senator from the state – one Edward Kennedy. When a joke he had spun from that bombed on the stump you knew there was no hope for the rest of the planet, and the only safe place was, indeed, Budleigh Salterton. For the fact is, the people in Montana didn't run Dick Cheney out of town for *his* joke about the pig wearing lipstick still being a pig.

Before he put down the phone Pewter wondered if he or Carrington would be the one to appropriate Kerry's still-good joke about Massachusetts being an old Indian name meaning the Land of Many Kennedys. (For that joke was too good for a man who had just lost an election it was his duty to win.)

And then they talked a bit about Arafat obviously dying in his expensive Paris hospital, and decided that neither Pewter in Sheffield nor Carrington in Budleigh Salterton was available at the moment to take on power in Palestine; so they might have to do the second-best thing, and write another big book together.

*

Pewter went back to bed and had an instant re-run of his conversation with Carrington. Including the business of drinking the extra glass of wine and pretending the little doctor wasn't watching. (In these dreams the doctor was always little, always female and always fanciable, usually with her tits out – or maybe, just one tit out.) Here, she's too busy to monitor the two friends because she's waking up in a sweat, not even bothering to cover her tits because of what's happening in Ohio, a place she thought was safe from capture; and there she is grabbing a few things and throwing them in the back of the old Packard and pointing the vehicle east towards the safety of Pennsylvania: at the back of her mind she's thinking she might just put her foot down – nice foot – and keep going, going, all the way into the furthest reaches of New York, if for nothing else (*to escape the hurricane?*) to put as much distance between herself and the Virginias, in case Maryland was too much like border country. And you know about the Virginias.

'Oh, I know about the Virginias,' Pewter said; for in a dream you know about these things. 'The Virginias and the Carolinas.'

'Oh, don't talk to me about the Carolinas.'

Pewter remembered a song about the Carolinas. 1960s. Someone like Doris Day. Or maybe it was the Dakotas. 'The Carolinas and the Dakotas,' he said.

'The Dakotas. That's on the other side. Jesus God. Is there no relief!' Reverend Carrington was the man in possession, he knew his geography. 'With the Dakotas on the other side of you, is anyone in Minnesota safe?' (And it was Gladstone and Disraeli all over again, in the Bond play at Windsor Castle, and the ceilings of the castle were high, like a cathedral.)

In the dream he had the map in front of him, so Pewter could easily check that there was nothing but red between Minnesota and Washington State. Nothing but enemy territory. No one normal could make it through Montana and those sorts of places unconverted: *and she's unarmed, she's unarmed: she's left her Bible and other forms of protection in the basement behind; the little doctor!*

In the dream Pewter didn't ask Carrington where he was calling from; instead there was the obligatory reference to C. J. Harris in St Caesare, as if that were an agreed safe house; and the Reverend and Pewter were doing their verbal jostling in the old man's room; and the old man was on his bed, either asleep or not attending, his face to the wall, with the boy from the grammar school sitting at the computer. And it was with the usual uneasy feeling of living in the past that Pewter woke up.

*

He was really more concerned with his own . . . things to resolve. He was giving up his harem in the summer after all these years. The girls were becoming too damn young; and he was a parody of the Sultan-figure, at any rate, too close to the Philip Roth vision of the old man professor and his young, young student doing the bedroom dance together; Pewter would have to learn not to panic when being forced out of his present life of denial.

That's why dreaming about C. J. Harris bothered him; because, awake, he couldn't be sure what he had dreamed: he had a feeling that the defrocked Carrington had said they should deny news of the American election result to old CJ. But how could they? CJ had access to the internet in his room, he had visitors every day who brought him news; presumably, he had a radio. It had crossed Pewter's mind that it was possible to write a play in which C. J. Harris had been given the wrong outcome to the election. (There was a '60s play, wasn't there? – was it Sartre? – where the son of the house, a German home, sat in his room in the attic and brooded over the destruction of Germany, of the culpability of Germany for the war; and he refused to believe that the reconstruction of the country was taking place. So he remained upstairs in his room as a sort of penance. And then one day he just came down from the attic – 'Hello, Dad' – and didn't over-react to finding Germany rebuilt.) But maybe this dream of cosseting CJ was just an obscure way of Pewter worrying about his own situation at the university. That was no more comfort to him than to be locked in some fruitless, wasting rivalry with his friend Carrington. At the end of the year he would be giving up what Carrington called his harem of twenty-year-olds (mostly women), firm-bodied, fresh-faced, high-breasted, and with near-perfect skin and teeth; and be cast out, perhaps for ever, among people his own age. (*Ah, Middle America among the Republicans!*) He would have to find ways to avoid becoming comic in having time on his hands, not having an office to go to. He would have to consult his little doctor on how to stave off bitterness and murder.

And then there was Carrington – the failed preacher; ungrateful man, biting the hand that fed it – Carrington, who was always going to punish Pewter for consigning him to the second division in the league table of world dramatists. (Was that what had unhinged him and turned him into a preacher?) Surely, anyone else, someone with a sense of perspective would be relieved to be put on a par with most of the Restoration and Caroline lot and, in our own time, with the kitchen-sink merchants, excepting Bond and Arden, who weren't really kitchen sink. What did the preacherman want: to be measured against Webster of *The White Devil,* rather than with Beaumont and Fletcher or Middleton and Shadwell? Did he want to be ranked up there with Ben Jonson?

So Carrington had first punished him with a portrait of Pewter at the university surrounded by an openly willing but inwardly pitying harem of twenty-year-olds you could kill a man for. And then Carrington had gone further and cashed in on Pewter's voyage to Mozambique.

III

On his last visit to England a very old C. J. Harris had made the trek up to Sheffield to see Pewter Stapleton; that counted for something; that was like saying that the roles of mentor and apprentice were reversed: Pewter chose a restaurant on the edge of town. Over dinner, having got over the news update thing, they began to talk in a way that both men would hold up as being characteristic of their late meetings. The talk was about dentists, about teeth. Years and years ago this special conversation might have been about drama – shouldn't they revive CJ's one-act play about mixed-race people, or together compose the play about Molière that CJ had always talked about? ('No man, that fella already did it. Fella they call Bulgakov. Mikhail Bulgakov. Russian fella. Born in Kiev. Doctor of medicine, man. Like Chekhov. And our friend over there in France, Rabelais.') Sometimes the talk was about novelists, about the unique role of the novelist not just to make us aware of the texture of a society – we could sense that for ourselves, we weren't stupid – but to make us care about nuance. 'I like that word, *nuance*. The community's nuance. A man might be a criminal, but if that man appreciate "nuance", you have to hand it to him, you have to take him seriously.' And they went through country after country round the world – ah, this was voyaging they both craved, this was the good side of globalization – ranking the grown-upness of a society by its ability to produce a novelist. And they would call him their 'nuancelist', a new word for the dictionary. And then have the society protect this nuancelist from ignorant people, so they could still live in the place and not have to go into exile – 'not like Solzhenitsyn or Rushdie or that fella in Cuba, who they say get his teeth fixed in America for free, in some college there, because he wrote an anti-Cuban novel that they like over there.'

But now, in the restaurant on the edge of Sheffield (the eventual bill was £70.00 for two, and worth it), the talk was about dentists, teeth. Pewter, having lost a tooth that morning, would not have another implant. And it wasn't just the money. The gap would not be particularly notice-able (except to a lover). *Except to a lover!* But that was not the point here. He already had four implants. Four, in the context of however many teeth, was a fair proportion, the overwhelming number of his teeth being not *planted*, his mouth hadn't become an artificial thing. One more im-plant could, perhaps, be interpreted as vanity, but not as a sign of desperation. Trying to roll back the years, sort of thing; of wanting to be forever young. Now, if CJ, at his age, were to have an implant – CJ, who has lost many teeth – this could be seen as an act of resistance; and as the conversation ranged – when did resistance become pathetic, sort of thing; and they drank to the ambience and toasted the meal – C. J. Harris, sitting in this cosy restaurant on the edge of Sheffield, began to turn into someone else; young, pretty, tooth-perfect; but the conversation remained the same.

Pewter was sitting in the canteen at Luton airport thinking that if the failed preacher were reasonable he would take up his friend's offer of Angola instead of Mozambique. (Each man would have to live to biblical age to clear their respective inheritance of landmines.) And from either side of the continent, Pewter's Mozambique and Carrington's Angola, they could sort out Africa, they could clean up Africa (*clean up in Africa?*), they could repossess Africa.

Pewter was sitting in the canteen at Luton airport scribbling a note about himself, Carrington and Africa when two women, his age, asked if they could join him. They were Americans, and maybe that's why they were more forthcoming – a lot more forthcoming – than strangers might normally be. Or maybe it was because he was the age he was that they felt the threat of inviting themselves to sit at his table, much diminished from the time when they were younger and afraid of black men: he was unlikely to leap up and overwhelm them when their defences were down. So though he wasn't pleased about the fact of his being considered safe – something he'd found more and more among women of all ages, now (didn't they read Philip Roth?) – he thought he would have to learn to get used to it.

They apologized, the Americans, who were on a flight to Budapest, for disturbing him, for Pewter had been scribbling in his notebook – his large, A4, 80-page door-stopper notebook, as if he had set up office at the airport. They had asked if they could join him; and he had said, yes, of course, and cleared away the office and resolved to be sociable: they seemed very old, the women, and he was in the mood to be gallant. They praised his accent; so he admitted to having gone to school in London in the Dark Ages of the 1950s. Inevitably, it soon emerged that the women, friends from schooldays in Philadelphia, were both the same age – sixty-five – and Pewter's exact age; and what exercised him (this is how his own sixty-five-year-old face must seem to others) – what intrigued him was that one of the women looked a good fifteen years older than the other, and he couldn't help himself speculating about what sorts of illnesses she must have had in her life; or whether this signified that one had had a harder life (more demanding husbands, lovers – and children perhaps?) than the other.

Their talk of grandchildren made him feel the opposite than intended: he began to fight the – if not exactly deprived, the subtly wronged – mood.

One of these women, *both* of these women could afford to drop dead this minute with the satisfaction that she had done her bit in the line of procreation; she was, one way or another, a legitimate part of the continuation of the species. Pewter was in the position that he was – he was reading, among other things, a book on cricket to pass the time – he was still, if you like, batting for himself, trying to defend his wicket: that was an undignified position to be in when your professional cricketer at thirty-six is thought to be selfish for not ceding his place to a younger rival. He thought of his friend Carrington, whose marriage had broken up, whose church had broken down but who was still in a position to say of his child, like Paul Simon in *Graceland*, that this was the son of my first marriage (in Carrington's case, 'daughter'), that first marriage being part of his considerable hinterland which even a bad presidential result couldn't take away from him. Ah, don't think about it.

Pewter had missed his EasyJet flight to Paris and had a six-hour wait for the next one; so he was relaxed about getting some work done. He had bought a *Guardian* – the big Saturday package – but wouldn't break into the seal (all this plastic, what of the pollution!) till he had done some writing, and he had the pages of his cricket book, which was Nasser Hussain's autobiography, *Playing with Fire*, a 400-page plus job, to relieve the boredom of the long wait for his next plane to Paris. If that didn't fill the time – the book wasn't terrifically well written, but not irritatingly bad – he could reach for a more sturdy text from his bag; Philip Sidney's *An Apology for Poetry*, or some other oddment long on his shelf that he had determined to read properly before leaving the university.

*

The Americans occupied a good hour and he felt better for it, more sociable; and went back to the notebook, to his note which he was determined to prevent turning into a short story, as what he was writing wasn't fiction. Then he was joined by a man who looked both relaxed and popping with energy.

This was good; people weren't avoiding his table (the rest of the canteen wasn't packed), so maybe he looked all right; maybe, too, he looked all right, after all, to his harem at the university. His new table-companion was a trim Jamaican maybe in his late thirties, sitting down to a big breakfast. (Not a very wholesome breakfast, but who was Pewter to query; he wasn't the man's little doctor.) He rather took to this man with his restless body language and healthy appetite, off to Munich where his friend, a dub musician, was going to do a gig. (He was to be the bouncer: he wasn't overly large but he had the posture of a bouncer – over-developed upper body, open chest; and arms a bit out at the sides: he looked fit.) For some reason Pewter had a thought back to those boxers of the past, those like Archie Moore and Joe Louis who had travelled to their bouts with the full entourage, including the priest; and he had a fleeting image of himself, accompanied by a bodyguard (the man did describe himself as a bodyguard rather than as a bouncer), as he, Pewter, moved around from place to place – not only from Sheffield to Edinburgh to London giving lectures and poetry readings, but nearer home, from his room to the photocopier to classroom to course committee meetings, sort of thing; but most specifically *on the trains* – his private bouncer/security man: he began to see this as a human right.

But this man, this high-energy Jamaican had a tale of woe impossible to make credible in a book. Let's say the man was nearing forty. His girlfriend had died of breast cancer; a first son had died of cot death; and all the in-laws – a shower of money-grubbing types who hated him and tried to turn the girlfriend against him – were, within two years, either dead or incapacitated, one by a stroke, another by an accident in the hospital – *accident in the hospital!* And here was this man with his appetite undiminished telling Pewter that he drew no comfort from the fact that all his tormentors had come so swiftly and completely to grief.

In the middle of it all Pewter was thinking of C. J. Harris; or maybe he was just thinking of a C. J. Harris view of the world that he (and Carrington) had helped to perpetuate: he had been thinking vaguely of that earlier when he had been interrupted by the Americans on their way to Budapest: he had recommended Pest to them as being more upmarket than Buda (meaning 'calmer'), thinking of their age; and then being ashamed of that.

Now the Jamaican with the healthy appetite set him back to revising certain things about C. J. Harris. This man, the Jamaican, was looking after his young son – a one-parent family scene – and dealing with the child's foibles. For the boy was, of course, missing his mother, two years on, demanding cornflakes at breakfast when the dad bought shredded wheat, and vice versa; and then he revealed that the dying woman had been put under so much pressure by her family in the hospital – to break off the relationship with him – that to this day, two years on, he hadn't dreamed of her. 'She don't dream me, yet,' was his phrase.

The man was still cheerful, eating a full breakfast, looking out for his friend, the dub musician, on the way to Munich.

And then Pewter began to wonder if his argument with Carrington wasn't a lot of nonsense. If he knew where the man was, and he had a mobile, he would ring him; and perhaps drop the joke about his having been a Reverend.

IV

Of course he knew the church would fail. He had pointed out to Carrington how very traditional it was to call his church the First Church of Christ, Biologist. Since all was biology, from the king to the beggar to the worm in the soil, there was something fundamentalist in calling your church after the Biological God; you'd be merely *confirming* the Americans in their fundamentalism. Now, if Carrington had taken Pewter's advice and called the church First Church of Christ, Artist. Or First Church of Christ, Poet, he might have got a result, as football managers say. At confession time you could have people kneel down to the god of Mrs Leaning of Manchester; and bemoan the fact that after their own death, there'd still be people in the town discussing something called Manchester United (or whatever sporting icon they'd be worshipping in middle America), and that criminal politicians and wife-beaters all over the world would continue to die peaceably in their beds. Pewter would have made a better fist of the church.

Though he decided to entertain the possibility that he was who the Reverend said he was; someone with an inflated sense of his own importance, someone cosseted and protected by years and years in the academy, someone who talked of 'blood on the carpet' meaning a slightly sharp disagreement in the English course committee meeting over new ways of assessing, or over the best way to respond to this or that student complaint. More worryingly, he wondered if the Reverend was right about his 'harem'. As he looked round the room of the twenty-year-olds in their third year, and preached the ideology of 'transference of power' (meaning shifting information from himself to them over the three years), and hoped that his method could be trusted to convert a mass of information into a little knowledge. If – to use another image – these were scales on which things could be weighed: access to information and the sharpening of the thinking process over here, gradually lifting the weight of knowledge on the other side; till by graduation time the thing would be held in balance. Tutor and the student in balance. He called it democracy. Or was this all bullshit? Did the fact of working in a pleasant environment, of having young, clean, fanciable bodies surround you, of being taunted by jutting, wayward, unattainable breasts – did that nullify the reality? – was it morality or pornography that this enterprise was all about? Did it make nonsense of saying that your assessment of any kind of imaginative writing would revolve round three broad categories; linguistic vitality, formal innovation and emotional truth; and that the learning process, seminar after seminar, the odd tutorial, would be demonstrating in practice how these aims might be achieved? Or was he, in fact, just persisting here in what the Reverend had called 'institutionalized wanking'?

So Pewter took a break – he still had hours to go for his plane; he had abandoned what he had been writing – and went to the food counter and liked nothing that he saw on display there, and decided against having anything to eat. But then he remembered: he was no longer to be cosseted by his harem for ever, he would soon have to face the outer world, and accept things that were not to his liking; he would have something to eat if it killed him.

And it killed him, of course: within three hours he was vomiting with food poisoning. That's what taking the other man's word had done for Pewter.

Naturally, in between visiting the loo you had to do something. The cricket book seemed the lightest option. Though he managed only two or three pages at a time. It was probably that that got him to thinking of a conversation that had taken place some time before, in CJ's room in St Caesare. At a bad time for West Indies. For West Indies cricket. Everyone had a theory of why West Indies were embarrassing themselves. The rival attraction of American sport was one answer. Baseball. Basketball. Sports scholarships to the US. Though most people in the know didn't believe that to be the real cause.

'The boys chigga-happy,' CJ had said, with something close to amusement. (Pewter remembered thinking that maybe one of the advantages of extreme age is that you didn't take anything seriously any more – a combination of old age and lack of religion.)

'Trigger-happy?'

'No man, chigga. You know, in your toe, in your foot. You don't look at the way they walking on the pitch, like these street-level fellas bouncing up, bouncing up and down pretend they walking, like the shoes don't fit, the shoes too tight? Like they have chigga foot. Not just in the toe, you know, but chigga in the whole foot. What foolishness is this,

I ask you, when you taking the field to play a Test match at the Oval or that place over there in Sydney? And then the way they do what they call the high fives. High fives were fine in the days when we were winning matches. Because then you celebrating not just the fall of one wicket that maybe don't matter, it was the whole movement towards the victory; that's what it meant. Now like they don't even know why they doing it. They doing it even when they losing; what foolishness is that! You have to ask yourself if these boys ever went to any sort of school; if they ever did their history; if anybody ever tell them that before Harry S. Truman it had Franklin Delano Roosevelt. I can't believe these fellas had any sort of mother at home to stop them playing the fool and to concentrate like normal children.'

So what, Pewter asked, was the answer; not really expecting an answer. Or expecting the usual answers. But CJ was characteristically robust.

'Latin, man,' he said. And then: 'As I say, philately won't get you anywhere.'

Nice one, CJ. So, the fellows were distracted from their cricket by stamp collecting. Then Pewter remembered – he hadn't really forgotten – the philately joke from years before. CJ had had a young son who collected stamps, and this was his joke at the boy's expense, almost a party piece. (The boy later ended up working at the Post Office, as if to punish CJ.) But Pewter also remembered that, in better days, he had heard CJ discourse on Francis Bacon's 'The Advancement of Learning', and on the Paris Commune of 1871. So you didn't write off the sage at any stage.

'Well, why not Latin?' Pewter tried to get back into the conversation.

'I remember reading the autobiography of that fella. Jamaican fella, you must know him.' Pewter searched his mind for a Jamaican whose autobiography he had read. Then he wondered if CJ was getting confused. CJ used to talk – in his old days as historian – about Simón Bolívar. Oh yes, and he talked about the work of C. L. R. James and Eric Williams. Apart from the weightier histories, Williams had written a little book on *The Negro in the Caribbean*; but that wasn't autobiography; and Williams was Trinidadian. Even someone as Olympian as C. J. Harris couldn't mix up his Trinidadian and his Jamaican. Or either with his Simón Bolívar.

'Louis Simpson, that's it. Poet fellow; not a bad poet. Live in America long time. Army man and all that. Wrote a book I used to have here. So our friend, Louis, talks of learning his Latin in this private school here in Jamaica. His Latin and his Shakespeare. Never looked back.'

'So we have to teach them Shakespeare as well.' The cricketers.

'Teach them lines, man, teach them lines.'

'Like "Now is the winter of our discontent".'

'Yes, man. Or: "I should not talk in class" a hundred times. Or something from the Bible as extra punishment. And make sure the handwriting good; legible.'

'Discipline.'

And just to make sure that Pewter didn't think that, having got through their Latin and their Shakespeare and their lines, the lads were ready for cricket, CJ informed him that the boys should then be sent to Pewter, to the university in Sheffield, to undergo an intensive course in creative writing.

Every time you started to doubt CJ he came up with something to confound you. So Pewter said: 'And if they still can't detect cliché in their own writing, they fail.'

'Yes, man.'

'They fail to get into the team.'

'Yes.'

That seemed to make sense to Pewter. And if it didn't make sense to Pewter it didn't matter. For during all this he was distracted, trying to remember a joke that he had found surprisingly funny, nothing to do with C. J. Harris. It was something about a teabag; about inviting someone out to tea, and then producing a teabag from your jacket pocket. A Tommy Cooper joke. Invitation to tea, then producing a teabag from your top jacket pocket. Thinking of CJ always seemed to produce that sort of mad spark, a sudden flare you couldn't control and didn't know whether to pursue before it went out. Carrington had pursued this to advantage. Ah, well.

So what had CJ been saying about West Indies cricketers and Latin?

*

She had been in the MA class the night they had discussed the campus novel, this woman, sitting opposite him in a restaurant on the edge of Sheffield. That must have been about eight years ago; she was married then and she was not married now; but no conclusions could be drawn from that. That night he had led the charge against what was called the English campus novel, the stuff produced by the C. P. Snows of the world up to the present David Lodge and Malcolm Bradbury. Even real campus novels, such as *Lucky Jim*, he hated. Now, the Americans, on the other hand, they knew how to present the academy. From Nabokov to Jane Smiley. And, of course, Roth. Someone took Roth to task for his portrait of old men academics and pubescent girl students; and he had found Roth hard to defend on that score. He was more concerned, though, that Roth's lecherous old men seemed not to live the consequences of their age. OK, one of them had had cancer, and another was taking Viagra; and yet no one says to the young girl before the bedroom scene: my dodgy stomach isn't up to it tonight, Amy-Lou. Or let me just go and do something in the bathroom, I'll be with you in twenty minutes. If I fall asleep on the, y'know . . . it's nothing you've done, darling. At the very least: hang on a second, sweetheart; I'm just going to put in my eye-drops before I forget. *Roth was a fantasist.*

So now, it was his girl students of the past who kept Pewter, however tempting the circumstance, from lapsing into a Roth-like old academic and young woman student caricature. *This was no harem.* So they talked about dentists and teeth. And they shared the £70.00 bill without guilt.

*

So Carrington had ruined Pewter's idea of a new religion; but he wouldn't be allowed to ruin Mozambique. The religion they had had in mind was based in Manchester. Pewter had lodged with a Manchester family, the Leanings, for a couple of years in the 1970s in Higher Openshaw, and he had tended to mythologize the experience somewhat. Mary and Stan Leaning, with the next-door neighbour, Em, who must have been in her late eighties at the time; and was taking care of Harold, a somewhat retarded house-bound son of fifty-four. And they were the basis, really, of the new religion. As far as Pewter remembered, the *Dramatis Personae* of the proposed play, informed by said religion, read something like this:

Dramatis Personae

LEANING (Mary) = a deity (55 years old; sense of humour)

EM = a priestess (warning against Planet America)

HAROLD (Off) = a 'house warning'

STAN = a stage-husband (aged 55)

SECULAR PRIESTS = Pewter Stapleton, Leon da
   Firenze, Lord Balham, Sally Goodman (poet), Paul
   St Vincent (poet), Maria Antoinette of Rome,
   Mixed-race Young Woman on a fruit stall in
   Shepherd's Bush, Helena of Kilburn, C. J. Harris of
   St Caesare, Mme de Sévigné, Crates of Pergamum,
   Marshal Louis-Alexandre Berthier (Napoleon's map
   reader), Robert Browning's Bishop Blougram,
   assorted biologists, Pliny the Elder, Pliny's sister
   Julia – *and many others.*

(Over the years 'Secular Priests' were added to the list to
suit the occasion. Carrington's included some Africans and
Americans no one knew. Pewter remembered arguing for the
inclusion of Ma Kilman, the obeah woman from Walcott's
Omeros – and now he would add the Cambridge poet
J. H. Prynne, and his old friend François Mitterrand of
France and Africa.)

The first scene would have been set in

Manchester (a place)

And this was Pewter's version of the start of proceedings:

ACT ONE, SCENE ONE

Higher Openshaw. Dinnertime. Knock on door. MARY
LEANING *goes to door. Pause.*

STAN (*to* PEWTER): Em. She always comes round just
   when we're sitting down to eat. Don't make sense.

(*shouts*) It's getting cold.

No answer.

STAN (*to* PEWTER): When these women priests get together, there's no stopping them. (*Shouts.*) Dinner getting cold!

No answer. Conversation (off) between the women.

PEWTER: Shall we put it in the oven to keep it warm?

STAN: Best put it in the oven to keep it warm.

Both men attempt to do it, but STAN *gets there first. Limps. Returns.*

Don't know what they find to talk about. Day in day out.

PEWTER: Oh, Galileo and the challenge to the Pope.

STAN: Better buck their ideas up.

PEWTER: Keeping the spirit of neighbourliness alive.

STAN: Better buck their ideas up.

MARY LEANING *returns and goes to the kitchen to get her dinner; comes back to the table, sits.*

Better buck your ideas up.

Pause.

What did Em want?

LEANING: Asked me not to tell you.

STAN: Typical of these priests.   *Etc.*

V

He was sitting in the tiny café Richelieu looking down on Mitterrand's glass pyramid, a triumph of malice and respect – respect, because you could see through it to the permanency of the opposite wall of the palace of the French kings; a building, they tell us, begun in the twelfth century; one of the mini glass pyramids remained in his peripheral vision. Pewter was having a glass of wine, and a glass of water, after visiting the king's apartments, the apartments of Napoleon III.

He was reflecting on having just visited the *grande salle à manger* in the king's apartments, the three large – got to use the right word – candelabra hanging over the long dining table, and the lashings of gold, everywhere gold; gold gold gold (*Oh, my Volpone!*) that somehow seemed in no way as off-putting and vulgar as, say, Versailles. He recalled reading somewhere that Henry James, on his deathbed, had had hallucinations about all that gold in the king's apartments.

Looking down on the glass pyramid Pewter thought of the ageing Mitterrand at last getting something into perspective. His library – his Bibliothèque de France – was a monstrosity. And the Grande Arche de la Défense? Of the *Grands Projets* maybe only the Eurotunnel worked; but these fragile triangles of glass seemed just right; right for a man of Mitterrand's age thinking of mortality instead of virility. For it's useful to remember that Mitterrand, when he came in as president in 1981, was diagnosed with prostate cancer, and kept it quiet, concealed it till he was safely re-elected seven years later. And how do you interpret these *Grands Projets* – in stone, in steel, in glass – of a man with prostate cancer? But the glass pyramid seemed just right. *Cheers!*

And Pewter was thinking, drinking his Badoit, sipping his Gantonet, making a note in his notebook – thinking less of François Mitterrand, now, than of C. J. Harris. He had had to assess a thesis on James Joyce, a D.Litt. thesis; and in the chapter on *Ulysses* the student had made the case for *Ulysses* as a reflection, a metaphor for *absence*, the absence of Parnell in Ireland after 1890. And maybe that was what got Pewter thinking of C. J. Harris as the shape of something absent in – what? In Caribbean literary history. But more than that. CJ had volunteered for active service in the Second World War and had been rejected (was he too old? did he have flat feet?), whereas others of his friends in the Defence Forces had been accepted and had gone abroad and fought, and had brought back stories. And CJ had written nothing about, well, about his disappointment in missing the war. And had said nothing about it, except in his role as concerned, dismissive historian. Was he angry, ashamed, relieved? Was it important to know? And Pewter was thinking, he knew so little about CJ's illnesses, except the one which laid him low, kept him in bed; and nothing about CJ's life accommodating those illnesses, with wit and defiance – with an acceptance that didn't dim his wit and lessen his defiance? And he understood that CJ's grand-daughter, who was said to be the closest one to him, would have a different view of CJ and his – what was it he used to go on about? – his 'Struggle'; was something closed to Pewter. Struggle without the inverted commas. Enough.

Before he left the Louvre Pewter went downstairs to the bookshop to see if there was a book, in English, on Napoleon III he could buy.

VI

And this, without contradiction, is the story of the Mozambique connection, which Pewter felt he had to record once and for all (for tomorrow, he would have to pass through Luton again, and might have to risk a cup of tea at the airport, and that would certainly kill him), and he couldn't trust the writing-up to Carrington. With that off his mind, he'd spend the fifty minutes or so of the flight finishing the Hussain book.

*

He read it over, what he'd written; it didn't feel right; there was something between him and the account he had presented. Too impersonal. So he had another go, this time in the first person.

I was in France, staying at our place in the Var, a house near Montauroux. I call it our place because we've stayed there on and off over the years, and got to know the village, the neighbours. It was Christmas time, just before Christmas, and I was alone in the house for a few days ahead of friends who would be joining me, old friends from America, a couple (mother and son) from Scotland and a woman friend from Sheffield. I was trying to make the best use of the time I had on my own, catching up on the reading, and getting some writing done, because in the New Year the marking would start with a vengeance. I was working on a new story and was so engrossed in it that I didn't mind the weather, which was wet and murky. (So much for the South of France at Christmas.) This probably led to a determination to get at least the structure of the story down before the houseguests started to arrive.

On this particular day I was invited out to lunch, to friends in Seillans, a village about twenty minutes away. Bill and Beatrice were old friends and wouldn't greatly mind my being late, but nevertheless you didn't want to be precious and delay lunch because you were writing a short story, because you hadn't got to a convenient breaking-off point. And it was always useful to remember Hemingway's old claim that to break off before running out of steam – to ease up on the narrative drive, so to speak, while you still had some gas in the imaginative tank – would make it all the easier to get started again after the break.

The story I was writing had one of those ironic working titles, 'A Muse from Home'. Through it I was depicting the activities – charting the progress, if you like – of a character who was conspicuously unlike myself. Having been criticized over the years by my (mainly women) friends for endlessly re-creating myself in fiction and poetry, portraying a main character whose characteristics I wished to have acknowledged in myself, I was determined to go the other way this time, to give up the safe ground, so to speak; to shift the norm towards greater risk – emotional, moral, physical, whatever – than I possessed. I'd been trying to do this for some time without success. In order to help effect this shift, I was allowing this character, in large part, to narrate his story.

Even though deep into the story – I was trying to manage a first, complete draft before the lunch – I was having difficulty in settling on his name. This wasn't necessarily unusual, this was part of the process. He was a man of an adventurous spirit, who would not put up with the nonsense I endured. He would still have a West Indian connection, as well as an English one (but he wouldn't have my biography). Personality-wise he would cut corners and not walk round them as I tended to do; he would take risks and not panic. Not being a *folksy* character he wouldn't have an old-fashioned name like Reginald or Winston or Cecil that would liken him to that 1950s migrant generation I was sometimes identified with. Though I couldn't pin him down to a specific Caribbean island I wanted him to have a larger perspective on things than your average islander or your average, what people call, black Briton: I wanted him, yes, to have come into contact with C. J. Harris, at a formative time in his life.

Already – and this was the beauty of it, this was what was threatening to delay lunch – he had shrugged off any suggestion of Reginald or Winston and was on the point of rejecting Cecil as well. He had by now become 'Not Cecil' while I vaguely searched for a second name, a surname.

As I was thinking of names I remembered that my Americans would be arriving in a couple of days, and of course, for them, Cecil would be pronounced differently; and though I rather liked saddling this tough character with girlie associations of an Americanized Cecil, he would need a stabilizing surname, like that of a *place*: Oldham, Newport. Cecil Washington? – if he wasn't going to be too ethnic. But then there was that American actor. This might be the place to break off for lunch.

But one last thought: I wanted him at the end of the story to end up somewhere different from the places I had been, no tame Tuscanies or New England. This was partly to prevent myself being too knowing and controlling, but also to have this character, theoretically at least, guide *me* through some physical or emotional thicket I would be too timid to negotiate in normal life. So, very hurriedly, late for lunch, I typed in the place where my character ended up late in the story. It was Mozambique.

I didn't know Mozambique: could you better that for a name? *Mozambique*. I put a question mark after Mozambique, saved the story and turned off the laptop.

After lunch I came back to the story. I'd thought a bit about it on the drive to Seillans, and more concentratedly, some hours later, on the drive back: it was early evening when I got back to Montauroux. The thing was to *write* rather than sleep off the effects of the lunch, and it wasn't the naming of the character that intrigued me now but the place where he had ended up. So I reread the story from the beginning, making the usual, light adjustments, striking out Washington as a possible surname, as that might sidetrack us into schoolboy irony.

Having reread the story I didn't have a problem with our man ending up in Mozambique. Why was this? Mozambique was in the news. Floods and landmines. But mainly floods. But lots of places were in the news; and I wasn't proposing to send him to Chechnya, say, or to the Middle East or to Zimbabwe. Despite the 'disaster' news Mozambique had a sort of uplift tone to it, one of those unsulliable names despite its difficult history. You could think of other countries changing their names for something more fitting – Zimbabwe or Tanzania, maybe. But Mozambique had a grandeur as well as a rightness to it. (What fun to be intellectually rebellious and bring in a revolution in France or Russia, and leave everything there as you find it, only change the name of France or Russia to 'Floraleas', say, or 'Borussia Monchengladbach'. But I couldn't be distracted now.) But you'd fight to preserve Mozambique. Mozambique passed the aesthetic test. And then all sorts of other 'rights' started to line up behind this. Angola – if one was going for the Portuguese connection – Angola had nothing as satisfying a resonance. Even though, from a literary point of view, I knew a little bit more about Angola than about Mozambique, having published, in the 1980s, some poems of President Neto of Angola in a magazine I edited at the time. But Angola somehow didn't appeal.

Angola was too dominated in the imagination with a monster called Savimbi: I wouldn't want to follow my character there.

I took out my travelling *Essential World Atlas* and checked out Mozambique, strung out along the edge of East Africa, the southern bit – nothing between it and Madagascar: that pleased me for some reason. Small things, that Mozambique seemed greener than anything else on the map, except the extreme coastal edge of Africa, reinforced the feeling of wholesomeness. (Later, when I looked more closely, I realized that the colour scheme related to the elevation of the land; and that Mozambique was green because it was largely below sea level. Ah, that explains the floods!) But the good feeling had already been generated: I wouldn't now change my vulnerable-to-the-elements Mozambique for the high posturing ground of Botswana or Zimbabwe or Zambia.

The map of Mozambique was small, without detail, with only a few towns marked in, that and two or three rivers, one of which was the Zambezi (in the news) in the centre of the country, which seemed to be coming down from Malawi. Of the towns, Maputo, the capital, seemed too close to South Africa: shouldn't the country free itself from that past connection and move its capital safer inland? In the middle of the country – beautifully, strangely shaped country, like a Y that a not very confident child might draw – was Beira, and a little aeroplane signalling airport. (On the news, about the floods, it said that the South African government had loaned the Mozambicans a couple of helicopters to rescue people trapped in the floods of the Zambezi.) Maybe the other towns didn't have airports: it was tempting to have to go by river. But that was tricky, that recalled – river journeying recalled, what, Conrad and the Naipaul of *A Bend in the River*. And the one river journey – I wasn't particularly into Mark Twain and his Mississippi – the one river journey you'd maybe want to emulate was the one that Wilson Harris charted, never to be bettered, in *Palace of the Peacock*, in 1960. So, I will pencil in Mr – what was his name again? – 'Cecil Oldham', somewhere in the vicinity of Beira. Too obvious to plump for the capital. Not being from the capital (a farmer, black-skinned, a foreign farmer?) would give him that little edge, something to kick against, bring out the *character* of the man (something of a role model for the worthless cricketers back home). It was a shame, though, having to reject more colourful-sounding locations for Cecil, like Xai Xai, in the south, just next to Maputo. Or Quelimane in the north.

*

I had some friends over in the Alpes Maritimes, Bill and Michelle, and I called them up because I wanted to consult Bill's library. Bill was a writer, an American, whom I'd first met in the 1970s when I'd had a spell working with a building cooperative there. And his library had always been a lifesaver. Though Bill was back in America, in Colorado, Michelle was at home in Spéracedes; and as I wanted to do some work on the story before the enthusiasm for Mozambique waned (and before the other guests started arriving) I arranged to go over to Michelle's the next day to consult Bill's atlas. I'd be back in England in a couple of weeks and yet it seemed urgent now, to pore over a bigger map of Mozambique.

(Oh yes, one thing I liked about the character going to Mozambique was that he wasn't joining the African-American pilgrimage to Ghana and Dahomey in search of 'root'. One thing our Cecil would not be was politically correct.)

Two weeks later, back in Sheffield, having read through a couple of guides designed to scare you off the country, and a couple of Heinemann books of stories – *that* was more like it: Mia Couto, top man! – the sense of inevitability continued to clear away all doubts. The process of clarification had started on the trip back from France. Because of the floods (in England) the rail system was disrupted and the train from St Pancras to Sheffield was diverted via Doncaster, instead of coming the usual route via Leicester, Derby and Chesterfield.

Changing trains at Doncaster, we made a series of short stops at local stations, one of which solved a problem. I looked up from my paper and saw that we had stopped at Retford. I'm not going to try and recall the process whereby that sign on that obscure station platform immediately communicated something both marginal and central, something nearly known but subtly different, the sort of thing you feel to be both native but perhaps in slight need of explanation: that was *Retford*; that was my man's surname. By the time I got to Sheffield Cecil Retford had become, by a series of aspirating shifts which would be easy on the speaker – a series of verbal exercises on the train that drew guarded looks from passengers – Cecil Retford had become, by trial and much error, Colin Retford. COLIN RETFORD. When I got to Sheffield I booked a flight to Mozambique, my mission to track down Colin Retford.

And I got to Mozambique before Michael Carrington did. No one's denying that he read the books, knew all about the great War of Liberation and the Civil War, and could lecture you on the virtues of the two great leaders of Frelimo, Eduardo Mondlane who had the university in Maputo named after him, and Samora Machel, the charismatic leader-statesman, who was murdered in South Africa in 1986, died in a still-unexplained plane crash. Carrington had the statistics; statistics of the numbers estimated killed in War of Liberation and Civil War, and had sorted out the blame game. *The Baddies:* the old Rhodesia, apartheid South Africa, the displaced Portuguese supported by the home journal *O Dia*; and all the rest. He knew about 'The Lusaka Agreement' of 1974, between Portugal and Frelimo and the transfer of political power to Frelimo, and even about the 1984 good-neighbourliness 'Nkomati Accord' signed by P. W. Botha of apartheid South Africa and Samora Machel.

Despite all that, our friend the Reverend Michael Carrington, late of the First Church of Christ, Biologist, won't know about Colin Retford until he reads this.

Select Bibliography of E. A. Markham

POETRY COLLECTIONS

Love, Politics & Food (Von Hallett Publications, 1982)
Human Rites: Selected Poems 1970–1982
(Anvil Press Poetry, 1984)
Living in Disguise (Anvil Press Poetry, 1986)
Towards the End of a Century (Anvil Press Poetry, 1989)
Letter from Ulster & The Hugo Poems
(Littlewood Arc, 1993)
Misapprehensions (Anvil Press Poetry, 1995)
A Rough Climate (Anvil Press Poetry, 2002)
Lambchops with Sally Goodman
Selected poems of Paul St Vincent and Sally Goodman
(Salt Publishing, 2005)

SHORT STORY COLLECTIONS

Something Unusual (Ambit Books, 1986)
Ten Stories (PAVIC, 1994)
Taking the Drawing Room through Customs
(Peepal Tree Press, 2002)

OTHER PROSE

A Papua New Guinea Sojourn: More Pleasures of Exile
Memoir (Carcanet, 1998)
Marking Time
Novel (Peepal Tree Press, 1999)

AS EDITOR

Merely a Matter of Colour
with Arnold Kingston (Q Books, 1973)

Hinterland:
Caribbean Poetry from the West Indies & Britain
(Bloodaxe Books, 1989)
Hugo Versus Montserrat
with Howard A. Fergus (Linda Lee Books, 1989)
The Penguin Book of Caribbean Short Stories
(Penguin, 1996)
Plant Care: A Festschrift for Mimi Khalvati
(Linda Lee Books, 2004)
Ten Hallam Poets
with Steve Earnshaw and Sean O'Brien
(Mews Press, 2005)

Acknowledgements

Versions of these stories first appeared in the following publications

'A Woman in Her Daughter's House' in *Ten Stories* (PAVIC, 1994)
'A Place to Hide' (*Stand*, 2002)
'Grandmother's Last Will and Testament' (*Ambit*, 1989)
'Irish Potatoes' (*London Magazine*, 2005)

Extract on page 80 taken from *The Thin Man* by Dashiell Hammett
(first published by Alfred A. Knopf, New York, 1934)